Bloodeagle

by the same author

Arnold Landon Novels
A SECRET DYING
A WISP OF SMOKE
THE DEVIL IS DEAD
MEN OF SUBTLE CRAFT
A TROUT IN THE MILK
MOST CUNNING WORKMEN
A GATHERING OF GHOSTS

Eric Ward Novels
A KIND OF TRANSACTION
A NECESSARY DEALING
THE SALAMANDER CHILL
PREMIUM ON DEATH
A BLURRED REALITY
ONCE DYING, TWICE DEAD
A LIMITED VISION
DWELL IN DANGER
A CERTAIN BLINDNESS

SEEK FOR JUSTICE
A RELATIVE DISTANCE
A VIOLENT DEATH
AN INEVITABLE FATALITY
AN UNCERTAIN SOUND
NOTHING BUT FOXES
A DISTANT BANNER
WITNESS MY DEATH
A PART OF VIRTUE
DOUBLE TAKE
A QUESTION OF DEGREE
etc., etc.

ROY LEWIS

Bloodeagle

An Arnold Landon novel

ST. MARTIN'S PRESS
NEW YORK

ISBN 0-312-10431-6

First published in Great Britain by The Crime Club, an imprint of
HarperCollins Publishers.

First U.S. Edition: January 1994
10 9 8 7 6 5 4 3 2 1

I do not now bid ye learn the sports of maidens, nor stroke soft cheeks, nor give sweet kisses to the bride and press the slender breasts, nor desire the flowing wine and chafe the soft thigh and cast eyes upon snowy arms. I call you out to the sterner fray of War.

Saxo Grammaticus, AD 1200

Bloodeagle

CHAPTER 1

1

There was thunder in his head.

The music swelled around him, beating at his skull, making the air tremble and causing the blood to pulse, surge in his veins. There was a red mist before his eyes and he blinked, trying to focus on reality, away from the vision of the African skies, the heat, the flies, the smell of blood and death. He could hear again, over the music, the insistent thudding of the boat engine pulling away from the fiery beach, and the sound enraged him, until the swelling music merged with the beat of the engine and he was on the beach again. The tight group was there with him, close and mutually protective, fighting together, cursing the escaping boat. There was blood on the sand and in the water and he shook his head, reliving the fury again, the despair and the hatred. Present reality slowly returned and the room took shape around him, the stone floor, the heavy drawn curtains, the long mirror before him.

On the crude wooden table lay the ceremonial brass-hilted sword with the mystic name etched into the blade: the curved guard and pommel, the sharply-shouldered tang, the gently tapering blade with its blunted tip, all glittered redly in the firelight. Designed as a two-edged slashing implement, the blade on either side held a fuller, the shallow, round-bottomed channel which reduced the weight of the killing implement.

The guard was of bone and the grip was covered in worn leather. The pommel was a single piece of metal in triangular form: victory runes had been cut into the mount. An old weapon, it had gained in value and virtue. He picked it up and hefted the weight in his right hand as the blood beat fiercely in his head.

He stood tall in front of the darkened mirror, the tip of the blade in his left hand, the pommel in his right. He raised the weapon above his head. He imagined the bearskin across his shoulders, stiff with blood.

Thrust into an iron-studded belt would have been the stabbing spear with its leaf-shaped blade and socket patterned with herring-bone design. He extended his arms, holding aloft the glittering swordblade, staring at his reflection in the mirror—imagining stocking breeches of wool, red tunic and a bronze-embellished baldric over his shoulder. As the music faded he heard the familiar words again, as he had heard them a hundred times.

'They went on board the towered ships . . . on one side lions mounted in gold were to be seen, on the other, birds on the tops of the masts showed by their movement the winds as they blew, or dragons poured fire from their nostrils. Here there were glittering men of solid gold or silver, there bulls with necks raised high, leaping and roaring like live ones. One might see dolphins moulded in electrum and centaurs in the same metal. The blue water, smitten by many oars, might be seen foaming far and wide, and the sunlight, cast back in the gleam of metal, spread a double radiance in the air . . .'

The music rose again and it had the power to transform him. He felt he was rising, magnificent, like King Sven with his invasion horde, and the tight muscles in his chest relaxed, confident in their power. The thunder still roared in his skull but it was an excitement, a passion that gave him the strength to contain the blood-lust, the berserk rage that had gripped him for five years, and which could be satiated only by the completion of the mission he had set himself.

He could hear in his mind the rhythmic beating of oars, the cries of men bent on war and destruction, the lycanthropic howl of the berserkers in frenzied battle, and he knew he was strong enough again, endowed with the power of the past, possessed by the strength that could blunt sword-edges and stop the flight of javelins, and give him the cunning that was necessary to exact the revenge. He had sworn his three-oath on that hot, murderous beach five years ago and since then he had planned and waited and exacted the penalties. His totem was the bear, and his release was almost over.

It was time again now, time to impose the penalty. No life-purchase, no atonement was possible.

In the blood feud, blood was the only release.

2

The warmth of the afternoon had made Arnold sleepy. He was seated at his desk at the Department of Museums and Antiquities in Morpeth with a pile of papers in front of him: they comprised lists of artefacts which had been lodged with the Department from excavations on sites scattered throughout the country. The Director of the DMA had ordained that it was time his department caught up with the twentieth century—all lists were to be held on microfiche and Arnold was deputed the task of undertaking the first sorting of lists. The fly that buzzed persistently against the windowpane seemed as irritated as Arnold at the boredom presented by the task, but Arnold felt too sleepy to get up and attack it with a rolled-up newspaper. Instead, he plodded doggedly through the lists, nodding occasionally as his eyelids grew heavy.

He did not hear the pert young girl from the outside office enter the room; he must have closed his eyes for a few moments. He came to with a start as she giggled. She was standing there in front of him, grinning.

'Better not let the Director catch you like this, Mr Landon!'

There was little chance of that, Arnold thought sourly: the Director rarely left his own office, except for the golf course.

'Busy?' she asked.

'Bored,' Arnold replied.

'Well, you're to leave that stuff now anyway, Mr Landon. Director wants to see you.'

Arnold's eyes widened in surprise. 'He's sent for me?'

'That's why I'm here. You're to go straight up. Message over, Mr Landon. Now don't go back to your snooze, will you?'

She turned and marched out, her neat little bottom swinging jauntily. Arnold was not particularly interested in bottoms and wrinkled his nose. The DDMA wanted to see him. That was not good news. The DDMA tried to keep well away from his staff and the only occasions when he called them to see him were to unload some particularly difficult or unpleasant task upon them, the kind of task that usually freed him to pursue his golfing interests. Arnold gathered up his papers with a sigh. He supposed the little clerk was right: it would relieve him of the boredom of this job, anyway.

Reluctantly, he made his way along to the office of the Director. The Teutonic Miss Sansom, personal secretary to the DDMA, was waiting in her office, female Cerberus to the Director, fierce-visaged and mannishly clad. She sat stiffly and disapprovingly behind her desk, her bristly grey hair emphasizing the air of Prussian menace she always seemed to exude when she caught sight of Arnold. She clearly disapproved of him, though he knew no reason for it: he sometimes wondered whether she kept a bullwhip beside her bed. He had never dared to ask her if she really did. You never knew with women: she might have taken it as an invitation.

'The Director wants to see me,' he offered.

Her scowl suggested she could think of no reason why he should. Nevertheless, she gestured towards the inner door. 'He's waiting,' she announced accusingly.

Arnold stepped forward and opened the door.

There were four people in the room. The Director, Simon Brent-Ellis, was lounging in his chair in front of the window. He was a big man, heavily built and wide-shouldered, with white hair that he wore long and a walrus moustache that tended to be cigar-stained at its tips. Arnold always thought he looked vaguely like pictures of General Custer before the massacre at Little Big Horn, though Arnold was reasonably confident that Custer had not worn a beige suit on that occasion, nor a floral tie and pale lemon shirt, such as Brent-Ellis had donned today.

It was one of the reasons the Director did not get on with the Chief Executive, Powell Frinton: rumour suggested the Chief Executive found Brent-Ellis too colourful for his management committee meetings. Yet Brent-Ellis hardly seemed to notice: he lived in a world of his own, dominated by his wife, succoured by his golf, but untouched by the anxieties of office.

He did not get up as Arnold entered the room.

'Ah, Mr Landon, please take a chair while I introduce you to our guests.'

His tone was languid as he waved an ineffectual hand towards the empty chair beside his desk. Arnold man-œuvred past the three other people in the room and struggled to the proffered chair. Brent-Ellis glanced out of the window and took a cigar out of his top pocket. 'Nobody mind, I trust?' Without waiting for an answer he lit the cigar from an automatic lighter on his desk. It was in the shape of a fat, nude, reclining woman. Arnold wondered whether Mrs Brent-Ellis knew her husband had such an ornament in his office: he suspected it reminded the DDMA of his wife, who was somewhat inclined to corpulence. Arnold was fairly sure she would not be flattered if she saw the lighter. Brent-Ellis was caressing the lighter now, his fingers lingering over the pendulous breasts.

'Now then, introductions,' the Director sighed. 'Mr Landon, this is Frank Lindley. I don't know whether you've come across him . . . same line of work, that sort of thing.'

Arnold had never met Frank Lindley but had heard of him. He stared with interest at the stocky, middle-aged man who half rose and extended his hand. Lindley had

craggy, tanned features, bright, honest eyes and a warm
smile; he was a little above middle height and his hair was
short-trimmed and curly, sandy in colour with a frost of
grey at the temples. He was dressed in all ill-fitting, rather
crumpled brown suit, and Arnold guessed he would be
more at home in mud-stained jeans, heavy boots and windcheater.

'I'm delighted to meet you,' Arnold said. 'I've heard
a great deal about you—your fieldwork in Cumbria and
Durham particularly.'

'And I've heard something of you, Mr Landon,' Lindley
said, with a smile. 'You've built quite a reputation for yourself as a non-academic historian. It seems to me you have
the advantage over many of us: it's one thing to slave over
books and work out theories that must be tested in the field
—it's another to have learned from the fieldwork itself.
Much more satisfying, in some ways, to gain knowledge at
first hand. Inspirational. I envy you your depth of experience. And technique. It can surprise old hacks like me.
Your dating of the Old Barn, for instance—'

'That isn't to suggest that one cannot gain from the writ-
ings of others,' the woman seated beside Lindley interrupted crisply. 'There seems little point, as far as I'm
concerned, in repeating investigations, other than for veri-
fication, of course.' She eyed Arnold coldly. 'I'm Jill
Ormond, Mr Landon.'

'I'm pleased to meet you,' Arnold murmured, aware he
was being addressed by a formidable woman. She was in
her late thirties, dark-haired, with grey eyes that held a hint
of steel about them. Her nose was straight, her mouth wide
and she was not unattractive, but she seemed either unaware of it, or determined to play it down. She would want
to be rated for her intellect rather than her looks, Arnold
guessed; she was dressed in a white blouse and grey skirt,
unfashionable and somewhat severe in cut. She was slender
in build, but there was a toughness about her that suggested
she would give first place to no man in a competitive situation. She did not smile when she introduced herself, and

Arnold felt she was slightly nettled at Lindley's comment about learning history from books.

'Dr Osmond is an expert on Roman coarsework and Samian ware, I believe,' Simon Brent-Ellis suggested. 'Not exactly within your competence, Arnold.'

'Indeed,' Arnold replied, offering the olive branch. 'I know nothing at all about such pottery. I wouldn't know the first thing about recognizing artefacts of that kind.'

Jill Osmond sniffed, as though she was not surprised, and made no reply. Frank Lindley gestured towards the man seated on her right. 'This is Mike Swindon—and his expertise is mediæval artefacts.'

Swindon was built like a bull. His features were florid, wind-tanned, and his hands were large and calloused. He was about forty years of age, narrow-eyed, and there would come a time when his body would turn to fat, but right now he was still heavily muscled, with the shoulders of a wrestler and his grip was hard and positive. He stared at Arnold competitively, with a barely concealed, red-rimmed contempt that left Arnold with the impression his presence in this meeting was not entirely welcomed by the expert in mediæval artefacts. Swindon's temper would be on a short fuse, always, and he would be a man unwilling to brook argument. The three in the group seemed to Arnold an ill-assorted gathering, but perhaps Lindley's charm would weld them into a working unit. Their skills would be undoubted, their compatibility unlikely.

'Well, now that introductions are over,' Brent-Ellis sighed, 'perhaps we can get down to business.' He drew on his cigar and inspected its end for a few moments. 'Mr Landon used to work in the Planning Department, so he'll understand the problem.'

There was a short silence. At last, Arnold asked, 'What problem?'

Brent-Ellis blinked. 'Well, you know, the problem you always have in Planning Departments. Building applications.'

Arnold frowned. 'I'm afraid I don't follow.'

Frank Lindley cleared his throat. 'You know Birley Thore?'

Arnold knew the village. It lay within the undulating farmland north of Morpeth, watered by streams tumbling from the Cheviots, sheltered by an ancient oak wood and overlooking the old turnpike road that had swept north through the valley in the eighteenth century, marking out the route to the Scottish border, and reincarnating the line the Romans had laid centuries earlier.

'Yes, I know the village.' Arnold thought back for a moment. 'There's an application for road widening there. It was made well before I left the Planning Department, but it's been held up for years. Is that the problem you mean?'

Lindley nodded. He glanced towards Brent-Ellis but the Director was inspecting his cigar. 'Partly. As you say, the application regarding the road has been before the Planning Department for some time: apparently the shortage of capital grants has made it impossible for the work to go ahead. The Government has now released some money, however, so work is expected to be completed within the year. The road widening scheme will involve the bridge—it was last worked on in 1834 and we have some interesting comments about Roman remains from that undertaking. Apart from that, an application has also been made to the county for a housing development. It's intended that new housing be developed in the field to the north-west of the village.'

'I'm not certain where you mean,' Arnold murmured. 'I don't know the village that well.'

'It's enough for you to know,' Dr Ormond burst in impatiently, 'that the south-western corner of that field is a Scheduled Area of Ancient Monuments because it contains part of the alignment of the defences of the village in mediæval times. It's also important because of its Roman connections.'

'I knew a Roman road had run through the valley,' Arnold admitted.

'More than a road,' Dr Ormond replied flatly. 'It coexisted with a line of small forts, one of which was sited at Birley Thore, together with an associated civilian settlement. The Roman activity there has been largely unexplored and there's been a tendency to interpret the topographical features as signifying that the *vicus*—the settlement—evolved into a walled town. But we don't know—'

'And we know even less of the development of the mediæval village,' Swindon interrupted, eager to emphasize his own specialism. 'The name of the village itself clearly indicates the influence of Scandinavian migration into the valley—it probably also signifies the renaming of an already well-established settlement.'

'We started excavations last summer,' Frank Lindley weighed in. 'We'd managed to get a geophysical survey by the Ancient Monuments Laboratory to assess the archæological potential of the field, and from that we developed our strategy. We opened up eight trenches and we found a hollowed trackway, filled with ploughsoil; there was some Roman and mediæval pottery present and in the higher part of the trench was a cobble surface—probably mediæval.'

'No sand and gravel?' Arnold asked.

Lindley smiled approvingly, realizing Arnold understood the significance of the lack. 'None. And that gives the surface a markedly un-Roman appearance.' He hesitated. 'Then we found a layer of clean, orange-brown sand that appeared to be the subsoil, a squared block of red sandstone and then maybe cultivation soil. It looks like a substantial ditch—but it could be a pit.'

'An extensive pit,' Dr Ormond said firmly.

'Used for extracting sand?' Arnold asked.

'Possibly, but there are cobbles, a wall, and aggraded ploughsoil with both Roman and mediæval pottery,' Lindley replied.

'And the mediæval stuff ranges from the twelfth to the sixteenth century,' Mike Swindon added.

Arnold glanced uncertainly in Brent-Ellis's direction. The DDMA hardly seemed to be listening: he was gazing in an abstracted fashion out of the window, towards the upper town. 'It sounds like a fascinating site,' Arnold said quietly. 'It could produce some interesting finds.'

'It could indeed,' Lindley said warmly. 'But that's where the difficulty comes in. We're short of time.'

'The planning applications?'

'Exactly.'

There was a short silence. The three visitors looked expectantly towards Brent-Ellis. As the silence grew around them it finally seemed to make an impression on the Director. He stirred, turned reluctantly to face the small group and made a defensive gesture with his hands, as though warding off criticism. 'I've done my best, you know. When the matter came up at the Management Committee I explained the problem. But Powell Frinton took the planning line. If we don't spend these capital grants this year, he argued, we could lose them, and the developments will be put back to some indeterminate time in the future. I agree time is of the essence for this dig, but what could I do? Appealing to my department was, after all, a last resort. Strictly speaking, it's the Planning Department you should be . . . ah . . . harassing.'

Dr Ormond's grey eyes glittered. 'I believe Mrs Brent-Ellis holds the chair in the Finance Committee.'

'I am in no position to influence my wife,' the DDMA retorted primly. 'I am merely an officer of the Authority.'

And a henpecked husband, Arnold thought to himself. He had met Mrs Brent-Ellis: she had a voice to match her figure and he could understand the Director's reluctance to do battle with the lady in question. She was a formidable woman and the fact that her husband was the son of a Lord Lieutenant cut no ice with her. She could get her own invitations to Buckingham Palace, and she ruled the marriage with a fist of iron and a tongue of fire and ice.

'So the most you can hold out to us is a month's delay —which gives us just three months to complete our investigations,' Lindley said.

'And some additional manpower and expertise,' Brent-

Ellis reproved him. 'The archival assistants in the department will be at your beck and call—and there's Mr
Landon, of course.'

Suddenly, everyone was staring at Arnold.

Arnold shuffled in his seat. 'I'm not sure what I can do
to help.'

Frank Lindley leaned forward. 'We're a small team:
we're fully committed to the site in the field. We simply
cannot spare the time to keep a watching brief on the bridge
we mentioned earlier. The road widening starts on that
bridge—but we've got to work like the clappers in the field
to make sure we get things done before the housing development gets the go-ahead. What we need is another pair of
eyes.'

'But—'

'The bridge is mediæval in construction, but the 1834
survey suggests that it follows the line of a Roman bridge
that spanned the river hundreds of years before. The 1834
watchers left us some information in their records, but omit-
ted facts we needed to know if we are to make an educated
summary of the importance of the bridge. This will be our
last chance to complete the survey—once the road bridge
is widened, that will be it. You know stone; you can date
timbers; you have an educated eye—'

'And we don't need you rooting around the artefacts in
the field,' Swindon muttered.

Arnold opened his mouth, then closed it again. He
glanced towards Brent-Ellis, but the Director seemed to
have lost interest in the conversation already, and was inspecting his cigar as though he had never seen one before.
Arnold shook his head doubtfully. 'As I said earlier, it's
an interesting dig you're involved in, and I appreciate the
time-scales involved, but . . . when would you want me to
join you? Assuming the Director gives permission.'

Lindley glanced towards Brent-Ellis. 'Permission is not
a problem, it seems. The Director himself suggested your
name. And as to when—it would have to be immediately.'

'Ah.' Arnold paused, and looked again at Brent-Ellis.

'I'm afraid we do have a problem in that case. You see, I start a period of leave next Monday.'

'Leave?' Dr Ormond's voice was gritty. 'I understood you were an enthusiast. We none of us allow leave to inhibit our work. I would have thought you'd have been delighted to spend your leave working on a project like this. It's an opportunity to make a valuable contribution to our under-standing of the nature of life in the valley over the centuries.'

Arnold shrugged reluctantly. 'Ordinarily, Dr Ormond, I would have been delighted. I spend most of my vacation periods in deserted village sites, or inspecting ancient ruins —one can never learn enough. But that's the point. It's not just that I have a vacation booked—I'm already committed to some work.'

'What work?' Ormond asked sharply.

'It's . . . ah . . . it's for a friend of mine.'

'An official survey?'

'Not exactly.' Arnold hesitated. 'She's a writer.'

Dr Ormond frowned. 'You mean you're helping her undertake academic research for a textbook?'

Arnold grimaced; there was an uneasy ache in his chest. 'Well, no. She . . . ah . . . she writes historical fiction.'

There was a long silence. Mike Swindon shifted in his seat, and Frank Lindley struggled to look sympathetic. Dr Ormond was made of more direct stuff. 'You're saying no to us so you can help a writer of . . . fiction?'

The atmosphere in the room was suddenly very cold, as all three of the visitors stared at him. Arnold wriggled uneasily. 'It's a longstanding commitment.'

'But hardly as important as the work at Birley Thore!' Dr Ormond glared at him furiously. She smoothed at her skirt with long, angry fingers: Arnold had the impression she would have preferred to wrap them around his throat. 'It really seems to me you should get your priorities right, Mr Landon.'

'I think that's right,' Simon Brent-Ellis said suddenly.

The Director was not a man given to making decisive contributions to a conversation but this occasion was an exception. He seemed relieved that the pressure was suddenly taken from him, and there was another who could be placed in the firing line.

'If I'd known you were needed at Birley Thore, Landon, I would never have agreed to releasing you on leave,' he announced coldly. 'And certainly I see the point of view of our friends here. I believe it's your duty to render assistance. In fact,' he added on a more cheerful note, 'I think I can propose a solution.'

Arnold's heart sank. He could guess what was coming. 'Director, this commitment was made some time ago and I—'

'The solution is quite simple,' Brent-Ellis beamed, waving his dying cigar, happy now that he saw a way out of the difficulty. 'We'll just cancel Mr Landon's leave. He can take his vacation—and still help his friend, no doubt—later in the summer. We'll cancel his leave, and I'll arrange for a secondment for him to your project. I'm not aware there's anything else so urgent in our calendar in the Department and I feel sure we can spare Mr Landon for as long as it takes.'

Lindley looked at Arnold with some sympathy, but it was tinged with relief, nevertheless. 'The work on the bridge will take about a month—'

'That's all right, then,' Brent-Ellis cut in. 'We'll make it six weeks, to be on the safe side, and then if you're still caught short on the fieldwork I'm sure Mr Landon won't mind helping out there too, isn't that right?' He glanced at his watch and tut-tutted. 'Oh dear, I have another meeting, I must leave immediately. So nice of you to all come in. I'm glad we've managed to settle things amicably. And . . . er . . . good luck with the dig, hey?'

Brent-Ellis heaved his bulk out of his chair. The others rose, and began to shuffle towards the door.

Frank Lindley paused, looked back to Arnold with troubled eyes. 'I'm grateful, Mr Landon. I hope this doesn't put you out too much.'

The other two seemed hardly concerned: they were

clearly much more direct in their objectives. Arnold shook hands with Lindley and said goodbye.

Brent-Ellis beamed and twitched at his moustache as the door closed behind the small group. He seemed to think he had behaved in a positive manner and had solved everyone's difficulties, particularly his own. Arnold hesitated, a little angry at the position he had been placed in. He was interested in what Lindley was trying to do, and wanted to help, but he disliked having his plans overridden in this manner. 'Director—' he began.

'No time now, dear boy. I'll get Miss Sansom to settle the vacation thing. She'll be happy to sort that out for you.'

Arnold had no doubt on that score.

When he left the office, with Simon Brent-Ellis close behind and bound inevitably for the golf course, Miss Sansom seemed almost pleasant. But then, she had every reason to be.

She was cancelling his vacation, and leaving Arnold in a most difficult position.

3

From the crest of the hill the road looped down across the fellside, twisting and turning away from the village of South Middleton where it lay basking in the late evening sun. Through the gathering golden haze the fields held long shadows thrown from the trees to the left, looking west. The setting sun marked out the field distinctly: the ancient village had long since been buried but shadows from the tumbled walls of long-vanished mediæval peasant houses showed up as rectangular earthworks in rectangular banked tofts. The limits of the ancient village were clearly defined by the ridge and furrow of the open fields, bisected by a modern hedge which cut across them.

A stream meandered to the right of the field, glistening in the sunlight, lazy and unconcerned by the activity in the declivity near the hedge of hawthorn, whitebeam and beech. The narrow gate at the top end of the field had been removed from its hinges to allow entry to the police cars and vans, and the area of the declivity was already staked out, prepared for plastic sheeting to be raised around the site, screening it from the inevitable Press attention. Journalists had already begun to intrude upon the field and a television crew had bustled their way on to the site.

Detective Chief Inspector Culpeper had been late arriving.

He had taken his wife, Margaret, for their usual break: the one they took every summer. They were both creatures of habit. He had taken a cottage at Seahouses and booked their evening meals in the Jolly Fisherman. He had hired a small fishing-boat from the man they had been dealing with for eight years, chugged out the mile or so to Coquet Island, and indulged in a quiet spot of fishing. Mrs Culpeper had hung her field glasses on her ample bosom, as usual, and was happy enough to allow her husband to indulge in his passion while she enjoyed hers—spending the quiet days rocking offshore in the tiny boat, watching the birdlife and the occasional seals on and around the island. At least twice during their stay they would normally take a trip out to the Farne Islands, where the wildlife was more numerous: John Culpeper went along with her on those occasions and left behind his fishing-rods.

She had said very little when the message arrived at the cottage: she had been a policeman's wife for a long time now, and even their only son had joined the police on Teesside, so she knew that holidays were always chancey affairs. It was with an air of resignation that she had started to pack, minutes after the messenger had arrived from the local police station at Seahouses. Culpeper had suggested she might wish to stay on at the cottage while he went off to South Middleton.

'I could pick you up at the weekend, drive you back to Morpeth.'

She had looked at him stolidly and shook her head. 'John, are you telling me you can guarantee you could get away for the weekend? If I know anything about anything, it's that I'm not likely to see much of you the next few weeks, let alone the coming weekend. Besides, it wouldn't be the same, being up here by myself.'

She had been born and raised in County Durham, daughter of a pitman, and he had met her when he was a young copper on the beat. She hadn't changed over the years, as he had been promoted: she was still a simple, relatively shy Durham lass, uneasy outside her own surroundings, committed to her home, resigned to the occasional social police function, but happier when there was just the two of them, spending time in County Durham, or up on the north-east coast near Bamburgh. Her waist had thickened, of course, and her bosom was more ample now in middle age, but her personality had changed little: she was placid of temperament, generally satisfied with her lot in life, and supportive of her husband. There were a lot of police wives who were not, so he counted himself a lucky man.

Travelling across from Seahouses, as he'd been forced to do, Culpeper was late, not least because they had been delayed by a caravan of some fifty-strong New Age Travellers—'bloody hippies,' the driver called them—and then got stuck behind a succession of farm tractors in the narrow lanes over the hills.

It had irritated Culpeper, and his normally placid temperament was also ruffled by the fact that he considered himself inappropriately dressed. A broad, thick-waisted man in his mid-forties, he liked to wear a sober suit when he was on duty: it set a standard for the men he worked with. They'd be inclined to dress more casually, but for his example, and now he was annoyed that he'd been forced to come to South Middleton in his holiday clothing: light slacks, open-necked shirt, loafers on his feet.

His soft, autumn-brown eyes were flecked with annoyance now as he stared down at the activity on the site. 'So what've we got?' he asked.

The detective-constable who had accompanied him cleared his throat nervously. 'Story came in early this afternoon, sir. Body found near the hedge—down in that declivity, over there. Farmer with his dog rounding up some stray sheep. Dog got excited, farmer went over. Apparently, he was sick.'

Farmers normally had strong stomachs, Culpeper thought to himself. 'Bloody, was it?'

'Hacked around, sir.'

'Hmm. Who organized the scene of crime unit?'

'Chief Constable called in Detective-Inspector Farnsby, sir, since you wasn't around. Then the call went out for you.'

Culpeper grimaced at the scene in the field below. 'It looks pretty chaotic down there. Let's hope young Farnsby's got it sorted out.' He grunted, then turned back to the car. 'All right, let's get down there.'

They skirted the hill, the shadows lengthening as they drove down into the narrow road that looped towards the field. The hedgerows had not been cut and rose briar lay tangled in straggling hawthorn, summer flowers thick in the long grass at the sides of the road. They'd stopped spraying pesticides, Culpeper thought, and there was more life in these verges now.

Even if there was death under the hedgerow.

The driver parked the car just inside the open gate. A couple of journalists recognized him as he came forward and, dragging a photographer behind them, advanced towards Culpeper, braying the usual inane questions. He cut them off sharply, and then frowned as he saw the television crew setting up just twenty yards from the screens that were being erected. Culpeper beckoned to one of the uniformed constables standing nearby.

'Sir?'

Culpeper jabbed an irritated finger in the direction of the television crew. 'Get them back.'

'Back, sir?'

'Way back, copper! And where's Inspector Farnsby?'

The police constable hesitated, glanced uncertainly towards the television crew, then looked wildly around.

'There he is, sir, near the tree over there. You want me
to—'

'Just get those television people the hell out of there!'

John Culpeper strode across the short, springy grass
towards the huddle of men near the ancient beech tree in
the hedge. As he neared them, one looked up and turned
quickly to say something to the others. The tall, lean man
in the dark grey suit immediately detached himself from
the group and hurried forward. He gave a surreptitious
glance at his watch as he did so, and an unreasoning, slow
anger moved in Culpeper's chest.

'Glad you're here, sir.'

'Don't you know better than to let that crew near the
scene of crime, Farnsby?'

Vic Farnsby was just thirty-two years of age now. He
had come in through the accelerated programme that was
available for young graduates, and had received two com-
mendations in the first three years. It had led to his quick
transference to plain clothes and a swift rise to the rank of
Inspector. He had been tipped for further promotion at an
early date, and was certainly seen by the Chief Constable
as a high flyer, but in the six months he had been working
with John Culpeper there had been little evidence of qual-
ity. The reports Culpeper had put in to the Chief Constable
had been so non-committal that the Chief had called Culpeper in.

'So what's the problem?' he had asked.

'You tell me, sir. I know Farnsby's got a good reputation,
but all I can say is what I've stated in my report. I can't
get to grips with the lad; there are times when his heart
doesn't seem to be in his work. His timekeeping's a bit odd
sometimes—and once in a while he seems to be miles away
when we're discussing a case. Some of his follow-up work
is . . . uncommitted, somehow. I just tell it as I see it, sir.'

The Chief Constable had leaned back in his chair, regarding Culpeper thoughtfully. 'You think there's a personality clash here, John?'

Culpeper knew what the Chief Constable was hinting

at: Culpeper, mid-forties, risen slowly through the ranks, envious of the smooth promotion of a younger man. He resented the suggestion, but bit his lip. 'Not as far as I'm concerned, sir.'

And though the Chief Constable had suggested he might go a little more easy on his colleague, Culpeper was not prepared to take that to heart when Farnsby transgressed, as he had now.

Farnsby's tanned features paled. He glanced across the field and grimaced. 'I was dealing with local coppers who were first on the scene. I didn't have time—'

'You haven't even got the screens up properly yet! Let that pack of wolves near the scene and they'll trample everything within sight!' Culpeper grimaced as he watched the police constable arguing with the television crew, insisting they remove themselves to some distance. They'd be complaining about the public's right to know, he could guess. He turned back to Farnsby, still disgruntled. 'What time was the body found?'

'We got the call about lunch-time, sir. But by the time the scene of crime unit arrived it was well into the afternoon, and we had to clear the site of gawpers from the village.'

'You didn't get the local bobbies to clear it?'

'There wasn't time, sir. I was out on call at Newcastle; Enderby and Sallis are on a case up at Berwick; it took me time to get out here. And you were not around, sir.'

Culpeper's eyes hardened. He stared at Vic Farnsby. His features were of a saturnine cast, and his eyes were a pale, washed-out blue. He was intelligent, sharp-witted, apparently, but there was a weakness about his mouth that Culpeper disliked. It was probably prejudice on his part, but he felt there was something hollow in Vic Farnsby, the kind of weakness somewhere in the man's emotional make-up which would make him ineffective in the long run, whatever the Chief Constable might think. But he had been asked to go easy: maybe he should reserve his judgement. Certainly he should not rise to the quiet gibe about his unavailability.

'What's the confab about over there?' Culpeper asked, changing the subject.

Farnsby's face was flushed. He nodded towards the small group he had left. 'It's two of the lads, sir, and the police surgeon. We were having a look at a piece of cardboard.'

'What?'

Farnsby made no reply but gestured to Culpeper and the two men walked across to the group. The others fell silent as Culpeper approached. They were staring at something lying on the grass at their feet.

'What the hell is that?'

'It's a piece of cardboard, sir. But there's something written on it.'

'Is this where it was found?' Culpeper asked, glancing across the thirty feet distance to the screens around the declivity.

There was a short silence. Farnsby cleared his throat, but it was the police surgeon who answered. 'One of the television crew picked it up, brought it across to us here.'

Culpeper felt a slow anger well up inside him. He put a clamp on his tongue and his temper. After a moment he said slowly, 'Where did they find it?'

The police surgeon looked at him with a quizzical expression, then raised his chin coolly, gesturing towards the hedge. 'Not far from the body would be my guess.'

'And it took a bloody television technician to find it!' Culpeper ground out. 'What the hell were *we* doing?'

No one answered. Culpeper glared at Farnsby but said no more: it could wait for his report, and damn the Chief Constable. He looked down at the cardboard. It was about eighteen inches square and a word had been written on its face in a large, sprawling hand; a damp stain had spread over almost one third of the card however, and the last few letters would seem to have been virtually obliterated.

'And what is supposed to have happened there?'

The police surgeon smiled thinly. 'The technician who brought it across to us held it delicately, between finger and thumb.'

'What's that supposed to mean?'

'My guess would be that the farmer's dog—the one who found the body—probably got over-excited and relieved himself over the card. Dogs have no regard for the proprieties.'

Farnsby shuffled uneasily, avoiding Culpeper's eye as one of the constables chuckled, unwisely. 'It should be OK, sir. Forensic will be able to make out the obliterated letters.'

Culpeper knew this was not going to be his day. He took a deep breath: it would not do to bawl Farnsby out in front of the other officers. But he had every intention of making his feelings clear at a later stage. 'All right, so what do the letters we've got amount to?'

Farnsby shuffled, and glanced around at the others. 'God,' he said.

'What?'

'G-O-D, sir. God.'

'So are we dealing with a religious slaying here? And has the identity of the culprit been pointed out to us already? Is that the theory?' Culpeper asked sarcastically.

The men around him said nothing. The police surgeon managed a hard-edged, unpleasant smile. 'Religious, who knows? Ritual—well maybe that's a line worth pursuing.'

Culpeper glared at the surgeon. 'You don't seem to be too busy this afternoon.'

'I've done all I can for the moment. We're just waiting now for the meat truck. I was called over here by your officers to take a look at the card.'

'Well, now you've seen it, perhaps we can get on,' Culpeper said emphatically. He caught the eye of one of the constables and gestured towards the card. 'Get that back to forensic, fast! And let's have no more clowns getting their prints on the bloody thing.'

He turned abruptly, stumped away from the group and as Farnsby followed he turned to face him, some distance from their colleagues. 'This is a right cock-up, Farnsby.'

'Sir—'

'You haven't kept the site clean. You've allowed civilians

to trample over the field. You let the bloody media in. You missed an obvious piece of evidence and let it be found by a bloody television technician. His prints will no doubt be all over it and I suppose we'll see that damned thing on the six o' clock news tonight!'

Farnsby bared his teeth in defensive annoyance. 'I've already explained, sir. The farmer phoned the police from a public phone in the village, at the post office. He was overheard, he told other people in the village. Some wise-acre busybody phoned the television people. And then there was our manpower situation, and your own unavailability—'

'Leave it, Farnsby, leave it for your report,' Culpeper cut in, breathing heavily. He glanced towards the screens. 'So what've we got?'

Farnsby paused, eyeing him uncertainly, unwilling to let the argument go. 'A messy one, sir. Male, mid-thirties, unidentified so far. Stripped to the waist.'

'Hey?'

'Trousers, socks and shoes, but no shirt. A lot of blood.'

'Cause of death?'

Farnsby shrugged. 'The police surgeon had a look around, and pointed out a couple of things—which were pretty obvious anyway—but he's non-committal of course, at this stage. There is a head wound, looks like a single shot. Could have been what killed him.'

Culpeper stared at his subordinate. 'So what's this about all the blood, then? A single head shot—'

Farnsby hesitated. 'You'd better take a look for yourself, sir.'

He turned away and began to walk towards the screens that had now finally been erected around the declivity. Men stepped aside as he and Culpeper drew close. One of the constables standing just inside the screen walked out as they entered the area: Culpeper noted the young man's face was pale: he looked as though he was about to be sick.

Next moment Culpeper realized why.

The dead man lay sprawled in the short grass of the

declivity, near to the ditch that ran below the ancient hedgerow. His head was turned to one side, his sightless eyes staring along the ditch, his mouth sagged open in a hideous death grimace. There was a gun wound in his right temple: the bullet would have exited messily at the other temple, but the shattered head was screened by the ground.

'What the hell is that?' Culpeper asked, pointing.

A piece of iron stood up from the dead man's throat. It had been driven fiercely into the neck, pinning the man's head to the ground, as though to prevent the thrashing of a body in agony. There was no way of telling which wound had been inflicted first—the neck wound or the shot to the head.

But it was neither of these wounds that had caused a farmer to vomit this morning, or a young constable to turn green within the screens.

'Good God,' Culpeper muttered as his glance travelled down over the man's torso.

The dead man's arms were sprawled wide as though welcoming the mutilations that had been visited upon him. A violent blow had been struck down through the centre of the chest, opening the chest cavity itself. It was possible the man had still been alive when the mutilations had occurred, for the blood flow had been copious, across his chest, over his arms, and on the grass surrounding the body. And at first Culpeper could not see exactly what had been done to the man. When it finally became clear to him he felt his own gorge rise.

The man's chest had been split open down to the sternum: the two parts of the ribcage had been thrust back, spread wide against the sprawled arms, opening up the chest cavity in a hideous mess of gore.

The corpse looked like some grotesque parody of a bird, carved for a hideous, cannibalistic table.

When Culpeper got home in the early hours of the morning, his wife was awake but Culpeper was disinclined to speak. He took a shower, then sat, clad in his shorts, in the lounge

of his small bungalow with a stiff whisky in his hand. He
was unable to get the image of the corpse in the field out
of his mind.

He'd seen enough blood and mutilations in his time to
become relatively hardened. It had all become part of the
job. There had been the suicides in his early days—des-
perate heads placed on the coal tram tracks that ran past
the pit village where he'd been the local bobby. There had
been three in the first two years he'd been there and he'd
had to do the cleaning up. He'd become inured to such
sights, though the abused bodies of young children could
still turn his stomach in a mixture of anger and nausea, and
there was still the occasional fear, when he was involved in
a dredging of the Tyne, that the corpse that came out would
be bloated and damaged by the depredations of fish.

The South Middleton corpse was something else, in his
experience.

The mutilations were extensive and horrendous, but it
was not even their extent that lingered in his mind and
his imagination. It was the fact that they had not been
haphazard, a wild slashing in a blood-frenzy. The man
had been dying, possibly dead, when the dissection had
occurred. It had been done coldly, deliberately, and even
with a sense of purpose.

The whisky barely helped. The image and the horror
remained in his mind.

There had been some tidying up procedures to be carried
out swiftly that day. He left Farnsby in charge of the field
and the scene-of-crime unit, confident that the Detective-
Inspector was now worried enough to be, if anything, over-
conscientious. Culpeper himself drove down swiftly to
Newcastle, after a quick word with the man in charge of
the television crew. He went straight in to see the studio
head and insisted that no mention be made of the card in
the field until it was cleared from police HQ. A quick call
to the forensic laboratories in Newcastle warned them about
what was coming in and the police liaison officer, Detective-

Sergeant Evans, promised him he'd keep a close eye on developments, reporting directly to Culpeper.

Thereafter he was kept busy with the detailed procedures that were necessary: talking to the scene-of-crime-unit officers, going over the statements of the farmer, the television technician, and others who had been present during the first hectic twenty-four hours.

It was two days before he received the first report from the liaison officer at the forensic laboratory. When he got the call, Culpeper drove down to Gosforth to the laboratory, and shut himself away with the detective-sergeant in a small, formaldehyde-odoured room.

'So what we got?'

Evans sniffed, and took a sheet out of a folder on his knee. 'Not a great deal, sir, but the preliminary findings—subject to usual confirmation, of course—are that the man died of the bullet wound in the temple. Neat shot, close range—and a Walther PPK. Very professional, is the view. Controlled.'

'The mutilations?'

'A heavy, sharp-edged instrument. It could have been a big butcher's knife, or maybe a chopper. But there's at least one view among the pathologists that it was something even bigger, longer and heavier. A sword, in other words.'

'A what?'

'A two-edged sword, sir.'

Culpeper grimaced. 'Bloody hell! You mean an ornamental one or a real one?'

'Very real, very heavy, sir.'

'Who the hell walks around swinging a heavy sword?' Culpeper wondered aloud. 'And as for carving the man that way . . . anything else?'

Detective-Sergeant Evans nodded. 'The object thrust through the man's neck—again, it was done probably after the bullet in the brain. They've run it through the usual tests, and it's clean as a whistle.'

'But what is it?' Culpeper asked.

Detective-Sergeant Evans had odd, mottled eyes. They

were cool and serious when he replied. 'It has an arrow-head, sir. It's not an arrow, exactly, it's almost like the bolt from a stable door, with the end sawn off and an arrow head fitted. Polished, but fairly crude in construction. Here's a photograph of it.'

He passed the black and white print to Culpeper, who stared at it for several seconds. 'Arrowhead, you said? This is sort of leaf-shaped.'

'It's how the medicos described it, sir. Arrowhead or not, it's a bloody weird thing to do to someone you've just shot. I mean, sticking a bolt through his neck, and then carving him up that way. I think we got a nutcase on our hands here.'

Culpeper was inclined to agree.

'What about that piece of card?'

'Ah-uh. Here's another print: you can see the lettering there. The forensic lads didn't have too much trouble over the stained area. There was an impression anyway, which they could trace. Dog's urine had stained the lettering, but it could still be made out.'

'God.'

'Not exactly. Two letters under the staining. A-R.'

'What the hell's that supposed to mean?'

'Godar? I've no idea, sir. Maybe someone's name.'

Culpeper shook his head. 'Well, not the dead man's, anyway. We got a preliminary identification this morning. There was a wallet in the back pocket of the corpse's trousers. We've managed to trace him from a credit card. The guy's not been home—so it looks as though what we have is a Mr James Lloyd, farmer, of Matfen. Vic Farnsby is conducting an identification session today.'

Detective-Sergeant Evans shrugged. 'Whoever Mr Lloyd was, someone didn't like him one little bit. Disliked him enough to carve his heart out.'

'Was that what he did?' Culpeper asked quickly.

Evans shook his head in embarrassment. 'Sorry, sir. Figure of speech. No, the organs were intact. Just the chest opened, and splayed back.'

Culpeper would have expected a liaison officer to be more precise. But he could guess that similar loose conversations would be doing the rounds of the stations after this.

He took a copy of the preliminary report and studied it back in his office. In the late afternoon a call came through for him: the Chief Constable wanted to see him. Culpeper sighed: the Old Man would be wanting a status report, but it was far too early for him to produce anything satisfying. But no doubt the Chief Constable would be concerned at media attention on this sensational killing. The television news had gone to town with the item on the last two nights —though they had kept quiet about the cardboard—and mention had been made of the horrific disfigurement of the body. They had not, fortunately, been specific, because although they had got pretty close to the corpse, they had been unable to see exactly what had been done. And the farmer they'd interviewed had been too incoherent to be of much use to them—he merely said it had been 'slashed about, horrible-like'. He had been too shocked to look closely at the nature of the wounds.

When Culpeper presented himself at the Chief Constable's office he was waved to a chair.

'Sit down, John. I thought we'd better have a chat.'

'About the status of the investigation, sir?'

The Chief Constable nodded. 'Something like that. What have you got so far?'

'Preliminary lab report is in, sir. I brought it with me. We've got a few things to go on now, but it's all a bit weird.'

'So I gather.'

'Sir?'

The Chief Constable smiled faintly. 'Hear rumours, even in this office, John. And the television news has raised a bit of a rumpus, like the newspapers. This is going to be a noisy case, my friend.'

Culpeper didn't doubt it.

The Chief Constable was watching him closely; after a long silence, he said, 'Farnsby didn't do too well.'

Culpeper shrugged. 'Things happened a bit too quickly

for him. It was all a bit chaotic. Press and locals got there almost before we did. Messy.'

'But there was a . . . signature found.'

Culpeper's eyes widened. 'Signature? Well, maybe, of a sort. There was a piece of card—'

'Godar.'

Culpeper was silent for a moment; a slow anger grew in his chest. This was his investigation: he did not take kindly to leaks, even to the Chief Constable. Men with loose mouths could cause problems in an investigation. Quietly, he said, 'How did you know that, sir?'

The Chief Constable leaned back in his chair and put his fingertips together. 'Don't get your bowels in a turmoil, John. I've not been having tittle-tattle behind your back.'

'Farnsby—'

'No, I'm telling you, there's been no chat up here.' The Chief Constable's glance strayed to an open file on the desk in front of him. 'Godar. A pinning of the head to the ground with an iron bolt. The opening of the chest cavity.'

The heat had not left Culpeper. 'Sir—'

'It's happened before, John.'

'What?'

The Chief Constable sighed. 'What we've got in our parish isn't pleasant. We've received a visit from a character who's done this before—and on an European scale.'

Culpeper frowned and scratched at his cheek. 'What exactly do you mean, European?'

The Chief Constable shifted in his seat and leaned forward to scan the report in front of him. 'We've not heard much about the European business because it's been kept under wraps, but Interpol have been keeping their eyes open ever since they hit the problem in France. They've built up a dossier already, however, and as soon as the news broke up here we had a fax through, via the Home Office of all places! It seems this has happened before—in France and in Switzerland. The first mutilation case was about three years ago; the Basle incident two years since. But, more to the point, maybe from our point of view, there was a killing in Suffolk eight months ago. A local politician—it made a bit of noise. It's how the Home Office acted so quickly: they've been holding a file after an approach from Europe over the other two murders. It seems they all fit a pattern.'

'Suffolk?' Culpeper wrinkled his brow in thought. 'Are you talking about that killing at Dunwich?'

'Michael Jenkins—the local mayor.' The Chief Constable nodded. 'He was found on the headland, carved about.'

'That didn't come out in the reports—even within the police. No mention was made of mutilation, not in detail, anyway.'

'Interpol wanted it that way. There was a lot of noise over the first killing—in France. After that, it was hushed up: I guess there's always the danger of copycat killings. And it seems they do have some leads.'

'The Godar thing, you mean?'

The Chief Constable shrugged. 'The report I have isn't specific. But there were enough indicators to suggest we need to consult. I've had a call. The co-ordinator at Interpol is suggesting you should meet the man in charge at the Suffolk inquiry. He has Interpol support—papers from the Sûreté and the Swiss police. They seem to feel that a meeting would be desirable, so that common matters could be looked at, cards compared so to speak.'

'You want me to go to Suffolk?'

'That's about the size of it, John.'

'There's a hell of a lot to do here, sir.'

'And there's Farnsby to do it.'

Culpeper opened his mouth to make a protest, but thought better of it when he saw the gleam in the Chief Constable's eye. And perhaps the Old Man was right. Culpeper knew he couldn't handle the whole investigation himself—and besides, the fact that this appeared to be a sequence of killings made him curious.

It might be possible to make some short cuts, if there was a similarity between the South Middleton murder and that in Suffolk. And he was curious to know just what sort of details Interpol might have come up with from the killings in France and Switzerland.

'I'll just clear up a few things, sir, and then I'll get down South.'

Thoughtfully, the Chief Constable passed the file on his desk to Culpeper. 'I'd like to see this one cleared up pretty quickly, John. I don't like the idea of a homicidal maniac running around our patch. The media will have a field day with it and we stand to get a lot of stick if we don't produce results.'

But wasn't that always the case, Culpeper thought gloomily to himself.

4

Arnold had known it was going to be an uncomfortable interview.

He had told the DDMA that he had other commitments, that he wanted to take his leave as planned, but it had been to no avail: the DDMA had cancelled his leave as he'd said he would, and made a formal assignment of Arnold's time to the Birley Thore archæological investigation.

Which meant that Arnold had to face Jane Wilson and tell her he was forced to withdraw from the agreement he had reached with her. She had invited him to dinner; he understood there were to be other guests, so he thought it best to call at her bungalow in Framwellgate Moor early, and explain the problem to her. It was not something he wanted to say to her over the phone.

She was surprised to see him, standing at her door. 'Arnold! I'm hardly ready for guests yet! You're at least an hour early.'

Her snub-nosed features expressed her concern, and she brushed back a lock of her errant, short brown hair. She was a no-nonsense kind of person, Arnold had long ago concluded: she had strong opinions and was not unwilling to express them, and although small of stature there were

times when she could be terrifying, as far as he was concerned. Since the death of her uncle, Arnold's friend Ben
Gibson, she had taken on the running of the Quayside
Bookshop in Newcastle—Ben had left the property and the
business to her since there were no closer relatives. Running
the business took up most of her time, which was why,
a few months earlier, she had approached Arnold with a
surprising proposition.

'I know you don't regard my writing very highly.'

'I've never said—'

'Historical fiction is simply not your scene, I know that,
but I think you've always been prepared to admit that the
research I do before I start the writing has been meticulous.
Indeed,' she had admitted, 'it's really the bit I enjoy most,
the research rather than the writing, which can be a bit . . .
arduous. Anyway, I want your help.'

'I'm really not certain what I could do to help,' he had
demurred.

'The fact is, since I took over Ben's business I can hardly
find any time to work on my next book. As you know, I
helped him out part time before, and that was pleasurable,
but since he died and I've been running the place full time,
I've realized it was a major venture taking it on. The
ordering, the invoicing, the packing, the bookkeeping—all
right, I can leave some of that to Gladys, the hired help,
but taking decisions! Well, I just don't seem to be able to
organize myself properly.'

'Have you not thought of getting in a manager?'

'The turnover wouldn't make it a feasible proposition. So
I'm closing the shop down in the summer, for two weeks.'

'That sounds a sensible plan.' He hesitated. 'But can you
write a book in two weeks?'

'Of course not. But I can make a good dash at the
research, and that's the first problem out of the way. And
that's where you come in.'

He had had premonitions, and warily had said, 'Book
research is not my line, as you know—'

'I want you to take two weeks' leave and help me,' she

had announced crisply. 'There's no way I can complete the research myself, I could employ some young researcher from the University during the summer vacation, but your own insight, your own background knowledge, your understanding of the period would be invaluable to me. So, what I propose is that we take leave together, get up into Northumberland, rent a cottage outside Warkworth—I have in mind one or two I've seen there—and we could spend two weeks working together on research for my book.'

Alarmed, Arnold had shaken his head. 'I don't think that's at all feasible. I haven't planned my leave—'

'You must be due some.' She had stared at him challengingly, her eyes narrowing. 'You're surely not worried about sharing a cottage with me? They have two bedrooms, you know. Safe enough for a crusty, middle-aged bachelor and an awkward, confirmed spinster.'

He had flushed. 'It's not that at all. I just don't see how I can really help you. The kind of books you write—'

'There you are!' she had said triumphantly. 'It's just what I thought. You're prejudiced. If I'd asked you to come with me to date some old ruin for an architectural project you'd have jumped at the chance to get out into the countryside and examine some old stone or timber. But because it's for one of my books you back off.'

'That's not so! It's the . . . the . . . idea of, well, you know what—'

'You haven't even checked with me what I'd be wanting you to do,' she snapped in an accusing tone.

'Well—'

'I want my next novel to be set in the time of Henry II. You know it's my best period. I've always been fascinated by Eleanor of Aquitaine—'

'And Arthurian legends,' Arnold had murmured.

She grinned at him. 'Anyway, in my next book I want to encompass the quarrel between the King and Thomas Becket. That would only be a sub plot, of course—the background against which I would weave my fictional plot. But there are things I need to know, need to check on—and you'd be able to give me first-class assistance. The plot centres on the activities of William Fitzstephen, one of Becket's retainers—and the time of the Scottish troubles Henry had to face. I need to look at places in Northumberland and the Borders, get the feel of what life was like at that time, learn about some of the villages and towns that lay along Fitzstephen's route north, and I can do it myself, of course, but your eyes, and your knowledge, are better than mine. You could help me enormously, Arnold. And it's only two weeks . . .'

Two weeks in Northumberland and the Border country looking at ancient villages and fortified towers. She was right: he was attracted by the proposal.

'And it's all expenses on me,' she said firmly.

'Under those conditions, no.'

'But it's only fair. I've asked you, you'd be helping me—'

'Certainly not. If I come, I'll pay my own way.'

So in the end they had settled it: he would join her, help the research, but would pay his own expenses, because of the pleasure he himself would gain from the fortnight. Yet afterwards, he had the vague feeling he had been manipulated. Nevertheless, he had to admit to himself now, he'd been looking forward to the two weeks together with Jane Wilson with a certain glow of anticipation.

And now he was forced to tell her it was no longer possible.

'Drink?'

'Gin and tonic would be nice.' Not a drink he usually indulged in, but he needed his sinews stiffening.

'Right, well, help yourself over there—' she gestured towards the drinks cabinet in the corner of the sitting-room —'while I put the finishing touches to the creation in the kitchen. Have I told you who else is coming tonight?'

'Well, no, you haven't but I wanted to—'

'I came across an interesting and very charming man the other day down at the University library in Durham.' Jane carried on the conversation from the kitchen. 'He's called Arthur Dennis—he's a professor in mediæval history at the

University, and you know, you're an awful snob, Arnold, because *he* doesn't turn up his nose at my books. Said he'd read one or two of them and enjoyed them. Congratulated me on my "feel for the period", as he put it. So I thought I'd invite him this evening.'

'That's more or less what I wanted to talk—'

'Then there's rather a clever young woman—well, I say she's young but that's because she's twenty-eight which makes her a few years younger than me—who works at a small shop in Durham, selling antiques. She's got a remarkable command of the provenance of Victorian and Georgian antiques, and she also knows a fair bit about much earlier stuff and she sort of taps into the antiques network, you know what I mean? I gather she served her apprenticeship, so to speak, at the British Museum. She's called Annette Dominick.' Jane came back into the sitting-room, wiping her hands on a towel. 'I thought if she joined us as well, we could all have a nice chat about elderly things, the kinds of things that interest us all: old jewels, old walls, old ways and old fashions. Terribly boring for most people, but fascinating for us. Do you think I've planned well?'

'Jane, I can't do it,' Arnold said desperately.

She stared at him, and frowned, half-smiling. 'Can't eat my dinner?'

'Can't come to Northumberland with you.'

There was a short silence. Jane Wilson folded the towel, turned, went back into the kitchen and came out again, smoothing her hair. 'The cottage is booked, Arnold.'

'I have to work.'

'You'd organized your leave—you told me so.'

'The Director has withdrawn permission. He's rescheduled my time. I'm committed to work.'

'Doing what?'

'I'm seconded to an archæological dig at South Middleton.'

'I see.'

'I've no choice about it, Jane. I'm terribly sorry—'

'Seconded, you say? It's not your Department's work, then?'

'No, it's an independent project and I told them I couldn't do it because I was taking leave and had other commitments, but the Director overruled me, said I had to do it.'

'Rather more interesting than researching for a piece of dowdy fiction, I suppose.'

'Jane, that isn't the reason,' Arnold said desperately.

'Doesn't sound to me as if you argued the toss very hard with your Director. Simon Brent-Ellis, isn't it?'

'Really, Jane, I couldn't do anything about it and I really am very sorry —'

'Your gin and tonic all right?' she asked, and without waiting for a reply, turned away and left the room.

The evening was a rather brittle one as far as Arnold was concerned. Jane barely spoke to him, concentrating upon her other guests, and although Annette Dominick asked him about his own interests and appeared interested in what he had to say about mediæval stonework, he was too depressed to display his usual enthusiasm, and soon lapsed into an uneasy silence.

After a while Annette Dominick gave up. She was a lively, bright young woman, slender, with a slight cast in her left eye which actually lent her a certain attractiveness. Her face was long and her mouth wide so she was not particularly good-looking, yet Arnold found himself watching her a great deal. She, however, seemed quite smitten by Professor Dennis.

He was tall, immaculately suited, about fifty-seven years of age, with a flowing mane of white hair which he wore long and thick to his collar. His skin was tanned—he had just got back from an historical expedition to Greece, he explained—and he had a white-toothed smile that came and went easily. His voice was deep and vibrant, an actor's voice, manipulated and confident, and Arnold could imagine young female undergraduates trembling when he spoke to them of the past. He was certainly aware of himself, and was clearly pleased that he had become the centre of attention this evening. He toyed with his glass of red wine and lowered his head, gazing at Jane with a slight smile.

'So are you working on a new book at the moment?' he asked her.

Jane nodded. 'Yes, I'm just about to make a start. That's one of the reasons why I asked you to dinner, Professor.'

'Please, call me Arthur. So it wasn't just the pleasure of my company you sought?' he asked teasingly.

'I wanted to pick your brains,' she replied. 'It's even more important now, in fact, since my plans for research have had a setback. I've been sort of let down—'

'It's one of the hazards.' Dennis nodded wisely. 'You simply can't rely upon research assistants these days.'

Arnold glowered at his glass. Annette Dominick shifted in her seat and leaned forward. 'What period are you setting the book in, Jane?'

'I'm back to the twelfth century again. As you know, I've written about that period before, using Eleanor's story, but this time I wanted to weave in the catastrophic events surrounding the murder of Becket. And that's why, I must confess, Arthur, I invited you to dinner. You're an expert on the Normans, I understand—'

'Not just the Normans—their predecessors, the ferocious Vikings, too. Ninth to twelfth century is really my period. And I've written a book about Becket,' he intoned, leaning back in his chair with a self-satisfied air. 'It's called *The Road to Glory*. Perhaps you've read it?'

'I haven't really started my research yet.'

'I'll let you have a copy. Signed, of course.' He smiled, confidently. 'So what do you want to know about Becket?'

Jane turned to Arnold and in a cool tone asked, 'Would you mind passing the wine, please? Professor Dennis's glass needs filling.'

Arnold, feeling humiliated at her tone of voice, complied:

Dennis barely acknowledged the courtesy beyond a brief smile. There was something patronizing in the smile that irritated Arnold.

'Well,' Jane was saying, 'it's not just about Becket, it's about his entourage. William Fitzstephen, in particular.'

'Ah, the arch-deserter,' Dennis said.

'Why do you call him that?'

Professor Dennis sipped his wine and glanced around the table, checking that all three were listening to him. 'Because of the way he blew hot and cold over Becket.'

'I understood he was close to the Archbishop. What was the problem?' Jane asked.

Professor Dennis leaned forward on his elbows, raising one eyebrow for effect as he stared at Jane. 'Well, you have to remember that the London merchant's son, Thomas, who clambered up the rungs of the ladder to become Royal Chancellor in 1155 was a complex character. A lover of good food, the chase, expensive clothes, wine and song— though apparently never women if we are to believe the hagiographies—he attracted the most vociferous criticism in his time, yet ended up as a saint.'

'I thought the criticisms were of his relationship with the King—the worldly way he behaved then. Surely, once he became Archbishop of Canterbury—' Annette Dominick began.

'No, that's not strictly true,' Dennis broke in. 'When he became Archbishop, he was still seen as the King's man and nothing changed initially. The appointment itself was much criticized by prelates throughout the kingdom. The man couldn't even speak Latin! For the King to put his own creature into the see was an action violently opposed by the Church dignitaries, not least because Thomas retained his simoniac attitudes. He put aside the robes of the Chancellor, but he retained the archdeaconry, and his love of finery was not set aside.'

Jane frowned. 'His tenure was a successful one, though, surely, in that he fought for the rights of the Church against the State.'

Dennis laughed lightly. 'Fought for his own self-aggrandisement, you mean. You must remember, all accounts of his life were written after his death and much of the criticism was then turned aside—I mean, John of Salisbury, and Edward Grim, and Benedict of Peterborough and the rest, they could hardly show a saint in a bad light! No, after he became Archbishop, Thomas kept up his princely ways and his finery—though at some stage he donned a hair shirt underneath his costly robes and it wasn't until 1164 that he began to wear a full length, dark mantle. And his battle against the State was as much to protect his own holdings and status and pride as anything else. Moreover, his methods and his antagonizing of Henry II—well, the rest of the priesthood were appalled by his behaviour and throughout the rest of his short life they pleaded with him to, as we would say nowadays, "cool it".'

'Do you mean his support was limited in the Church, before his martyrdom in the cathedral?'

Dennis sipped his wine thoughtfully. 'That is certainly the case. Most people considered him a proud hothead and thought he should reach a compromise with the King; Henry himself felt the man was treasonous in leaving England to seek help and succour from the French court. They had been close friends—Thomas was almost a mentor to Henry—but the rift could have been mended had Thomas been prepared to compromise. But he resisted the pressures, and stubbornly went his own way, supported by his *eruditi*.'

'Who? I've not heard of that term,' Annette Dominick said.

'We have the names of twenty-two young men who were his close confidantes, his *eruditi*, his wise counsellors. They were the men who adored him, supported him, advised him to stick to his guns, and who influenced him in most of the bad decisions he took. Some of them stayed with him, right up to his death: Edward Grim, for instance, was still there at his side when he died. In fact, when Reginald Fitzurse swung the first swordblow at the Archbishop it was Grim who thrust out an arm to protect Thomas, and had his arm hacked off for his pains. Your William Fitzstephen, on the other hand, he was there too, but just watched. And he hadn't been around for a while, anyway.'

'How do you mean?' Jane asked.

'It's clear there were jealous divisions in Thomas's clique: his court was like any other, with dissension, petty squabbles, favourites, and comings and goings. A number of the *eruditi* abandoned their master when he went into exile in France, but William Fitzstephen in a sense was the worst. It's to him we owe a great deal, for his account of Thomas's life—Fitzstephen's *Vita*, written in 1174. But he was quite a turncoat, for all that. He was Thomas's friend, a *dictator*, or drafter, in his chancery, his subdeacon and occasionally his advocate in court. But he deserted Thomas after 1162, and returned to the King when Thomas went into exile. Do you think you can work this into your book, Jane?'

'It's fascinating,' she breathed, maybe for Arnold's benefit. 'Do go on. You'll be making my research so much easier. So Fitzstephen abandoned Thomas?'

'That's right. He made his time with Henry again. But, oddly enough, he was back with Becket towards the end of 1170 and was actually in the cathedral when de Morville and the other murderous knights burst in.'

'He didn't try to prevent the murder?'

'Well, let's be fair about this. They were all scared to death. They had warning of the murderers' intentions and pleaded with Thomas to run to safety, in fact, but the Archbishop was a stubborn man. There's a school of thought that thinks maybe he was by now actually seeking martyrdom. Fitzstephen certainly saw the killing. And then, guess what? He went back to court and made his peace with Henry. He must have had something about him, because he was welcomed back again, to become Sheriff of Gloucester from 1171 to 1189, and an itinerant justice as well.'

'How did he get away with it, bouncing back and forth between King and Archbishop?' Annette Dominick marvelled.

'Who knows?' Dennis mused. 'But it was probably this

second "apostasy" that would explain the suppression of his name and role in Thomas's life by all the other early biographers. He wrote his own *Vita* independently of all the others, and with quite a different slant. And this is the man you want to use in your book?'

Jane nodded. 'That's right. I think maybe I could work the climactic murder and Fitzstephen's part in it into the last section. But I also want to use him in the period before he was in Henry's service again. In between the first and second apostasy.'

'In what sense?'

'There is a tradition in the north that Thomas's position was secured at one stage, in some way, by Fitzstephen. It's supposed to have occurred in Northumberland.'

'It doesn't appear in his *Vita*,' Dennis replied solemnly, 'and one would have thought he'd have taken the opportunity for self-aggrandisement.'

Professor Dennis would know all about that, Arnold thought sourly.

'So you don't give it credence?' Jane asked.

Professor Dennis shrugged deprecatingly. 'I have a feeling you've got the story wrong. There's another version— it was the life of the Bishop of Durham, Hugh le Puiset, that Fitzstephen saved. It's more likely: he could have been in the area on the King's business, summoning Hugh le Puiset to the coronation of the King's son. Durham and York were used for the coronation, you see—a mortal insult to Thomas who claimed the ancient privilege for Canterbury.'

'He could hardly exercise the privilege when he was exiled in France,' Jane murmured.

'That was one of the bones of contention. Henry wanted his son crowned, to ensure the succession, but Thomas wouldn't come out of his abbey bolthole in France.'

'And the Bishop of Durham story?'

'The story has it that Fitzstephen came north to summon the Bishop of Durham, who was on pilgrimage to Lindis-farne. Then, when Fitzstephen was making his way back through the county he was ambushed by a band of Scottish raiders. He escaped, to warn the Bishop that the raiders were in the area, though he is reputed to have lost most of his baggage and other valuables in the skirmish. But we have only one source for the story, and its provenance is doubtful.'

Arnold leaned back. Professor Dennis was well launched now, and he was clearly about to spend the rest of the evening talking about William Fitzstephen, Thomas and the quarrel with the King. Arnold was interested, but also somewhat miffed. Jane was sitting chin in hand, gazing almost adoringly at Dennis in the way the Professor's female undergraduates undoubtedly would. Arnold was annoyed: he thought better of Jane—she seemed to be behaving like a starstruck adolescent. He had a vague suspicion she was doing it only to irritate him, to repay him for his seeming disloyalty and weakness, but that made him no less disconsolate.

He poured himself another glass of wine and ignored Dennis's half-empty glass. It was a hollow, petulant gesture, and Jane glanced at him with a thinly veiled contempt in her eyes.

For Arnold, the evening dragged unbearably.

It was almost midnight when the dinner-party broke up. To his surprise, Jane put her hand on his arm as he was about to leave. 'You've a long drive ahead of you, back to Morpeth. Why don't you stay the night?'

Arnold was reluctant, but she seemed to take his assent for granted, said good night to Professor Dennis and Annette Dominick and closed the door. She went back to the living-room and poured herself a brandy, offering one to Arnold. 'You won't be driving, so you can indulge yourself.'

Little mollified, Arnold accepted the drink. 'You sure it's OK for me to stay?'

'You've used the spare room before now. You were drunk then too, as I recall.' Then, suddenly, she seemed to hear

the sharpness in her voice and she smiled. 'I'm sorry. I
don't think you enjoyed the evening.'

Arnold lifted a shoulder. 'I thought your friend Professor
Dennis was . . . interesting.'

'I can use his knowledge,' she replied quietly. 'But I'm
afraid I was a bit rude this evening. You also were my guest
—and a friend as well.'

'I consider myself so,' Arnold heard himself saying.

'You're getting quite gallant, Mr Landon.' She flopped
into an easy chair. 'Anyway, you deserved the treatment.
You've let me down badly. But, I suppose I know you well
enough to believe you couldn't help the situation. So, let's
call a truce, hey? You let me down; I've treated you rudely
all evening. We're quits, all right?'

Still somewhat glum, Arnold nodded. 'I'll settle for that.'

'Now you tell me about this dig you're to be involved in.'

Arnold told her about Lindley's team and Birley Thore.
As he did so, some of his tension was smoothed away, and
he became more like his usual, enthusiastic self.

'It sounds interesting,' Jane said. 'In fact, that valley—
where the old Roman road ran—would have been the main
route north in the twelfth century. My William Fitzstephen
could have taken that road. So perhaps your eye will not
be entirely lost to me yet, Arnold. Would you keep me
informed about the progress of the dig?'

'I'm involved with bridge-watching rather than digging.'

'Even so—'

Arnold nodded. 'I'll keep in touch, and if there's anything
that might interest you, I'll let you know.' He settled back
in his chair to savour the brandy. Jane Wilson always had
the capacity to make him feel uncomfortable, but he valued
her friendship, and he was pleased that the evening would
now seem to be ending rather better than it had started.

'So, you tell me about the plot of your book,' he suggested.

'That,' she replied crisply, 'would be taking friendship
much too far.'

CHAPTER 2

1

John Culpeper waited uneasily in the sitting-room of the manor house in Matfen. He had driven across from Morpeth, leaving Farnsby to get on with other checking back with the scene-of-crime unit, but he felt it best that he should interview James Lloyd's widow personally. She had already made a statement, and had been taken by Farnsby through the trauma of identification, but now that a little time had passed he thought it would be possible to seek answers to some general questions he felt were necessary.

A grandfather clock struck hollowly in the hall. The sun shone brightly through the mullioned windows of the seventeenth-century manor house. Culpeper could see out of the windows, way across to the rolling meadows that were part of the farmholding, to the wooded slopes beyond. The Lloyds had had a good lifestyle, he thought. He heard the door open behind him.

Mrs Lloyd was of middle height, handsome, thickening somewhat now in her early forties and in tight control of herself. She was dressed entirely in black. He had seen a photograph of her as a young, smiling blonde woman with someone who was presumably her father: he was in the uniform of a brigadier. If she really came from a military background, some of it had rubbed off on her. She was controlled and dignified, stiff-backed: there were dark hollows around her eyes, but she kept her head high, and her features were composed.

'Detective Chief Inspector Culpeper,' he introduced himself. 'I'm sorry to come here bothering you with further questions.'

'I can understand that it's quite necessary. Please sit down.'

Quietly, he took her through the same old routine. She answered calmly. When he got around to asking her about the day her husband had died her answers were short and direct. No, there had been no signs of anxiety in her husband. He did not appear to be worried by money matters. She was not aware he had been under any pressure or in receipt of any threats. There had been no suspicious strangers in the neighbourhood. No, she hadn't seen her husband after breakfast that day. He had told her he had a business meeting in Morpeth.

'This business meeting—it was with a Mr Clem Stevens . . . ?'

'That's right. They had been considering certain investments together. I believe Jim was interested, but reluctant: he felt the business was possibly shaky. Certainly, he committed no money to it. They were still talking about it.'

'According to Mr Stevens, your husband didn't turn up for the meeting. Five hours later Stevens rang here, but there was no answer.'

'I had some shopping to do. I went into Morpeth, had lunch there, generally sort of wandered around—visited the hairdresser's. I would have missed the call—didn't get back until six.'

She had gone to bed early with a migraine—she suffered occasionally. She had not heard her husband return, and had not been unduly worried when she did not see him next morning. They slept in separate rooms—no, there was no marital discord—it was merely convenient. Accordingly, since he was often up early about the farm she was not surprised he did not appear at breakfast. By lunch-time she had become curious—by the evening she had begun to make inquiries. And then the police had come.

'Do you know of any enemies he might have had?' Culpeper asked.

She shook her head. 'I can't imagine any. My husband was—well liked, I believe. We had a narrow circle of acquaintances—we kept very much to ourselves, in fact. Jim looked upon this farm as . . . as a sort of peaceful haven. He'd had a fairly adventurous life, he'd lost some of his best friends over the years, and he enjoyed the relaxation and the peace of the Northumberland countryside.'

'He bought this farm about four years ago, I understand?'

'That's right. He'd accumulated some money during his service—and I had a certain amount from my own family. There were no money troubles.'

'He was in the Navy previously?'

Mrs Lloyd hesitated, then nodded.

'Is that a photograph of him when he was in the service?' Culpeper asked, gesturing towards a framed photograph on the mantelpiece.

'That's right.' She rose stiffly, took it down and showed it to him. 'That's Jim, there.'

He was standing, bare-chested, grinning into the sun, squinting slightly, a tall, broad-shouldered man with his arms around two other men standing beside him. It had been taken on a tropical beach: they were wearing shorts and no shoes.

'This was taken some time ago?'

'About eight years, I would think.'

'Where was it taken?'

She wrinkled her brow in thought. 'Malaysia, I believe.'

'Was he still in touch with his companions? The ones here in this photograph?'

Mrs Lloyd shook her head. 'No, he left all that behind him when his service was over. The life, and the acquaintances. All he kept were some medals; but he never looked at them, never dwelled over them. He'd been decorated, but he didn't even want to talk about it to me. It was a chapter of his life he closed, when he came here to Matfen. He did tell me once, though—'

'Yes?'

'He did tell me that this man here—' she pointed with her finger. 'He was killed in the Gulf War, Jim said.'

'Did he mention his name?'

'I think so, but I can't remember it now.'

'And the other man?'

She shook her head. 'As I've told you, he never talked to me about his service days. I never questioned him: I understood.'

Understood what? Culpeper thought. He remembered her family background—maybe it was traditional in her family not to talk about service records. Reticence was not unusual in servicemen, conditioned to keeping quiet with outsiders, tied into their own tight, clubbable world. He hesitated. 'Do you think I could take this photograph—get it copied?'

She stared at the frame in his hands. For a moment he thought she was about to refuse. Then she gave a small shrug, as though in the circumstances it was unimportant. 'I see no reason why not, though I cannot think it would be of much help. Jim had no contact with the friends of his service days. But provided I get the original back—'

'I'll see to that, Mrs Lloyd. I've troubled you enough. You've been most helpful, answering my queries. And . . . I really am very sorry, about your loss. We'll be doing all we can, I assure you, to arrest the person who—'

'Yes. No doubt. Can I offer you a coffee before you go, Inspector?'

Vic Farnsby was waiting in the small ante-room to Culpeper's office when the Detective Chief Inspector arrived. Culpeper caught sight of him through the glass panel in the door: he was standing in front of the window, staring out. His shoulders were drooping dejectedly and his face was lined. When Culpeper entered he straightened up, turned, and composed his features. He followed Culpeper into the room and took the seat in front of Culpeper's desk. If he really had been dejected, the emotion was now masked and he was in control of himself.

In two hours' time Culpeper would be on his way south, as the Chief Constable had suggested. Before he left, he wanted to check what Farnsby had found out. The

Detective-Inspector sat with an open notebook on his knee.

'All right, let's start with the dead man himself,' Culpeper suggested.

'All pretty straightforward,' Farnsby replied crisply. 'Bought the Matfen manorhouse about four years ago: prior to that, lived in York. Brought up at Beverley, in fact, so he was a Northern man. Not an experienced farmer, so he used a manager—'

'Checked on him?'

'Yes, sir. No problems, far as I can see. He was out in the west pasture most of the day with two other men . . . The farm itself makes a small profit, it seems, though Lloyd was more of a gentleman farmer than anything else. Served in the Navy—'

'Yes, I've got a photograph from the widow, so you'd better get it copied. You'd better check on the others in the photograph. Any problems about Lloyd's service record?'

Farnsby shook his head. 'Not that I'm aware of.'

'You contacted the Ministry of Defence?'

Farnsby's eyes were hooded. 'Well, no, not really.'

'We need details of his record,' Culpeper sighed. 'Get on to it.'

Farnsby nodded reluctantly. 'I've been spending my time checking on this so-called business partner, Clem Stevens.'

Culpeper ignored the defensive tone: a copper had to keep several balls in the air the same time. 'Have you got anything?'

Farnsby shrugged. 'There's a sort of smell about the guy. It seems he and Lloyd were having discussions about opening a riding school and racehorse stables in Yorkshire. Stevens is a good talker. He insists he's got a good thing going, but there's something odd about him. He drives a flash car, but it's like it's front, you know? I've got the impression he's a bit strapped, really, and was hoping his deal with Lloyd would go through to help him over a hurdle.'

'You running a check on his financial status?'

'Trying to.'

'Do it. The two could have quarrelled—if he needed the money and Lloyd had promised it . . .'

'He'd certainly been pressing Lloyd to put some money into the stables, but so far there was no commitment.'

'They were due to meet the day Lloyd died, I understand,' Culpeper said.

'That's right. They'd arranged to meet at Stevens's office in Morpeth, but Lloyd didn't show at the scheduled time. Stevens says he had another appointment—I checked that, and it was true—up in Alnwick, and that kept him out most of the day. He rang the Lloyd house in the late afternoon, but there was no answer.'

'Mrs Lloyd says she was out.' Culpeper paused. 'How long was Stevens in Alnwick on business?'

'Over lunch, I think. After that, I'm not sure.'

'Why not?'

Farnsby hesitated. 'I . . . I didn't ask him how long the meeting went on.'

Culpeper rose and stretched. He walked around the office, stared at the back of Farnsby's head. The Detective-Inspector worried him. He had a good reputation, yet his work was slapdash. 'You'd better complete the investigation of Stevens's movements. And get Lloyd's service record. What about the lab reports?'

'Preliminary still.'

'Chase them up.' Culpeper hesitated. Maybe he was being too demanding, too hard on the young man. 'Farnsby, is everything all right with you?'

The man's back stiffened. 'What do you mean, sir?'

'Are you OK? In yourself, I mean.'

Farnsby turned his head, stared at Culpeper with cool, narrowed eyes. 'I'm fine. No problem.'

But there was something there. Culpeper frowned. It was probably none of his business—Farnsby's touchiness suggested that if there were any problems, they were personal. Even so, Culpeper had to make sure it had no effect upon the investigation.

'All right, that's good,' he muttered, dismissing the matter for the moment. 'I'll be off now, got to get home and packed, then down to Suffolk. You get on with the Stevens thing and find out what he was up to during the afternoon. We don't have a positive time of death yet, so check his movements closely.' He began to walk towards the door. 'I'll be back in a couple of days. You need me, you can get me through the Suffolk HQ.'

The police driver took an unclassified road leading off the Blythburgh to Westleton road and took them through a dark forest area, passed the Victorian church and the ruined chapel of the twelfth-century leper hospital and entered the one straggling street of the village. The driver stopped outside the Ship Inn, and Detective Chief Inspector Castle grunted.

'Come on, let's take a break. I could do with a beer and a sandwich before we go any further. They do great fish and chips here, if you prefer something more substantial.'

'Sandwich will be fine,' Culpeper replied.

Castle was about Culpeper's age and of a similar background, having risen through the ranks slowly, with no short cuts to promotion. He had a soft Suffolk burr, heavy features and a completely bald head, apart from some reddish fur above his ears. His mouth was friendly, his speech a little dogmatic, but that could have been the job: there was a tendency, Culpeper knew, for men to develop such a trait almost as a defence against uncertainty.

They entered the pub and took a seat against a wall hung with fishing nets and photographs of old Dunwich, emphasizing the tourist interest that would fill the bar during the summer months. Castle ordered a couple of lagers and some beef sandwiches. He took his seat beside Culpeper, heavily, grunting as he eased his weight on to the narrow wooden chair. 'First time in Dunwich?'

'That's right.' Culpeper smiled. 'Not much to it, is there?'

'Just the one street, me old son, and that leads straight down to the shore—fishing boats, shore winches, a smokehouse and that's about it. It was once a great port, of course.'

'Really?'

'The Romans built the first port, and nine hundred years ago Dunwich was the capital of East Anglia. In the twelfth century it stationed as many galleys as London. But from then on, the sea took over.'

'Erosion?'

'That's about the size of it. The harbour silted up, the sea reached the market place, refused to stop and eventually engulfed eight parishes and nine churches. Must have left a few unemployed vicars. The last to go was All Saints— they took the roof off in the late eighteenth century and dismantled the tower in 1923. The cliff was unstable, you see: once the rock has been undercut by the waves, the cliff comes crashing down. So now, all Dunwich amounts to is a small village crouching behind a shingle bank and a crumbling cliff.'

Culpeper bit into his sandwich. 'But a centre for tourists, I've no doubt. I suppose there'll be the usual stories of bells tolling under the water and all that sort of thing.'

Castle nodded and grinned. 'Of course. But that's old wives' tales. The parishes would have been dismantled and the stone re-used. And the shingle covers everything, anyway. But they still dredge up Roman coins and other bits and pieces from time to time. You'll get the chance to see the way it happens, the erosion, I mean. We'll be going up on the cliff top.'

'That's where the killing took place?'

Castle leaned back in his chair and took a long pull at his lager. 'That's where we found the body. As to where the actual killing took place, that's another story. My guess is the guy was shot somewhere else, and the body brought up to the cliff top, and dumped near the monastery walls.'

'Why?'

Castle shrugged. 'Your guess is as good as mine.'

'What do you have on the dead man?'

'Nothing that helps very much. I mean, he was a public figure, so we know a lot about him. He was called Michael Jenkins. He was born in Bishops Stortford and made a living as a solicitor in the town—a good living too, it seems, because he ended up pretty well off, though his wife brought some money into the family as well. Anyway, he ended up in a large house just outside Southwold and became very much a local politician: had a stint as mayor, that sort of thing. A few years back, after his wife died—no children— he stood for Parliament as a Liberal, but didn't make it. Even so, he was a pretty well known character in this area, and his killing caused quite a stir.'

'Any obvious suspects?'

Castle shook his head. 'No one likes politicians; no one believes them, or trusts them—and we always assume they've got skeletons in their closets. But our friend Jenkins, he must have been the exception. A blameless life, it would seem.'

'What about his practice?'

'You mean did he help put away any villains who might have borne a grudge? Naw, he didn't have that sort of practice. It was mainly conveyancing and matrimonial. And though disappointed wives and violent husbands can get a bit awkward when divorce cases don't go the way they like, they don't end up shooting people and then carving them up.' He paused, eyeing Culpeper for a moment. 'I gather your candidate was pretty badly mauled, like ours.'

'That's one way of putting it.'

'You got any thoughts about it?'

Culpeper shook his head. 'Not at this stage. Why the hell anyone should cut a corpse about that way I've no idea. And you?'

Castle took a deep breath. 'When I saw the body up on the cliffs, I gagged. And it seems it's not the first time— you'll see the reports when we get back to my office. But though the killings are pretty identical, everyone seems to be at a loss. Even so, there are some unusual features.'

'Such as?'

Castle heaved himself to his feet, draining his glass as he did so. 'I'll show you later. Let's go take a look at the place we found the body, first.'

The driver was still sitting in the car. Castle jerked his thumb to signify the constable could get some lunch while he was waiting and then led the way, walking down the single street of the ancient port. It was a grey morning and gulls whirled above their heads, moaning in the wind. Castle pointed out a narrow track that wound its way between the backs of the houses. The lane rose steeply, through straggling briar and hawthorn, and they climbed with the smell of bruised dock leaves in their nostrils, up the hill until they came to a level area on the cliff top. They paused at a small, fenced off, grassed area with a Suffolk County Council notice board inside the wire-fenced cliff edge. It explained the history of Dunwich and the depredations of the sea since 1250. Castle pointed to the edge of the cliff. 'Some friends of mine put a seat there, in memory of their parents. Just four years ago. Gone now. Like it will all go, in time.'

He turned and plunged back along the track. They wound their way through a thick wood of scrub and thorn and beech, catching occasional glimpses of the sea at the cliff edge, some twenty feet to their left. Among the scrub Culpeper caught sight of what appeared to be an ancient carved slab of stone, half buried, leaning sideways just ten feet from the cliff edge.

'What's that?'

'Seventeenth-century tombstone. We're actually in St James's graveyard. The church itself was swept away. The graveyard's all but gone. You can still find bones in the cliff, sometimes.'

He pushed on through the thickening undergrowth until they emerged in a clearing where he turned in to a wicket gate. Ahead of them was an open, grassed area, dominated by the ruins of a mediæval building and a wall that stretched either side of it parallel with the cliff edge. 'We've taken the direct track up, but there's a road over there which gives access by car.' He pointed to the ruin. 'Grey-friars Monastery. The shell is thirteenth-century, but there'll have been older buildings here. It'll go, like every-thing else, in time: the cliff erodes at anything from three inches to a yard each year.'

Culpeper closed the gate as Castle strode off across the greensward. He followed him until they were standing beneath the arch of the ancient monastery gateway. The facing stone had crumbled, exposing some of the rubble and flint construction behind, and scaffolding had been erected for renovation to be carried out. Culpeper pointed to a slab of stone in the entrance itself.

'That's where he was found?' Culpeper asked.

'The exact spot.' Castle stretched his neck, looked about him, sniffed at the sea breezes. 'Not a bad place to die, I suppose, but better ways to achieve it.'

'But why dump the body here?' Culpeper wondered. 'I mean, it wouldn't be long before it was found, I imagine. This would seem to me to be a fairly popular spot with visitors, tourists, men walking their dogs.'

'That's what I asked myself,' Castle replied. 'Your ordi-nary killer, he'll try to hide the body, conceal it so he's got time. Time to cover his tracks, get away from the scene, sort himself out. The longer the body's concealed, the less chance we've got of tracing the killer. Forensic work is more difficult; witness statements are less easy to come by; people's memories of events deteriorate. But this guy, he dumps the body out in the open.' He glanced at Culpeper curiously. 'What about your corpse?'

'In a field, under a hedge. But not concealed. And found within twenty-four hours, by a farmer.'

'Hmm.' Castle considered for a few moments. 'Anything special about the field?'

'How do you mean?'

'Well, is it just a bit of farmland? No tourist attractions there?'

Culpeper shook his head. 'Not that I can think of. Except . . .'

'Except what?'

'Well,' Culpeper said slowly, 'it's not a tourist place, but it is a site of special historical interest, I suppose.'

'What's there, then?'

'Not a lot to see, actually, but there are mediæval earthworks, I understand. It's the location for one of the north's deserted mediæval villages.'

Castle stared at him and nodded slowly. 'Yes . . . That doesn't surprise me. It sort of fits, really.' His glance strayed towards the crumbling mediæval walls of Greyfriars Monastery. 'I think we'd best go back and go through the files in my office.'

2

Detective Chief Inspector Castle rang through for some coffee to be sent in to his office while he waved Culpeper to a seat. The room was warm: clearly, its occupant liked to have central heating on even during the summer months. Castle put the phone back on its cradle, sat down and opened his desk drawer. He took from it a thick manila folder.

'So,' he said slowly, 'here it is. Confidential, top secret, kept under wraps. Interpol stuff—they like the cloak and dagger bit, you know, but in this situation I guess it's the sensible way forward. We don't want to show our hand too clearly: some details we need to keep to ourselves for the moment. We certainly don't want any copycat killings to start—muddies the waters. It also helps weed out the nutcases who want to claim credit for the killing.'

'Have you had many of those?'

'Three so far, for the Dunwich killing. None of them measure up. You?'

Culpeper shook his head. 'It's one problem we haven't hit so far, I'm glad to say. We don't want to waste time and energy.'

'I know what you mean.' Castle eyed the folder in front of him. 'It's a bastard, this one, though. Interpol were quick to get on to us once the Dunwich murder hit the wires. They recognized the treatment quickly, and their computers were humming. They'd had similar killings over there. I had a call from the Home Office—cooperate with the French police. I had to go over.'

'And *I* get to come to Dunwich. There's no justice,' Culpeper said, smiling.

'I'm not so sure about that. I didn't get to see much of low Parisian life—not the kind you can enjoy, anyway. The first killing was at Saumur.'

'I've been there,' Culpeper said. 'On holiday, some years ago. Magnificent castle on a promontory, overlooking the Loirc.'

'That's where they found the first body. On the lawn, in front of the gateway.' Castle paused. 'Should I go through what we got at Dunwich though, first of all?'

'That would be helpful.'

'OK.' Castle took a deep breath, leaned back in his chair and looked at the ceiling. 'Michael Jenkins was found stretched out on a slab of stone near the mediæval gateway at Greyfriars Monastery. He was sprawled out, arms wide. The cause of death was a bullet through his left temple. Neat job; short range, while he had his hands tied behind his back—marks on his wrists. Ropes removed before the corpse was dumped.'

'I've no lab report on the Lloyd killing yet, so I don't know if he was wrist-bound,' Culpeper said.

'We've identified the gun as a Walther PPK. Unusual weapon. Very professional killing.'

Culpeper nodded. 'And the mutilations?'

'First of all there was a piece of iron, like a stake driven through his throat, thrust deep into the earth—his head was slightly to one side of the stone slab.'

'What sort of point did the iron bolt have?'

'You say a bolt,' Castle replied slowly, 'and that's not far from the truth. Hand fashioned, from a piece of iron, about half an inch diameter. Quite heavy, about two feet long, and as for its point, well, a leaf-shaped piece had been welded to the end of the bolt. It could have been designed as a stabbing spear, or a crossbow bolt, or an ornamental arrow. Not really like anything we've come across before .'

'But that wouldn't have been all you found,' Culpeper said.

'Damn right,' Castle growled. There was a tap at the door and a young constable walked in with two cups of coffee. Castle waited until he had gone before he went on. Dragging his cup towards him, he said, 'It was a bloody mess—the man's chest, I mean. He'd been split open, carved right down to the sternum and opened up like a turkey at Christmas.'

'Or Thanksgiving,' Culpeper murmured.

'Eh? Yes, suppose so. God, it was a mess, the ribcage splayed out, blood all over the place.'

'But deliberate, not a wild slashing?'

'That's right. It matches what was done to your man?'

Culpeper nodded and sipped his coffee. 'Was there anything else?'

'Ah-uh. There was a tag tied around the man's neck. Sort of luggage label, almost as though Jenkins was being parcelled up to go through the post. It had one word written on it.'

'Godar.'

'That's the word.'

'Have you got anything on it?' Culpeper asked quickly.

Castle shook his head. 'Not a thing. No idea what it means; don't know if it's someone's name; maybe it's a biblical reference or something. Don't know. Suffolk coppers are not recruited for their detailed knowledge of the Old Testament. Maybe that's a failing in our recruitment policy.' He grunted. 'Some of these homicidal nuts think they hear heavenly voices—or say they do when they come to trial. You got any theory about it?'

'None.'

Castle opened the manila folder and extracted a plastic

cover . . . 'Well, here's the details. I've summarized them, but there's the photographs. Don't let them put you off your coffee.'

Culpeper studied the papers and the photographs in silence. The room seemed to get hotter, and he loosened his collar. Impassively, Castle watched him and sipped his coffee. At last Culpeper looked up. 'Much the same,' he said. 'Details tally, except we got a large calling card rather than a luggage label. Had the same word, though not so easy to make out—a dog had pissed on the bloody thing.'

Castle snorted. 'Some animals have no respect for the police.'

'What did you get from Interpol?'

Castle turned to the rest of the material in the folder. 'It's all here. Two other cases—single shot in the left temple; an artefact driven through the throat; horrific carving of the chest cavity; signature card of some kind, with the word Godar written on it. Oh yes—as I began to tell you, in Saumur the body was found in the castle grounds. In Basle, it was in a small wood, close to a rune stone.'

'A what?'

'You know, one of those thousand-year-old stones with carving on them. No one knows really who put them there, but they were probably memorials, sort of tombstones set up in honour of dead warriors. But you see the significance?'

'The locations?' Culpeper frowned. 'In isolation, with the Lloyd killing, I wouldn't have. My corpse was found in a field—I wouldn't have attached much significance to the location. But with Dunwich, the Basle site, and the mediæval castle in Saumur—it's like our murderous friend wants to lay his artwork out for display on ancient sites.'

'Kinky. Or maybe something else,' Castle suggested.

'Something else?'

'A message, maybe. But I'll come to that later. These are photographs of the men killed in Basle and Paris.'

Culpeper studied them. They were both elderly, and on checking the file details he found that one was sixty-three, the other seventy. 'How old was Michael Jenkins?'

'Sixty-four.' Castle frowned. 'And your guy?'

'Forty.'

'Doesn't fit the pattern.'

'Do the others have something in common?' Culpeper asked.

'All three in the same age bracket, as we see. But we didn't find that surprising. The guy killed in Saumur was called Everett Chesters. He was the seventy-year-old—a retired banker who lived in a house at the edge of the town, nice place, overlooking the river. He had a French wife and had retired to the area, living close to some of her family. It was the deal, apparently: she'd spent their married years in London, while he clawed his way to a vice-presidency in a City bank. Retirement was to be in France. He only enjoyed three years of it. Somebody then opened his chest.'

'Did they dig up anything on his background?'

'Like Michael Jenkins, a blameless life—if it's possible to say that of a banker. Next to lawyers, they must be the most hated men on earth. No, there were no skeletons rattling around. Rather a boring character, really.'

'What about the Basle killing?'

'Identified as one Samuel Conor. Born in Bermondsey in the late 1920s. He set up a small travel agency business after the Second World War and did well in the post-war travel boom. Really made a bomb in the 'sixties and opened up a chain of agencies: he was eventually bought out by a large Swiss-based travel combine, and they gave him a seat on the board, along with a million in cash. Once again, he didn't live long to enjoy it.'

'Equally blameless?'

Castle grimaced. 'Well, I wouldn't say that. He appeared in court a few times in the early days—usual stuff, holidaymakers dissatisfied with non-existent hotel rooms and salmonella in their egg and chips. As the business got bigger he was able to distance himself from such trifles. There was a bit of a scandal in the late 'seventies: a flurry over some share dealing activity he was on the fringe of but he got away with it. Those complicated fraud cases, they're hell to prove. So, really, if not blameless, well, nothing criminal that was proved. And neither of these characters seems to have transgressed, bimbo-wise. Maybe banking and travel agencies take up all your available energies.'

'And Michael Jenkins had no background, either?'

'Pillar of the community. Dry little lawyer, really, pretty humourless but hardworking. In the 'sixties got married, wife died of cancer.'

'So what connections have you been able to make between the two European murders and the Dunwich killing?' Culpeper asked.

Castle shrugged. 'First, the obvious one. Conor, Chesters and Jenkins were all English. Second, they were all three successful businessmen in their own right. The one made his pile in travel; the other in banking; and my man was a successful solicitor cum politician.'

'Is that all?'

'Beyond that, nothing. And your man?'

Culpeper thought for a little while. 'He doesn't really fit the pattern. He had a fair bit of money, but wouldn't have been in the same bracket as Chesters, Conor and Jenkins. He couldn't be called a successful businessman. He was trying to be a farmer, and maybe tinkering with the idea of setting up in a horse stabling operation. As for other links with your three, he wasn't the same generation. He wasn't retired. And he spent some time in the Navy. We're still checking on his service record. So in a sense, he doesn't quite fit the pattern.'

Castle sighed with a hint of despondency. 'If there is a pattern. We could be dealing with a random killer here. Maybe the only key is that he doesn't like Englishmen. If that's the case, we got a hell of a lot of people who would fit that description. We could start with the Welsh and the Scots. But it's not the thought we've been dwelling on.'

'What line have you been following?'

Castle put a thick finger on one of the photographs. 'The bullet to the head. It's a clean, professional killing. This guy knew what he was doing. The throat wound, and the chest carving bit, that's for show. It's an indulgence. Maybe meant to throw us off any scent we've got; maybe to suggest a nutcase, a homicidal maniac; maybe just to give us a trademark, like the label with the word Godar. Don't know. But we've been working on the theory that these guys were killed by a professional hit man. If that's the case there could be a pattern—the killer's been paid by someone. But who? The three killings before yours could have been linked in some way, by their backgrounds for instance, so we're still digging on that one. But we've come up with nothing so far. Nothing except that, like I said, Chesters, Conor and Jenkins were successful, retired businessmen, well respected heads of their families.'

'If it's random killing, we've got a hell of a job on our hands: it'll be more difficult to track our friend down.'

'That's so. And that's why I hope it isn't random—that there's a pattern to it. And I've got a gut feeling that there is.' He glanced curiously at Culpeper. 'You run a hotel check in your area yet?'

Culpeper's surprise came through in his voice. 'Hotel check? Looking for what?'

'Names in the registers.' Castle grimaced and rattled his coffee cup in its saucer in an irritated gesture. 'I have to admit, we didn't give that a high priority ourselves. But you know what the Froggies can be like—they can be damned efficient, sometimes. And they like to keep tabs on all the foreigners who use their sleazy hotels. Anyway, they did run a check, and they came up with an odd piece of information.'

'Yes?'

'There's a hotel in Saumur called the Anne of Anjou, right on the waterfront, directly below the castle itself.'

'I know it. It has a good restaurant listing.'

'It has more than that. They found a registration there that had been crossed out. It said Godar.'

'You mean the killer had had access to the register at the hotel?'

'Better still—he stayed there. Wrote Godar, and crossed

it out. Then, in the same hand, he wrote a name, underneath. Robert Dreng Baillehache.'

Culpeper frowned. 'You mean he was going to register
himself as Godar, maybe, then changed his mind, and sub-
stituted the other name. False, of course. The French ran
a passport check, I imagine.'

'*Bien sûr*, as they say. A week in France and I could speak
it like a native! Yes, they ran a check, but no joy. It was a
pseudonym. And the hotel management could remember
little about the guy—middle height, dark, that's about it.
They hadn't asked for his passport when he registered—
they're a lot less careful in that respect than they used to
be. Euro-travel, I suppose.'

'Credit card?'

'Not so careless. He paid cash. Stayed just one night.
Anyway, when the killing took place in Basle, Interpol put
through the information—because the details of the slashing were the same, and the little gnomes also ran a hotel
check. They came up with an odd coincidence.'

'Godar again?' Culpeper asked.

Castle shook his head. 'Not this time. But they did come
across an hotel entry in the name of John Dreng Hagger.'

Culpeper sat back in his chair. Absent-mindedly he
removed his tie, slackened his shirt at the throat, stuffed
his tie in his pocket. 'So what the hell's that all about?'

Wearily, Castle said, 'Could have been just a coincidence, but I have a say I've never come across the name
"Dreng" before, as a family name or a first name. But then,
of course . . .'

'Dunwich?'

'Precisely. Once we got the information from Interpol we
did our own trawl. Sure enough, the signal turned up in
Southwold, just four miles from Dunwich. Popular enough
with tourists, get a lot of visitors staying in the local hotels.
But no one remembers anyone turning up with the name
Dreng, before.'

'Before you found Michael Jenkins's body.'

'Right enough. We did our check after we got the word

from Interpol, and there it was. The night before Jenkins died someone had stayed at Adnam's Hotel in Southwold and signed himself in with the name Dreng. Except in this case it was Peter Dreng Crocker.'

Culpeper was silent for a little while. 'I don't understand the point of it.'

'Neither do we. Why should the murderer—if that's who it is—take the trouble to sign the hotel registers in that way. He uses a different name each time, but uses the middle name Dreng. What's the point? For that matter, what's the idea behind the Godar sign on the bodies, and its single appearance in the hotel register at Saumur?'

Culpeper shook his head. 'You're throwing that at me? You've been with this problem longer than I have. Haven't you come up with any thoughts on the matter?'

Gloomily, Castle muttered, 'Nothing at all, because it doesn't fit. To start with, the bloody body carving caper doesn't square in with a professional killer's approach—a hit man does the job he's paid for and gets the hell out of there. He doesn't mess around with dramatic gestures like calling cards, and bloodthirsty carvings of the guy's chest. And he certainly doesn't start going through some teasing routine, like leaving pointers in hotel registers. So I've no idea what the hell he's playing at.'

'And there's no thoughts from Interpol?'

Castle stood up, pushing his coffee cup aside, and walked across to the window. Moodily, he stared out at the grey skies, darkening with rain. 'Looks like we're in for a bit of a blow. Take away a bit more of the Dunwich cliffs, no doubt . . . Interpol? Well, there's a guy there called Lorraine. Calls himself a criminal psychologist. You know the kind: they'll work like hell to give you a profile of a killer, talk about his motivations and all that guff, and then when you've caught a guy they turn up in court and come out with all sorts of expert reasons why his psychological profile doesn't fit and is all to hell now they've talked to him. They even take voices from the sky seriously! Those characters get me steamed up. Anyway, he's had a talk with me on the phone. Speaks good English, even if most of it is jargon. He's got a theory. It's a real giggle.'

'What's he say?'

'M'sieur Lorraine believes our killer wants to get caught. Isn't that a laugh?'

Disgustedly, Castle returned to his desk. 'Our psychologist friend reckons that leaving the calling card is a cry for help; writing the names in the registers is an echo of that cry. The killer doesn't want to be identified by name, but by leaving a clue he's telling us that if we chase hard enough, if we apply our intelligence, we'll catch him, get hold of him before he can do any more mischief! Can you imagine!'

'There might be something in it,' Culpeper suggested cautiously.

'The hell there is! It's a load of rubbish.' Castle shook his head violently, took a pipe out of his desk drawer and stuck it, unlit, into his mouth. It seemed to plunge him even more deeply into gloom: probably because there was no tobacco in the pipe. He sucked at the stem, noisily, then plucked it out again in disgust. 'I could take the idea that the guy was laughing at us—but a cry for help! If he wanted help, why make it so obscure? And why be careful to stay only one night in a hotel, keep himself to himself, leave little behind by way of descriptions, and use this unusual Dreng name just to prove he'd been in the vicinity? And why the different names otherwise? No, our friend Henri Lorraine is barking up the wrong tree.'

Culpeper was not so convinced, but kept the opinion to himself. 'I suppose at this stage we should throw nothing out.'

'I suppose so. I'd even call in the clairvoyants if I thought it would help.' Castle dumped the unsatisfactory pipe back in the drawer, recovered the contents of the manila folder and refiled them. 'You'll want copies of these?'

'I do indeed.'

'I'll arrange it. They'll be available at your hotel by six this evening. You staying to eat at the hotel?'

'That's my intention.'

'It's not bad fodder there,' Castle admitted. He hesitated for a few moments, a wary expression on his face. 'You married?'

'Yes.'

'Then you'll know what life's all about. I'll join you for a coffee and brandy in the lounge bar when you've finished, but won't join you for a meal.' He winked at Culpeper meaningfully. 'Got to get home tonight, or my wife'll do to me what our guy did up at Dunwich. I've seen her wield a cleaver on a leg of lamb: I wouldn't want her to get ideas. So though I'll join you, I won't stay long—just get your views when you've read all the details in the file. Other-wise—'

'Yes?'

Castle heaved himself to his feet and gestured towards his desk. 'You can use our phone here at HQ to get on to your support in Morpeth. I think the sooner he starts a register search in the vicinity, the better.'

'Looking for an entry using the name Dreng?'

'Exactly that, me old son, exactly that. But where on earth that will get us all in the long run, who in hell knows?'

3

Arnold started his secondment to the Birley Thore project on the following Monday morning. Out of curiosity, and partly to inform Frank Lindley he was in place, he visited the fieldwork site first.

A small hut had been erected in the south-west corner of the field to serve as headquarters for the project and several tents were located near the hedgerows, high on the sloping ground. Arnold had parked his car in the pub car park down in the village, and had walked the short distance up the hill to the field. There were some cars parked in the lane leading to the field, however, a few of them relatively battered vehicles which suggested that Frank Lindley had already begun to employ labour on his dig—they were often impecunious students who were keen to make a pittance while taking part in an investigation of the past. Some would be archæology students, but many would be merely interested amateurs, sixth-formers from local schools.

There were about twenty people on site, as far as Arnold could make out. They had been split into three groups, each working on a different trenching site. As Arnold stood there watching them undertake the preparatory work Frank Lindley came out of the hut and caught sight of him. He raised a hand and walked across to Arnold.

''Morning. Glad to see you. No problem in getting away, then?'

Arnold shook his head.

'I wondered whether the Director would have changed his mind,' Frank Lindley said. He glanced at Arnold quizzically. 'Or whether you might have.'

'I didn't really have much choice in the matter.'

Frank Lindley looked somewhat sheepish. 'I'm sorry we put you in such a spot.'

Arnold relented. 'You weren't to know I'd made other commitments. It was the Director's doing, not yours. Besides, the problem's gone away, really. I've made my peace.'

'Your friend—the writer—she wasn't too upset, then?'

Arnold managed a smile. 'She was upset all right—but we've made up again. It's one of the reasons I'm up here this morning. I came partly out of curiosity, of course—I'm interested in what you're doing up here at Birley Thore and I wanted to tell you I'm starting the watching brief at the bridge this morning. But she also asked me if I could keep her informed of the work—tell her if you find anything interesting. So I thought I'd better have a word, to make sure you don't object to me mooching around up here from time to time.'

Frank Lindley's features split into a beaming smile. 'Hell, no, always glad to see you at the site. Any time you can spare from your watching brief down at the bridge, come on up. You'll be welcome. That goes for your friend too—Miss . . . ?'

'She's called Jane Wilson. She may well come up if there's an open invitation.'

'Fine. Anyway, would you care to have a look around now, and I'll explain where we've got to?'

'I'd like that.'

Frank Lindley gestured towards the north-western corner of the field. 'We'll make a start there. OK if I call you Arnold? Bit silly sticking to formalities.'

'Feel free.'

'The workforce is mainly made up of kids at the moment, few University lads and lasses, half a dozen sixth-formers from the comprehensive school,' Frank Lindley said as they strolled across the field, 'but we'll be losing them in a couple of weeks, and we'll have to draft other people in. The funding from the Department of Environment Ancient Monuments Branch will be in by then, so we should be OK. Right, if we just stop a moment, I'll lay out the plan for you.'

He pointed out to Arnold where he and his team had planned a series of trenches. There was a raised plot east of the original road line, laid by the Romans as part of the North Way through Birley Thore, which had later been extended by a narrow section of an associated road.

'That's where we started a new trench, to link up with the three we'd already investigated—the ones we were telling you about in the Morpeth office.'

'That's where the pit is.'

'Correct. But we're doing no more work on that for the moment. I thought it better—with inexperienced labour—to get the extra trenches dug so we can get a stratigraphical link. We'll be opening the pit thereafter, and I must admit there's a feeling of excitement about that. We feel we might make some significant finds there.'

'You've evidence?'

Lindley shook his head. 'Not really—but the gut feeling is strong, and it's not just me. As you know, Jill Ormond's picked up some Samian ware near the pit, but we have a feeling there's something more important in there. So we're eager—but it's best to wait.' He gazed around the site,

waved his hand. 'I've had to split the work force, of course
—Jill Ormond is down there, supervising that group . . .'

She was in windcheater and jeans, and had a woolly cap
on her head. He would not have recognized her from this
distance, and now she was in her element, doing work she
enjoyed, she seemed a happier person, laughing and joking
with the young men she was supervising. 'She's all right, is
Jill,' Frank Lindley remarked reflectively. 'She can get a bit
uptight in situations like that in the Director's office, but
her heart's in the right place. She should relax more—she'd
make a good wife, and I think she'd like that, but the right
man hasn't come along.'

He turned and pointed towards the trenching area in the
south-west corner. 'There's a sort of box area down there
which looks interesting. Mike Swindon's in charge. What
did you make of him, Arnold?'

Arnold shrugged. 'Seemed a very positive personality,'
he replied guardedly.

'Tough character. Bit of a chequered history, really. Brilliant mind—real expert on mediæval pottery. But he's . . .
well, a bit wild, you know. Violent temper. If things go
wrong for him, or if he's crossed, he's not above taking a
swing at you.' Lindley hesitated, glancing shamefacedly at
Arnold. 'I wouldn't normally talk about a colleague this
way, to a virtual stranger, but since you're almost one of
us, and your path will be crossing his from time to time,
it's as well to warn you. He can be subject to sudden shifts
of mood—gets surly if the work's going badly. And then he
can hit out, verbally or even physically.'

'Isn't that a liability on a dig like this?'

Frank Lindley shrugged. 'Maybe. But I know how to
handle him. And he does have solid experience and, like I
said, a brilliant mind and eye.'

Slowly, they walked across to the area Swindon was
supervising. It lacked the cheerfulness of Jill Ormond's
trench. Swindon had his head down, but the young men
working with him seemed sullen: Arnold had the impression

they had just recently been given the rough edge of Mike Swindon's tongue.

'Hi, Mike, Arnold's come up for a while to see how we're getting on,' Lindley said.

Mike Swindon straightened. His eyes were red-rimmed and his mouth was grim. He glared at Arnold. 'How we're getting on? We'd get on a bloody sight faster and better with some intelligent workers and fewer interruptions! I thought you were supposed to be down at the bridge.'

'Work's only just starting there,' Arnold replied coolly.

'Like here, then,' Swindon said disgustedly, glancing around at the young lads working with him. 'Some people don't know their backsides from their elbows! I really will have to get some other people in this trench, Frank—these kids are useless.'

Arnold wondered whether all they really needed was a little encouragement: they were unlikely to get it from Mike Swindon, he concluded. As they walked away from the trench he asked Frank Lindley, quietly, 'What's the problem with Swindon? He seems perpetually bad-tempered.'

Lindley shrugged. 'He feels undervalued. He was up for a professorial post at Bristol recently—he wanted the chair badly. He didn't get it—and he feels slighted. He reckons the successful candidate was less well qualified.'

'It may have been a personality problem in the interview,' Arnold suggested.

'Knowing Mike, that's very possible. He's got time off from Exeter University—he lectures there—to work up here on this dig, but he's niggled, can't get the failure at Bristol out of his mind. Makes him a bit . . . explosive. He'll get over it, in time . . . Meanwhile, everyone suffers . . .' He turned, and began to walk to the third trenching area. 'Come on, there's one of the team you've not met yet.'

A small group of students were working near the boundary fence removing a thin layer of topsoil and a scattering of small stones, recent accumulation over the last hundred years. In charge of the group was a youngish man in a green sweater emblazoned with the words 'Head Gardener'. He

was about six feet tall, thin, with a fresh-faced, cheerful
expression. He had light blue eyes that lit up easily, and a
welcoming smile. Though slimly built, he was well-muscled
and he moved smoothly, light on his feet. There was a
devil-may-care lift to his mouth that women would find
attractive, Arnold guessed. The lads working with him were
laughing at something he had said, leaning on their spades
and giggling at him. As Frank Lindley and Arnold approached he stood upright, smiling, and raised his hand.
'All right, lads, break time. The big boss has arrived, so we
don't want him to see what a mess you're making of the
site.'

He stepped forward to meet them, wiping his right hand
on his jeans. He grinned at Arnold. 'Colin Marshall,' he
said, and stuck out his hand.

'Arnold Landon.'

'Ho! Heard of you. In a roundabout fashion.' Marshall's
grin widened. 'They were all moaning about you, after seeing you up at Morpeth. I had the feeling they didn't want
to be saddled with you, but it could have been just an
impression.'

Frank Lindley laughed. 'That's a defensive attitude,
Arnold. Colin's the one we don't want to be saddled with
—but seems we have no choice!'

'Ah well,' Marshall replied, 'if I wasn't around who'd
make your coffee? Who'd organize your lives and sweep
up behind you? And correct all the mistakes you so-called
experts make!'

Frank Lindley clapped an avuncular hand to the young
man's shoulder. 'Quite right, what would we do without
you? Get on faster, maybe. Mr Marshall here, Arnold, is
our general factotum. No particular skills, of course, but
you know the saying, jack of all trades—'

'—master of none.' Marshall grinned. 'That's me, Mr
Landon. I organize the site, hire the labour, order the supplies, check on the security, keep the local authority sweet,
get the necessary permissions, supervise the preliminary
digging, arrange tourist visits, keep the vandals away, sell

photographic rights, liaise with local museums and keep the records of artefacts. And make the coffee. Otherwise, my time's my own.'

'Including Wednesday afternoons!'

'A guy has to relax,' Marshall protested.

'What exactly do you do to relax when you disappear every Wednesday?' Lindley inquired. 'Play bowls?'

'Too energetic. I just sort of . . . play around. Gives me the energy to undertake my responsibilities here.'

'To moan, and niggle and generally make a nuisance of yourself,' Lindley said fondly. 'Anyway, tell Arnold what you're up to here.'

Marshall glanced back to the resting lads and ran his fingers through his short, curly, fair hair. 'We dug an exploratory trench at the far end there and hit cobbles, so now we're stripping the area of the topsoil. It's the only way we can determine, sensibly, the area of what we think is a cobbled yard. Then, we'll get some idea of the extent of the structural remains.'

'There you are,' Lindley said approvingly. 'You've learned something from your association with me, after all.'

'Other than bad habits, you mean?'

Lindley laughed, and gestured towards the exploratory trench. 'Show Arnold what you've got there.'

Marshall walked across to the end of the area. Arnold followed. He was able to make out a cobbled surface, made of local boulders, deeply embedded in dark brown earth and sealed by a layer of sandy orange clay.

'We found some sherds in here,' Marshall said. 'We think the cobbled surface runs down for about ten metres, and there's probably a revetment with a terrace wall—see that mound over there? Mike Swindon took a look at the sherds and he reckoned they were sixteenth- and seventeenth-century, but in the deeper clay there are certainly remains of a much older village site. Dr Ormond thinks it's probably twelfth-century, but Mike Swindon is non-committal at the moment. This area doesn't seem to have any Roman remains anyway, not in relation to the Roman road.'

'What are the darker stains there?' Arnold asked, pointing.

'Carbon deposits, Mike reckons,' Marshall replied. 'The guess is that the later village houses were built on a site that had been fired at some stage.'

'Burned out?'

'Looks like it happened on a large part of the site,' Lindley intervened. 'Once you get past the sixteenth-century layers there's evidence of some kind of conflagration. We're only best-guessing at this stage, and we'll have to refine our theories, but what it looks like is some kind of catastrophe —twelfth, thirteenth-century—when the larger part of the village was burned out. It could have been accidental, of course, we can't tell yet, but equally it could have been a firing by raiders.'

'The reivers.' Arnold nodded.

'You'll know well enough that they were constantly harrying in this area, down from the Scottish border . . . They'd have come roaring down the valley, burning and looting at pretty regular intervals.'

'The Border raiders,' Arnold murmured.

'That's about the size of it,' Frank Lindley agreed. 'Anyway, back to work, young man. I'll show Arnold the rest of the site.'

They moved away and walked down to Jill Ormond's trenching area. She looked up as Arnold approached, and her face was flushed, her eyes happy. She looked almost beautiful. She nodded affably enough, but showed no inclination to speak as Lindley explained their interpretation of the trench site—the working part of a hearth, later demolished, a kitchen and a yard.

'Some burned flagstones,' Arnold pointed out.

'We don't think that's evidence of the conflagration,' Lindley demurred. 'More likely evidence of the fact it was a kitchen. What pottery have you found here, Jill?'

'Fifteenth-century,' she replied shortly. 'A few iron nails; not a lot else.'

'We expect to find more when we excavate the pit,'

Lindley said as he turned to walk away. 'Coffee back at the hut?'

'I'd like that,' Arnold replied. 'Then I'd better get down to the bridge. They should be starting excavations this morning.'

'Time enough.'

Lindley led the way to the small hut. Inside there was a table and six chairs, with a small cooking stove. 'We eat here in shifts—use the tents if it rains. We send down to the village for food, or go down to the pub,' Lindley explained, 'so all we need in here is something to heat water for coffee. Damned things . . . I always have trouble making these paraffin stoves work.'

Arnold lent a hand.

When the water boiled, Lindley made the coffee. 'Partly true what I said,' he explained. 'Colin usually breaks off to organize the coffee.'

'From what he recounted to me of his duties, he must be a good organizer.'

'Pretty good. Inexperienced, but learning fast.' Lindley handed Arnold his mug of steaming coffee. 'I've known him for years—his father was a manager with Shell, but often came on digs with me at weekends when we were young men. Colin . . . well, he was a bit of a disappointment to his father. Bright lad, but . . . lacking a bit of balance, you know? He went to university, started taking a Sociology degree of all things—his choice, didn't please his father, who wanted him to take a vocationally orientated degree, like engineering. Then, things got worse and they quarrelled badly. Colin got in with the wrong lot when he was away at the university.'

'Wild oats,' Arnold suggested.

Lindley squinted into his mug, thoughtfully. 'Well, maybe so. There was a young nursing student . . . he got her pregnant, I believe, and his father had to sort things out. But it was a bit more than that. There was a prosecution . . . drugs, you know? His father managed to hush things up, and there was no prison sentence, but it was a near thing. Suspended. Colin didn't get his degree and then dropped out of sight for a while after that: he spent some time wandering on the Continent, I understand, Germany, France, Switzerland, and when he came back to England he became one of our New Age Travellers—living off social security. Seemed to think the world owed him a living, as they say.'

'He seems to have pulled himself together now.'

Lindley sighed. 'Yes . . . The fact is, his father died three years ago—his mother had already passed away when he was a kid. Colin came into a reasonable amount of money— the house alone was worth three hundred thousand, and there was a fair bit apart from that. The trouble was, Colin's worst side came out. He blew the lot. It only took him about fourteen months and he had nothing to show for it at the end —not even friends. That's when he got in touch with me.'

'How did he think you could help?' Arnold asked curiously.

Frank Lindley frowned. 'I think he began to realize he needed a stable figure—a father figure, if you like. He'd resented his own father's control, but more recently came to realize that he needed someone to . . . set him right? I don't know. Anyway, he came to me, I took him under my wing—he's a bright chap, you know—and sort of got him involved in my digs. Basically, he's a bit weak in character and needs guiding.'

'He'll hardly make a living in archæology,' Arnold suggested.

Lindley nodded. 'That's right. But he spends a fair bit of time with Dr Ormond and Mike Swindon—he's a good listener, he learns quickly, and he's started working up a fair knowledge of artefacts. We've had a chat—I think what he has in mind is to develop his expertise, and maybe go into the antiques business in a small way. He's already built up contacts—goes to all these antiques fairs, that sort of thing. I've hopes for him. But . . .'

There was something in the way Frank Lindley's voice trailed off that left Arnold with the impression Colin

Marshall still had a long way to go, as far as his mentor was concerned.

Arnold finished his coffee. 'I'd better go down and see what's happening at the bridge. I'm not being paid to sit here drinking coffee, relaxing though that might be.'

'You're not being paid by us at all,' Lindley replied, smiling. 'And we really are grateful for your assistance. Call up and see us, whenever you can. And anything interesting we find, we'll keep you informed—you and your writer friend.'

The main road outside Birley Thore had been marked with cones and yellow diversion signs to send the traffic down a side road, through the back lane that ran behind the village, over a narrow one-way bridge to emerge on the north side of the village. Most of these small mediæval towns had back lanes: in the eleventh-century Norman burst of town planning they comprised the original main roads that tended not to enter the towns but to skirt them: accordingly they were narrow and winding between Saxon field layouts.

In later centuries traffic had started to move through the villages and towns, causing restrictions in the market squares that had never been built for traffic. The Roman road, however, had always run straight through Birley Thore as the main thoroughfare north, and the nineteenth-century road had followed the same line.

The construction traffic was already in place around the old bridge as Arnold walked forward. Agricultural contractors had been called in with their JCBs to do some earth shifting, clearing an area where lorries could turn, short of the bridge. Scaffolding was being erected, building materials stockpiled and various men in hard hats and bright yellow jackets were moving around the site with surveying equipment, notepads, site plans and airs of importance.

Arnold stood watching them for a while and then caught sight of a face he knew. Nick Summerby worked for the Planning Department at Morpeth and had been one of

Arnold's erstwhile colleagues. He was standing at the bridge end, arms folded, gazing abstractedly into the muddied, slow-flowing water. Arnold walked across to him.

'Hello, Nick.'

'Arnold! What are you doing here? Haven't seen much of you since you left the Department.'

'Oh, I've been out and about a bit. At the moment I'm holding a watching brief.'

'For the DMA? What's their interest in this widening scheme?'

'No interest really, it's just that I'm on secondment to the Birley Thore archæological project. They want to be kept apprised of what's happening on this site.'

Nick Summerby pursed his lips. 'There's been nothing said about any controls here.'

Arnold shrugged. 'The Management Executive at Morpeth decided apparently that the work has to go ahead . . . come hell or high water.'

'While the money's available.' Summerby grinned. 'Aye, that'll be it. So what are you expecting to see?'

'I'm not sure . . .' Arnold peered over the bridge into the swirling water, and glanced towards the nineteenth-century piers. 'As far as I can gather there was an earlier survey of the bridge in the nineteenth century.'

Summerby nodded. 'This bridge was built in 1834. It replaced a stone bridge that was in danger of collapse. I had a look at the old reports, in fact, before I came out here this morning. The stone bridge had been made partly redundant, apart from its dilapidated state—or maybe that's why it had become dilapidated. You see the course of the stream now?' He pointed to the far bank. 'See the declivity over there? That's where the stream used to run, I guess. In the old days it ran quite a different course, and consequently the position of the fords and bridging points would have been different.'

'Have you got a copy of the 1834 survey?' Arnold asked.

Summerby waved his hand in a mock courtier's flourish. 'Since when did the Planning Department not come always fully armed? Yeah, I got a dog-eared copy in my van. You want a look at it?'

He led the way back to the departmental van parked just short of the bridge. He opened the back and rummaged among the document cases he stored there. 'Here we are. Gilbert Stoneleigh. *Survey of the Birley Thore Bridge Reconstruction*, published April 1834.' He flicked through it dismissively. 'Not a lot of interest, really—bit of an amateur, our Gilbert. But you're welcome to have a look at it. You going to be around all day?'

'More or less.'

'OK, have a read. Let me have it back, this afternoon maybe, before you leave. Can't have outsiders walking off with valuable departmental archival material.'

'Outsider!' Arnold took the material from his former colleague and, armed with the board-bound document, walked away from the bridge to a wooden seat placed at the water's edge as a memorial to a former parish councillor. He sat down. The sun was hot now, but he was shaded by an old alder tree that sent its long arms out across the river bank. There were some ducks up-ending themselves in the stream, heedless of the bustle and noise emanating from the construction workers at the bridge itself and Arnold watched them for a while. Then he turned to the survey.

Nick Summerby had been right: Gilbert Stoneleigh had left out rather more than he had put in. The intentions of the survey were sound, but Stoneleigh's amateur investigation made the document less valuable than it could have been. It recounted that when the stone bridge was demolished a concreted mass of Roman artefacts had been exposed, built into the fabric of the bridge's eastern pier. The objects were listed: coins, brooches, implements and small statuettes, and some iron objects were also present. The discovery was unusual and important, and recognized as such by Stoneleigh, who was unable to provide any simple explanation for the mass but had left few clear clues for the modern archæologist. The precise location, description and later whereabouts of the artefacts were not given.

It was not clear from his account whether the old bridge had been completely demolished in 1834. That left open the question whether all the artefacts had been recovered from the structure at that time.

Arnold checked the mapping Stoneleigh had attempted, and shook his head. The amateur archæologist, or surveyor, had not shown how the new bridge had been positioned relative to the older structure. His notes remarked that the old bridge had been 'ill placed', but that could have implied it was not in alignment with the existing road and was therefore in a different location from its successor.

Arnold looked up to the work in progress. The road-widening operation might well give some answers to the questions posed by the 1834 report. As far as Arnold understood, the idea was now to widen the existing 1834 construction by some three metres. They would be adding reinforced concrete piers and beams to the southern side of the existing structure. It would call for the laying of new foundations, the raising of new piers and buttresses, and considerable excavations around the existing piers of the bridge.

Arnold explained what was happening to Jane a week later when he called to see her at the Quayside Bookshop, in response to her invitation. She intended leaving for the cottage the following day: she had cancelled one week of their projected programme because of Arnold's absence and pressure of work at the bookshop with summer visitors.

'They've already started work on the sheet piling,' Arnold said, 'driving it into the banks and the bed of the stream.'

'What's the objective?'

'They aim to create several cofferdams adjoining both piers of the bridge. Once they've enclosed the wet areas with the cofferdams they'll drain, and then they'll be able to excavate them. They'll then pour in the new foundations. After that, there'll be the associated kerbing and walling and road resurfacing, but while they're digging within the cofferdams it will give me a chance to keep an eye on what they turn up.'

'I would have thought the opportunity for observation will be limited,' Jane suggested.

'That's right, but it's better than nothing, and there's no way they're going to hold up the operations for a closer look. That's already been made clear at Morpeth. Still, it will give me the chance to check whether there are any traces of preceding bridge structures—either wood or stone. I might also be able to see whether there was any paved or metalled ford just there. My guess is, though, that such crossings were probably to the east of the bridge—the river will have moved so much from its original route in Roman times.'

Jane Wilson looked at him quizzically, with a slight smile on her face. 'That's interesting . . . You're beginning to enjoy this watching brief, aren't you, Arnold?'

He bobbed his head, a little embarrassed, still aware that he could have been working with her in Northumberland rather than undertaking his watching brief at Birley Thore. 'I suppose so. How are you getting on with William Fitzstephen?'

'Ah, I thought you'd never get around to asking,' she said primly.' Your letting me down—'

'Jane, I told you—'

'—your letting me down,' she repeated insistently, 'meant that I had to settle down to some checking at the bookshop. In doing so, I found a copy of Jeffrey's *Chronicles of the North*, you know, that nineteenth-century regurgitation of facts, old legends and stories, all mixed up with historical anecdote?'

'I know it.'

'Well, I came across an account of the William Fitzstephen northern venture there. It appears that Professor Dennis was right: I'd got my stories mixed. Or partly so, anyway.'

'How do you mean?'

'Fitzstephen was still in the service of Thomas Becket when he rode north—his objective really was not to summon anyone—he was trying, on behalf of Becket, to dissuade the Bishop of Durham from taking part in the coronation ceremony down south. He failed. Even so, he was able to warn the Bishop that the reivers were in the area. It allowed Hugh le Puiset to scurry back to Durham, and later to the south.'

'After which, presumably, Fitzstephen turned coat again?'

'I guess so. He probably thought this was the right time —when he'd got into Durham's good books and helped the King too, over the coronation. However, something equally interesting turned up.'

'You've been having an exciting time,' Arnold observed drily.

'Fitzstephen was riding north, right? The natural route lay along the old Roman road—indeed, Jeffrey's account specifies that. He met the reivers along that road—and there was quite a skirmish. He got away, lost most of his belongings, and there were quite a few killed. But tradition has it—according to Jeffrey—that all this took place in the valley you're working in!'

Arnold considered the matter. 'There would have been a number of villages along the floor of the valley in those days.'

'Jeffrey mentions no names, but says it was quite a skirmish.'

'Frank Lindley pointed out to me that there's evidence of a twelfth- or thirteenth-century burning of the old village at Birley Thore, but that's hardly conclusive. I mean, the Border raiders in Northumbria were always burning and looting—right down as far as Stainmore, which they claimed as the real border up till Malcolm's time.'

'I'm not suggesting your colleagues' excavations are linked to William Fitzstephen's ride north. But it's the same route, towards Berwick, isn't it?'

'If we can believe the *Chronicles of the North* . . .' Arnold pursed his lips thoughtfully. 'Frank Lindley will be opening the pit shortly, I understand. They're getting pushed for time, and they're also eager to do that dig. I think Mike

Swindon is getting impatient. So, who knows what they'll find when they start removing that soil cover?'

'All the more reason why you must keep in touch,' Jane insisted. She hesitated for a moment, looking at him sideways. 'Will you come up to the cottage at the weekend, tell me all about what might have been found at the dig?'

'I shouldn't think that would be a problem,' Arnold said carefully. 'Things tend to close down at the field site over the weekend, and they suspend work up at the bridge as well. People like to get home to their families from time to time.'

'I look forward to seeing you then. Meanwhile, I must have another chat with Professor Dennis, to check with him on detail of this *Chronicles* story.' She caught the sour expression on Arnold's face and added mischievously, 'I've come across a second-hand copy of one of his books here.'

'Not *The Road to Glory*, complete with signature.'

She grinned, 'No—*The Viking Age*. Would you like to buy it?'

Arnold grunted, displeased.

He certainly would not.

CHAPTER 3

1

Lying among the rugged moorland fells of south-east Redesdale, Elsdon had been the capital of the Middle Marches during the Border Wars that had flared continually during the mediæval period. Cattle had once been herded on the spacious green at the centre of the village in times of danger; an old pinfold still stood at one corner of the green. But over the centuries Elsdon had declined in importance. Now it was only a place visited by tourists, who came to gape at Winter's gibbet on the main Newcastle road, and drove on to Elsdon's offering of the pinfold, the stone slab of a bull-baiting ring, and a few eighteenth-century farmworkers' cottages, apart from St Cuthbert's Church with its three-hundred-year-old bellcote and stubby spire.

And the Bird in Bush Inn.

'He certainly tucked himself away this time,' Culpeper remarked grimly.

They had got the breakthrough only that morning. When he had returned from Suffolk, Culpeper had ordered the inquiry to start. Two constables had been placed on the job to make telephone inquiries at all hotels and guest houses within the immediate vicinity of South Middleton, but they had drawn a blank. They had then tried the Morpeth area but luck seemed against them, until finally Vic Farnsby came rushing into Culpeper's office in a state of some excitement.

'We've got another Dreng!'

Culpeper had informed Suffolk immediately and set out for Elsdon. He took Farnsby with him on the drive out to the village. He was beginning to feel a little sorry for the man: since the murder inquiry started Farnsby had been pinned to HQ, rarely getting home, sleeping in the cells a few nights, following up the detailed inquiries that were necessary. It had taken its toll of the Detective-Inspector: his features had a pale, haggard look about them, and his eyes had darkened with fatigue. He was clearly not sleeping well—the investigation was getting to him.

Culpeper had seen it with other men in the past. They became committed to an investigation; it became almost obsessive. Time began to have no meaning, the only important thing was to follow up all leads, dredge out all the facts, narrow down the list of suspects—and then make the arrest. And if the arrest was slow in coming, a man could deteriorate, in terms of morale, and physically as well. It was time then to pull him away, give him some other task in spite of his arguments, and his sense of failure.

Farnsby hadn't reached that point yet, but he was

looking as though he could crack. A drive out from HQ to follow this lead would do him no harm. They spoke little in the car, nevertheless. Culpeper might feel sympathy, but he did not find Farnsby an easy man to get on with. The Detective-Inspector had too many secret thoughts behind his hooded eyes, and when his attention strayed, as it often seemed to, Culpeper was left impatient and adrift.

The police driver parked near the church. Culpeper looked up at the stubby spire: he had heard that when the fourteenth-century church was restored in 1810 they'd found more than a hundred skeletons under the north wall —grisly relics of the battle at Otterburn in 1388. The Scots had hammered the English that day. Culpeper grunted— fat lot of good it had done them. Too much death, that was the problem.

The same applied to the man Northumberland and Suffolk Police were hunting.

The landlord was waiting for them at reception. They found the signature in the red-covered Visitors' Book.

Laurie Dreng Hirder.

It was written in a neat, deliberate hand. Somehow, although in one sense he should have been elated, the sight of the name depressed Culpeper. It brought home the reality of the fact that the man who had written in the book had probably been responsible for several killings.

He sighed. 'We'll have to take this book in, get it checked at forensic, do the whole thing on it.' He turned to the short, sandy-haired landlord. The man was looking slightly scared, not understanding why the police were interested in his register and probably worried about his licence. 'Do you remember anything about the man who used this signature?'

The landlord scratched his sandy hair nervously. 'Only stayed one night. The missus booked him in, like. Maybe she'll remember something about him; I just can't recall him at all. Don't think he came into the bar. But it was pretty full that night: lot of tourists around this time of year.'

Culpeper groaned inwardly. That would make things even more complicated for the investigation—chasing up a whole range of people who might have been drinking in the bar that night. And the chances that they might come up with useful information was slim. Even so, it would have to be done. 'Is your wife around at the moment?'

The landlord nodded. Culpeper glanced at Farnsby. 'Over to you. I'm going to take a walk.'

He hefted the book in his hand and then walked out to the waiting police car, stowed the book in the back seat and looked about him. The man who had killed James Lloyd could have stood here recently, on this green, while he was planning, making his preparations. He might have walked through the wooded ravine, sat down beside Elsdon Burn in the sunshine, and people might have seen him, unaware of the obscenity that lay in his mind: the planning of a murder, and a mutilation.

Farnsby would have to send a squad up here now to do a house-to-house investigation, interviewing everyone who lived in the village, everyone who had been in the Bird in Bush over that few days, everyone who might have driven into Elsdon and possibly seen the man who called himself on this occasion Laurie Dreng Hirder. Culpeper sighed and looked up at the scudding sky: grey and white storm clouds tumbling and whirling against an expanse of blue, the close humidity of an impending storm making his shirt collar damp against his neck.

He looked uncertainly at the church. St Cuthbert had had his own problems with murder and mutilation—and his followers even more so. In Cuthbert's day Lindisfarne had been under the threat of the Norsemen constantly; after his death the monks had had the task of transferring the holy bones from the island all the way to Durham, to the relative safety of Chester-le-Street, to escape the depredations of the Vikings rampaging through the North.

But those wild Norsemen had had a mission—plunder. Their own land had become too small for them, over-populated, so they swept out seawards, coming to raid and

pillage, eventually staying to farm and raise families. Elsewhere they had spread into France, down into Sicily—but
always with the same mission: wealth, land, power.

But what was the mission of the man who had killed at
Dunwich and South Middleton, Saumur and Basle? What
madness lay in that man's skull?

Culpeper sat on the low stone wall in the hazy sunshine
and waited, while the thoughts churned around unpleasantly in his head. For a moment, something drifted into his
mind and out again. He shook his head, irritated, trying to
recall the momentary thought, but it was gone. He dismissed it then, aware that the more he struggled for recall,
the more irritated he'd become. He sat there, motionless in
the sunshine, waiting.

It was an hour before Farnsby emerged from the pub. He
looked uncertainly about him, caught sight of Culpeper
sitting on the wall and made his way across the green
towards him. Farnsby seemed down in the mouth, tired,
and there was a weary stoop to his shoulders as he trudged
over the grass to join Culpeper.

'What did you get?' Culpeper asked, not expecting much.

Farnsby shook his head. 'Not a lot.'

'Let's have the bad news.'

Farnsby stared at his notebook gloomily. 'This guy
turned up at the Bird in Bush about six in the evening.'

'Had he made a booking?'

'Ah-uh. The day before. Lucky to get in, apparently,
because most of the small hotels are fully booked this time
of the year. The landlady was of the opinion he would have
had trouble getting a room in the area: they've been pretty
swamped, with tourists—time of year and the good weather
lately.'

'She remember him booking in?'

Farnsby shook his head. 'Not really: it was a busy time,
it seems, and though she has a vague recollection of someone about middle height, maybe five ten or so, dark—that's
about it. He came in at the same time as a group of other

people, she recalls, but he wasn't with them. Went straight to his room, didn't eat in the hotel, and took no breakfast. Paid in cash next morning and was away.'

'What luggage was he carrying?'

'Just hand luggage—a small case.'

'Car?'

'She didn't see it—neither did the landlord. He'll have parked near the church, they think.'

'Odd,' Culpeper mused.

'How do you mean, sir?'

'Why did he bother staying at the Bird in Bush at all?'

'He needed a room, I guess.'

'Why? He can't have planned the killing in the short time he stayed at the inn. And where were the implements he uses for the mutilation? You can't stuff a sword or an axe or a spear into a small case.'

'Left in the car?'

Culpeper shook his head in irritation. 'No, there's something odd about this. South Middleton's quite a distance from Elsdon. Why stay here?'

'Maybe he couldn't get in anywhere else.'

Culpeper nodded, and squinted up into the sunshine. 'That's possible . . . But why would he need to book a hotel room at all? When I spoke to DCI Castle, down in Suffolk, we went over this whole thing—the names in the registers. He thought it was all a bit of a game on our friend's part. An attempt to show off, create a puzzle for us. And maybe it is. But it gets a bit elaborate when he uses an hotel out in the sticks like this—and some distance from the murder. It could be, of course, that he's getting more careful.'

'How do you mean, sir?'

'I've been thinking about it.' Culpeper eased himself from his perch on the low wall and began to stroll across the village green. Farnsby followed him. 'Let's assume this is a calling card game,' Culpeper said. 'He started it in the Anne of Anjou, in Saumur—only a few hundred yards from where the body was found. I don't know the precise situation in Basle, except again, it wasn't too far away. Now for the Dunwich killing, he stayed at Southwold—that's about four miles distant. In each case, he stayed for only one night—to plant his calling card, that's all. But maybe he's beginning to get a bit more cautious. He must realize the links are now known—so he wouldn't want the signature found too quickly.'

'There could be another reason, sir.'

'Let's have it.'

Farnsby thought for a moment, struggling to phrase his suggestion in a logical manner. 'You stress he stays only one night at these hotels, to leave a calling card. You also mentioned he couldn't have planned the killing at the hotels —unless they're purely random.'

'I have a gut feeling,' Culpeper growled, 'they're far from random. We've got someone here who plans very well, I think—and there's got to be some kind of link between these killings. What the hell it is, I've no idea, but I just don't believe they're random. DCI Castle, down in Suffolk, thinks it might be a professional hit man, killing for payment. I'm not so sure. But you were saying?'

Farnsby shrugged. 'If you're right, sir, and they aren't random, the man we're looking for has to go through a planning stage. Where does he do that planning?'

'How do you mean?'

'If he stays at these hotels just the one night, he's got to have some sort of base in the locality.'

'So?'

'He travels, sir. Switzerland, France, Suffolk, now up here. All right, it's over a four-year period, but he can't do these killings, surely, from one base. He must come into the area, seek the hit, and plan how he's going to organize it. I mean, we know he doesn't always kill at the place where he dumps the body. So he's got to be staying somewhere in the area.'

'He could be long gone from the north already,' Culpeper murmured.

'Even so, sir. I mean, if he came into the north to kill James Lloyd he must have stayed somewhere.'

'A hotel?'

'That could work out to be expensive, over a period—and my guess is he wouldn't want to stay somewhere long enough to have connections made. He clearly takes pains to avoid identification so we can assume he'll do the same away from the hotels, at his local base. When he comes into an area he could buy a house, of course—but that's hardly feasible—imagine the problems of shifting houses between three countries! My guess is, sir—'

'Go on,' Culpeper said, as Farnsby hesitated.

'I think he must rent a place, sir, near enough to his victim for him to do the necessary planning. He's a professional, we all think that: he'll plan carefully, and that means a base.'

'One where he won't get snooped on,' Culpeper agreed thoughtfully.

'Where he can keep his gear; where he can feel safe.'

'His gear is certainly peculiar enough to attract attention.' The thought that had earlier escaped Culpeper danced into his mind again, and was gone almost immediately. Irritated, he went on, 'But rented property! How the hell are we going to check on all the property available in the north-east—without even knowing what we're looking for?' Culpeper shook his head, unconvinced.

Farnsby shuffled along beside Culpeper. 'I don't think he'd stay in a flat, or a boarding-house, sir. We could make a start by checking on cottage rentals. Who's come into the area during the last three months or so: probably alone—I think it's unlikely he'd bring company, he's got to be a loner. There'd be too much blood around for him to keep his activities quiet if he's got a woman with him. I think he'd want something quiet, few neighbours to spy on him. In his position, I'd be wanting some place where too many questions wouldn't be asked because there'd be no one around to ask them.'

'It would be a long haul.'

'We could start with estate agents, sir, and remote cottages.'

'I doubt we can spare the manpower,' Culpeper growled.

'What else do we have to go on, sir?' Farnsby said in a quiet voice.

Culpeper stared at him for a moment then stopped. He turned, began to retrace his steps to the car. 'What else indeed?' he agreed sourly.

Back in the car he made a call to HQ in Morpeth. He told the scene-of-crime unit that they had to get a few people out to Elsdon urgently to make the necessary house-to-house inquiries: that exercise shouldn't take too long but there was the much bigger task of trying to identify everyone who had visited Elsdon over the relevant period. Statements would need to be taken; eliminations would have to be made.

Culpeper was not at all confident that the inquiries would produce results, but it was activity that had to be under-taken. They couldn't afford to miss anything.

'Farnsby, you'd better stay on here, make a start. Get detailed statements from the landlady and her husband, and check off the names and addresses of locals who are regulars in the Bird in Bush. I'll take the book back to Morpeth, and we'll get going on the task of tracing all the people mentioned in there—we've got their addresses from their entries.'

'What about Hirder's address?'

Culpeper smiled thinly. 'You really believe it's genuine? I hardly believe that's going to give us much of a pointer. The address is in Warrington—but I bet the street doesn't exist. Anyway, the squad will be out within an hour or so —you stay on here now and you can get a lift back with them.'

Farnsby nodded despondently. He opened his mouth as though about to say something but thought better of it, and Culpeper wondered whether the Detective-Inspector had been hoping to get home at a reasonable hour that night. Fat chance, he thought to himself, and instructed the driver to make his way back to Morpeth.

The driver spoke over his shoulder to Culpeper. 'I think it would be sensible to take a different route back, sir. Avoid those narrow lanes where we hit that farm traffic. Bit longer, but probably faster.'

'Take whichever road you think best,' Culpeper replied, 'so long as we get back in reasonable time.' He settled comfortably in the car and opened the Visitors' Book from the Bird in Bush. He stared at the name written there: *Laurie Dreng Hirder.*

An odd prickling started at the back of his neck and he felt cold. He had taken part in a number of murder inquiries, as well as the usual run of assaults, beatings, rapes that were the lot of any detective squad. But this was different: this man who had written the name in the book was being sought by police forces in four different areas. And there was nothing to suggest that he would not strike again: the odds, in fact, were that he would.

Laurie Dreng Hirder.

What were the other names . . . ? Robert Dreng Baillehache; John Dreng Hagger; Peter Dreng Crocker. What was the significance of the middle name? What the hell was this madman playing at?

He closed his eyes and let his head drop back against the seat. Images flashed through his mind—the field at South Middleton, the cliff top at Dunwich, the mutilations on the body, the matching photographs Castle had shown him, the stained cardboard square in the grass. He was getting nowhere; Castle was getting nowhere. They were floundering, following behind the events, unable to make any predictions, failing to even guess what was going on.

And yet, Culpeper was convinced, there were links that were there to be teased out—it was all too deliberate, set in a pattern that mocked at them, maybe. That was Castle's theory . . . Culpeper wasn't sure.

He heard the driver groan.

'What's the matter?'

'Looks like we've gained nothing, sir. Diversion up

ahead. And there's a bloody lorry jack-knifed. They're clearing it, but we could be here for half an hour.'

'Can we back out?'

The driver glanced in his rear-view mirror. He shrugged. 'There's vehicles behind us, sir. Difficult. I could walk down to the accident, get the coppers on duty there to help us back out, but I don't think we'd gain much. It's a long detour to go the other way.'

'Where the hell are we?'

'Just outside Birley Thore, sir.'

Culpeper leaned back in his seat. 'The hell with it. We'll just wait it out. Shouldn't be too long.'

He stared ahead, over the driver's shoulder. The problem was that the lorry had come too quickly into the narrow lane of the diversion—it was a road-widening operation, it seemed, and traffic was being routed around the village along a road that hadn't been built for heavy lorries. The long vehicle had failed to take the bend, ploughed into the hedge, and jack-knifed. It must have happened some time ago: the police already had a JCB on the scene—probably called up from the road-widening scheme—and it was attempting to shunt the lorry out of the hedge.

Culpeper got out of the car. 'I'll walk on down, stretch my legs. I'll be back before they shift that lot.'

The driver's estimate of half an hour was unlikely: it was going to be some time before they got the lorry disentangled. Culpeper walked along the lines of cars, passing men leaning in shirtsleeves on car roofs, watching the attempts of the JCB to shunt the lorry. Culpeper strolled on towards the village itself, and in a hundred yards came upon the reason for the diversion.

They had sealed off the old bridge and erected scaffolding on either side. Sheet piles had been driven into the bed of the stream and anchored against the piers, and electric pumps were draining the cofferdams that had been erected alongside the bridge buttresses. There were excavators working against the line of the bank, gouging out great gouts of mud and shale, outside the cofferdams themselves, in preparation for the construction of new piers. Culpeper didn't give the fish in the stream much chance of survival while this work was going on. The ducks downstream didn't seem very much concerned, however.

He joined the inevitable group of work-watchers.

They were a mixed group—a few elderly, retired men, no women, some younger, farming characters in jeans and flat caps, and a few sub-teenage children, larking about. Culpeper leaned on the parapet at the end of the bridge and watched with them, as the excavator manœuvred and dug, and the water sloshed about in the grey mud thrown out by the pumps in the cofferdams.

When he looked up, he saw Arnold Landon.

Landon was standing at the far end of the bridge, inside the roped-off area, watching the work intently. Culpeper stared at him for several seconds, wondering what he was doing there. Then he realized it would have something to do with his work at the Department of Museums and Antiquities in Morpeth: Landon wasn't the kind of man to take time off in the working day to stand idly watching work on a bridge.

Not like DCIs, Culpeper humphed self-critically.

Landon would be here in some official capacity, looking for something to do with timber or stone, mediæval stuff, the kind of things he was always interested in, and more committed to than ever now that he worked for the Department of Museums and Antiquities.

Antiquities.

The errant, butterfly thought that had drifted into his mind several times now came back, as though triggered by Landon's presence. Culpeper stared across the bridge thoughtfully, wondering, but saw nothing as his gaze became fixed: he tried to refine the niggle in his mind, log it, file it, inspect it critically, but it was too vague to be defined, too hazy to be categorized.

He'd thought about it when he had waited at St Cuthbert's Church at Elsdon—he'd been thinking about the wild Norsemen. The sites where the mutilated bodies had been dumped had all had mediæval connections: the château at Saumur, the runic stone at Basle, the monastery at Dunwich, and the mediæval deserted village at South Middleton. The mutilations had been done with a two-edged weapon, and there had been a spear, or an arrow-head, thrust through the corpse's throat. It was a primitive way to kill and mutilate—apart from the pistol shot. Primitive rituals, mediæval locations, the wild violence of another age.

Culpeper ducked under the blue and red plastic line that blocked off the bridge to unauthorized visitors. A man in a hard hat and a yellow jacket came forward. 'Please, sir, you're not allowed—'

'Police,' Culpeper said shortly and pushed past him.

When he was half way across the bridge Arnold Landon looked up and caught sight of him. Culpeper saw the recognition dawn in his eyes and saw the reluctance too. Culpeper was not surprised: few people seemed to be able to meet a policeman without some tremor or other. And the previous occasions on which he and Landon had met had not been happy ones—but that was Landon's problem. Culpeper had just been doing his job.

'Mr Landon,' Culpeper said affably as he grew close, raising his hand in greeting.

'Mr Culpeper.' Landon's tone was more wary.

'On business?' Culpeper asked, glancing around at the bridge.

Landon nodded. 'More or less. I'm on secondment. A watching brief on this road-widening scheme.' He hesitated, gestured down to the arches below them. 'The bridge is nineteenth-century, but there's a mediæval and probably Roman construction underneath. I'm watching to see what turns up, in the course of the rebuilding.'

'You won't see much in that mess,' Culpeper suggested, looking towards the excavation.

'It's a bit cruder than I'd expected,' Landon admitted, 'but I'll be able to do some sifting of the pile, and once the water's pumped out of the cofferdam I'll be able to get down there and have a look around before they start tearing it apart too seriously. And then I'll get down at intervals once they removed some of the top shale.'

'They'll let you?'

'It's arranged.'

Culpeper took a deep breath. He was uncertain how to bring the matter up. They stood side by side, looking down over the parapet, while Culpeper struggled internally. At last, casually, he looked at Landon and asked, 'You're reckoned to be a bit of an expert on mediæval things, aren't you?'

'I wouldn't say expert,' Landon replied cautiously. 'I . . . have some experience.'

'What about weapons, things like that?'

Landon shrugged. 'Not really. My expertise, if it's anything at all, concerns timber and stones, constructions, mediæval buildings, that sort of thing. I have some knowledge of the rather more esoteric uses to which buildings are put, I suppose—but weapons, well, only in the context of military building, and the slighting or destruction of such buildings.'

Culpeper hesitated. He was on tricky ground, not sure how far to go. The murder investigation was in its early days as far as he was concerned, and the strict instructions were still to keep details under wraps. On the other hand, he reasoned, Landon wouldn't know what he was talking about if he kept things vague. 'I came across something the other day,' he said slowly, 'but couldn't place it. The meaning, that is. I have a feeling it might have something to do with . . . mediæval matters.'

'Yes?'

'Godar.'

'What?'

'G-O-D-A-R.' Culpeper spelled it out.

Landon stared at him. 'What's the problem?'

'No problem,' Culpeper replied hastily. 'It's just I came across it, wondered what it meant. Do you know?'

Landon shook his head. 'I can't say I've ever come across the word. Is it important?'

Culpeper shrugged, and looked around at the cofferdams. It had been a long shot, he thought, born of his reflections about rampaging Norsemen a thousand years ago—there was no reason why he should have expected Arnold Landon to be able to help. Diffidently, he asked, 'What about the name Dreng?'

'Name?'

Culpeper turned slowly to look at Landon. He nodded.

Landon was frowning. 'You mean someone using it *as* a name?'

Culpeper's heart began to beat erratically in his chest, and his mouth was suddenly dry. 'That's right. Have you come across it?'

Landon shook his head. 'Not as a name. In another context . . .'

'What context?' Culpeper asked, more sharply than he'd intended.

'Is this part of some investigation?'

Culpeper hesitated. 'No,' he lied, and turned away again, fingers quivering slightly as he tried to appear casual. 'Just a matter of interest. But what do you mean about context?'

Arnold Landon was silent for several seconds. He frowned, as though he was trying to recall something that was eluding him. Then he nodded. 'Runic stone,' he said.

'What?'

'Runic stone,' Landon said positively. 'You know, those ancient, carved stones, usually Scandinavian in origin. They were set up as memorials—to the dead, or to commemorate some event, a battle, the death of a comrade, that sort of thing. You find them all over the place in those areas where the Vikings stormed in—Ireland, the North Country, France, Italy, Sicily . . .'

'And you've come across the name Dreng on a runic stone?'

'The word,' Landon corrected him, 'not the name.'

'All right, word. So what does it mean?' Culpeper rasped, unable to keep the impatience out of his voice.

Landon stared at him, considering. 'Boy, I suppose. Or young man. That sort of thing.'

'Boy?' Culpeper glared at him, puzzled. 'Is that what it means?'

Landon wriggled. 'Well, something like that. Let me think . . . There's a stone just outside Kirkby Stephen, in the Mallerstang valley towards Uldale—that means Valley of the Wolf, you know, in old Norse—'

'Go on.'

'There are runes on it which have been translated as "Drengs raised this stone in memory of their brother"— there are strong Scandinavian influences in the Eden valley, you see, Viking settlements—'

Culpeper shook his head. 'I don't understand the use of the word *drengs* as "boys" in that context. Are you saying that kids—'

'No, no, it doesn't mean children.' Landon was casting around for a better explanation. 'Perhaps the word "lad" is a better translation. *Drengs* in that context means "the lads"—to be a *dreng* was to be one of "the lads", you understand?'

Culpeper shook his head.

Arnold Landon frowned. 'It's about usage. The English word "gentleman", for instance, has various connotations. I believe *dreng* literally means "boy" or "youth" but . . . well, in the collective sense it could mean a group of young men, and the natural connotation then would be the crew of a fighting ship, members of an army unit, or a fraternity of merchants. They were all lads together when they were *drengs*. They were . . . comrades. Do you see what I mean?'

As Culpeper stared at him, Landon went on cheerfully, 'I suppose the singular could have a technical sense also— a brother maybe, or someone who was in service to another. But my own guess is that *drengs* was a term normally applied to the young men who formed a ship's crew for fighting service. They were lads who could be spared from the home toil of summer food production—they formed the war fleets. And I guess the word also developed among young men as a suggestion of camaraderie, particularly on adventurous or dangerous service.'

'All lads together . . .' Culpeper murmured, almost to himself.

'Something like that.' Landon was watching Culpeper curiously. 'Is that any help?'

'What? Oh yes . . .' Culpeper hesitated. He forced his attention back to the work being undertaken below them. 'Runic stones, you say? You an expert on those too, then?'

'Not really. I've come across them,' Landon explained, 'because in the course of my work—and interests—I have to date stones, and runes are a good source of evidence, naturally. Better than tooling, because they can often date a stone precisely—link it to written records.' He eyed the policeman. 'I didn't know you were interested in runic stones, though, Mr Culpeper.'

Culpeper shrugged diffidently. 'It's just something that's come up.' In a careful tone, he added, 'Could the word "Godar" have the same kind of origin?'

'I don't know. It's not a word I've come across. It could be old Norse, though. I wouldn't be able to confirm that, however.' He paused, considering the matter for a moment. 'I think I know someone who could.'

'Confirm it? You do?'

Culpeper was on awkward ground. He did not want to expose his hand; he had already given Landon words that were central to the killings, not just here in England but abroad as well. If the man became suspicious and let others know what had been asked it could cause problems— details that had been kept out of the public domain so far could be screamed from the newspapers.

On the other hand, Culpeper knew Landon: he wasn't given to talking to newspapers.

'I wouldn't want to make a big thing about it,' Culpeper said carelessly. 'It's just a matter of personal interest. But I'd quite like to find out a bit more . . . about Godar, if possible . . . and about *drengs*, too. You say you know someone?'

Landon nodded. 'I'm no expert. He is. He's written a book about the Vikings. I met him recently through Jane Wilson. You remember her?'

'I do.' Culpeper felt he was walking on eggshells. 'I wonder whether it would be possible to meet this . . . ah . . . expert?'

'Professor Dennis. He works at the University in Durham. You could contact him there.'

'Nothing formal,' Culpeper said hastily. 'I wouldn't want to get in touch with him out of the blue—you know how it is, if a copper starts asking questions, there's always the thought that . . . well, people begin to sweat . . . I'd rather it was . . . informal. Just a friendly chat. Maybe you could arrange for me to meet him—sort of off the record, nothing to do with business.'

He had the feeling Arnold Landon wasn't fooled.

'I could probably arrange it through Jane,' he said. 'She's the contact. Would it be all right if she and I sat in on it? She's writing a book on the Normans and—'

'No problem, no problem at all,' Culpeper exclaimed in mock enthusiasm. The last thing he wanted was this to be seen as part of a murder investigation. But he still wasn't sure Arnold Landon had been fooled.

2

On the Saturday morning, Arnold Landon rose early. He had been surprised by the meeting with DCI Culpeper at the Birley Thore bridge, and had been even more surprised by the request the policeman had made. Arnold did not dislike Culpeper: the man had an honest, blunt directness about him and Arnold felt he was a man to be trusted. At the same time, it was clear that the meeting at the bridge had been one where Culpeper was being less than honest and Culpeper was unable to dissemble successfully: he might feel he was being devious, but his real feelings and intentions shone through.

Arnold could no more believe that Culpeper was interested in mediæval history than that he had a belief in fairies: on the other hand, Arnold was not inclined to inquire further. If Culpeper wanted some information and did not wish to explain the real reason why, that was his business. Moreover, though Arnold did not care for the rather pompous Professor Arthur Dennis, he had to admit that the historian had had some interesting things to say at Jane's dinner-party, and the man was clearly an expert in his own field.

Jane had been almost enthusiastic when he had mentioned Culpeper's request to her. 'I'm sure it can be arranged—and I'd like to be there. I haven't really had time or opportunity to talk to Professor Dennis since last we met. Did I say talk? I really meant listen to . . . he *is* a bit overweening, isn't he?'

Arnold had smiled at that.

'If Mr Culpeper wants to tap him for some information for whatever reason,' she went on, 'that's fine with me. Gives me a chance to listen, and you know how it is, when an expert gets launched, all sorts of things come out that can be useful. You know, stuff I could use in my book by way of background.' She had looked at Arnold mischievously. 'You'll want to sit at the feet of the oracle as well, of course.'

'I wouldn't miss it,' he intoned solemnly.

She had made the arrangement, and Professor Dennis had been so gracious as to invite them for coffee at his college. Arnold was pleased about that: although he often used the University library he had never had an invitation to visit any of the colleges, and he looked forward to it. The University was an ancient foundation, and while some of the more recent colleges were housed in modern buildings on the slopes overlooking the city, the older colleges in close proximity to the cathedral had a mediæval atmosphere about them. Till now, he had savoured that atmosphere only externally.

The appointment had been fixed for Saturday morning, at the Professor's rooms.

Arnold had some shopping to do and decided he would do it in Durham itself, rather than go into Morpeth. There was nothing he needed that couldn't be kept in the back of the car for a few hours while he was with the Professor at his college.

He drove down the A1 and was in Durham by ten. He parked near Durham School and enjoyed the walk down the narrow cobbled road towards Silver Street, with the steep-sided bank to his right with its fine view of the castle, Durham Cathedral and the bend of the river. At the entrance to Silver Street there was a shopping mall: a modern area which was, he supposed, inescapable these days but which had been tucked away insignificantly enough, away from the castle and cathedral towering on their rocky promontory.

He managed to complete his purchases quickly and calculated he had time to spare before he needed to stow his shopping in his car, and then walk back down to Silver Street, cross the bridge and make the short, stiff climb up the hill to the college.

He was idling in front of a camera shop when someone collided with him. Stepping back, an apology on his lips, Arnold turned to see a face he recognized. 'Ah! Mr Marshall!'

Colin Marshall stopped in surprise. For a moment an expression almost like consternation crossed his features, then he recovered, smiled and said, 'Mr Landon. Long way to come to shop, isn't it?'

'I've an appointment here this morning.'

'Ah.'

There was a young woman with Colin Marshall. She was slight, pretty, with dark hair and a disconsolate, sulky mouth and dissatisfied eyes. She was standing half hidden at Marshall's side and she seemed displeased at the meet-

ing, reluctant to speak or meet Arnold's glance. Arnold had
the impression she was somewhat older than her com-
panion.

Colin Marshall looked at her hesitantly, then turned back
to Arnold. He smiled. 'This . . . ah . . . let me introduce
you,' he said with a breezy self-confidence that did not
appear forced. 'This is Fanny. And Fanny, this is Arnold
Landon.'

She made no attempt to shake hands, but nodded off-
handedly and looked away. Her mouth was tight, and she
seemed angry about something. It might be that she and
Marshall had been quarrelling before they'd met Arnold
and the vestiges of that quarrel remained.

'Arnold works up at the Birley Thore project. Not exactly
with us, but down at the bridge.'

She made no response. She was clearly disinclined to
carry on a conversation.

'How are things down at the road-widening scheme, anyway?' Marshall asked cheerfully. 'You sloshing away successfully in the mud there?'

'The work's proceeding slowly—like all road construction projects. But I should be able to get down into the
cofferdam on Monday. And the fieldwork?'

'Ah! Everyone's getting a bit impatient.' Like the young
woman at Marshall's elbow, Arnold thought. 'Mike Swindon wants to get his teeth into that pit—if that's the right
expression,' Marshall continued. 'And I think Frank's now
of the same view. We're losing the youngsters on the site
next weekend, so we'll use them to do the first stripping,
but after that I'll be hiring some rather more mature people,
if I can get them. We're hoping for big things, once we open
the pit. Frank wants it left for a while: he's away with Dr
Ormond at a conference for a few days.'

There were two red angry spots in the young woman's
cheeks. 'Colin,' she interrupted, touching his sleeve with
her left hand, 'time's pressing. I think we'd better be getting
on.'

She was wearing a wedding ring, Arnold noticed.

Colin Marshall managed a surreptitious wink in Arnold's direction. 'Yes I suppose so. Nice to bump, into you, Mr Landon. Will we be seeing you up at the field soon?'

'If you're opening up the pit, I'd like to come up and see what you find.' He glanced at the girl. 'Nice to meet you.'

She nodded, raised her left hand to brush back her hair. Then, as though conscious of the ring on her finger, she dropped her hand quickly, covering it with her right. As they walked away, she began to mutter angrily at Colin Marshall. He seemed unconcerned; he tucked his hand behind her elbow and steered her into the coffee shop on the bridge. He was smiling carelessly, but there was a stiff anger in every line of her body.

Making his way back up the hill to his car Arnold guessed that she had not enjoyed being introduced to him. Durham was a long way from Morpeth. Distant enough for an assignation between a young married woman and her lover to be deemed safe—so long as her lover didn't introduce her to his acquaintances

Arnold recalled that Frank Lindley had told him there'd been girl trouble in Colin Marshall's past. Maybe the young man hadn't learned his lesson. Arnold smiled to himself: he was probably being fanciful—and romantic.

He arrived at the college promptly at eleven.

It was a fine morning, and the streets were thronged with tourists and shoppers, but the precincts of the college itself were quiet, mediæval in structure, and imposing in a calm, non-theatrical way. The entrance to the college was modern, an excrescence on a sixteenth-century building, but inside the main doorway the carved arch above the worn steps was imposing, and Arnold paused there for a few minutes, admiring the stonework, and the carving of the college arms. The mason of old had cut his own tool-mark into the stone but Arnold was not able to make it out clearly in the dimness of the hallway.

The door swung to behind him.

Arnold turned to see Jane entering. She smiled warmly

at him. 'I think I saw Culpeper parking his car, outside, Arnold. He'll be in to join us shortly.' She stepped closer to him, conspiratorially. 'Have you had any further thoughts about what this might all be about?'

Arnold grinned. 'I really don't know. Culpeper wants to get some information from Professor Dennis but is playing a bit cagey. He says it's just personal interest, but I doubt it. It'll be some police business or other.'

'And he thinks Professor Dennis will help?'

Arnold shrugged. 'I wouldn't really know. He wants to talk to a mediævalist, that's all I really know about it. What have you told Dennis about Culpeper?'

'Just that he's an amateur enthusiast.' Uncharacteristically, she giggled. 'Do you think Culpeper can play the part?'

'If he wants to pretend it's just idle curiosity rather than police business, he'll have to. But why all the secrecy and cloak and dagger, I don't know.'

'Well, once he joins us I'll take us up to Professor Dennis's rooms.'

'You've been before?' Arnold muttered suspiciously.

'Just once.' She looked at him, and smiled. Arnold felt himself flushing, and cursed himself for a fool.

The door opened behind them and Culpeper marched in. Arnold greeted him, reintroduced him to Jane and the two men then followed her up the curving, balustraded staircase towards Professor Dennis's room. 'Jane has told the professor that you're just an amateur enthusiast—but also that she wants to tap him for information she can use in her book.'

Culpeper nodded; he seemed tense, slightly anxious, perhaps overawed by the atmosphere in the college. Jane tapped on the door at the top of the stairs and when invited to enter, opened the door. The others followed her in.

Professor Dennis was sitting at his cluttered desk in front of the mullioned window. He was dressed in corduroy slacks, a check shirt and a blue, long-sleeved cardigan. He was smoking a pipe. Arnold was left with the impression that the Professor wanted to give the appearance of the academic at ease in his ivory tower retreat, surrounded by his books. He was, of course, immaculately groomed, as usual, and he rose to his feet as they entered, to shake Jane's hand between both of his own, and to be introduced to Culpeper.

'Arnold you know,' Jane explained, 'and Mr Culpeper is . . . an acquaintance who is very interested in mediæval history. He . . . he asked if he could sit in on our discussions and maybe ask a few questions.'

'Always delighted to meet an enthusiast,' Dennis said cordially. 'Are you a member of the Northumberland Antiquarian Society?'

'I . . . er . . . I used to be,' Culpeper mumbled, out of his depth immediately. 'My . . . er . . . membership lapsed.'

Arnold smiled inwardly. That answer ensured Culpeper couldn't be asked about current members of the Society, who might be known to Dennis. Always the cautious policeman, Culpeper.

'Doing some private research, hey?' Dennis pressed him.

Culpeper swallowed nervously. 'That's about the size of it. My . . . ah . . . my family go back a long way. I'm trying to find out about their Norman or Viking predecessors.'

'Viking?' Dennis wrinkled his nose. 'That's a long way back.' He hesitated, looking at Culpeper carefully: it was clear he was suspicious of the explanation he'd been offered. But then he shrugged it aside as inconsequential. Turning to Jane, he said, 'How's your book coming along?'

'Well enough. I checked up on your correction of my Fitzstephen story, Arthur, and you were right. He *was* involved in a skirmish in Northumberland, and went on to warn the Bishop of Durham.'

Dennis nodded, pleased. 'Yes, good. I think as a result, Hugh le Puiset had cause to be grateful. The likelihood is he commended Fitzstephen to Henry, and that's how the turncoat got back into the King's good graces. Tradition has it that the skirmish was on the old Roman road, in the Birley Thore area.'

'Really?' Arnold exclaimed. 'I'm working up there at the moment, on the bridge-widening scheme. There's also a dig just outside the village. In fact, it was up at Birley Thore bridge that I was talking to . . . Mr Culpeper. He asked me about *drengs*.'

'Ah yes.' Dennis glanced at Culpeper, his eyes sharp. 'In what context have you come across them?'

'Ah . . .' Culpeper was at a momentary loss. He looked wildly at Arnold. 'Ah . . . rune stones,' he said quickly.

Dennis nodded. His voice was solemn. 'Yes, there are many runic inscriptions, referring to the "fine young men". Vastergotland, Jutland, Skane—and quite a few in northern England. There's a well-known one which was a double cenotaph—in Denmark and in England—commemorating one Karl, who had crossed with Knut for the invasion in 1016. As I recall, it ran "Thorir raised this stone in memory of Karl, his comrade, a very fine *dreng*." But which stones in particular—'

'I was able to explain *dreng* to Mr Culpeper,' Arnold broke in hastily, to save Culpeper embarrassment, 'but he asked me about another word. I wasn't familiar with it, but I said you might be able to help, as an expert on Viking and Norman periods.'

Dennis raised his chin, pleased. 'What word was that, Mr Culpeper?'

'I don't know whether it really is Norse in origin,' Culpeper replied uneasily, feeling he was already out of his depth and half wishing he had not exposed himself in this manner. 'I just asked Mr Landon . . .'

'The word?'

'Godar.'

'*Godar*. Oh yes,' Dennis said blandly. 'It's Norse in origin, of course.'

There was a short silence. Culpeper's breathing was heavy in the room. At last he asked, 'What does it mean?'

'*Godar?*' Dennis put his head back and stared at the ceiling for a few seconds, thinking. 'Well, you have to know a little about the organization of society under the Vikings to

understand. You see, they had no central administration—
they came from a sort of republic of farmers—though
maybe one with oligarchic tendencies. But there was no
military organization as such, no hereditary commanders,
and no national leader. They had their *Logmann*, their
"Lawspeaker", but he hardly counted as a national leader.
He was the person who pronounced the law in the *Logretta*,
the legislative assembly, where the *Godi* were gathered.'

'*Godi?*'

'Plural of *Godar*,' Dennis explained loftily. 'I suppose you
could describe them as sort of local chieftains—but they
were really rather more than that. The name also meant
"priest"—a man in special relationship with the gods, pos-
sessing divine powers. Their chief functions were secular,
but they had special rights accorded to them, and obligations. They served in the *Logretta*, they nominated the
judges, and they sat in judgement. To some extent also they
were responsible for the execution of justice.'

'I thought blood-feud meant that the execution of justice
was a private initiative,' Arnold questioned.

'That's so,' Dennis replied, rather cool at Arnold's interruption, 'but the *Godar* was expected to take action where
private initiative was not possible, or unwise, because of
the nature of the offence. In cases of great importance, for
instance—such as a crime against the public weal.'

'The execution of justice,' Culpeper murmured, almost
to himself.

'That's right,' Dennis said, warming to his subject. 'Mr
Landon is correct about private initiative. Justice—or re-
taliation—was often carried out by the *hird*—that was a
word borrowed from the Anglo-Saxon *hired*, around about
1000. Its English meaning would be "family" but in Norse
it was used to designate a group around a king, or leader.
A father would send his son off to the sea, with a *hird*, to
earn his living by plunder. As part of the crew in a longboat,
that young man could well then soon become a *dreng*—one
of the lads, one of the comrades in arms within the *hird*.'

'So the *drengs* were really members of war parties,'

Culpeper said slowly, frowning. 'And the *Godar* was like an executioner.'

Dennis sighed, nodding reluctantly, as though he was dealing with an unintelligent student. 'I think that's an over-simplification, Mr Culpeper. The functions of the *Godar* were rather more extensive than mere execution. The execution of justice was merely one of his functions. He had administrative and legal functions also—and as a local chieftain he might also be one of the *drengs*, of course—if he took part in the sea-crew as a leader.'

Arnold glanced at Culpeper. The policeman was leaning forward now, heedless of the slighting tone employed by Dennis, concentrating as he stared at the Professor. It was clear he was getting information that was important to him. 'When these . . . *drengs* sailed in a war party, what weapons did they use?'

Dennis gestured vaguely. 'Not really my field, actually, but in general the Viking raiders carried several weapons —the sword, of course, pattern-welded, with the pattern believed to have magical properties. Then there was the *spjot*, the spear. Iron spearheads are the most common weapons found in Viking graves, as a matter of fact, and they used two types—a throwing spear, which tended to be a fairly simple implement since it was lost to its owner once thrown, and the stabbing or thrusting spear. The plain iron points we find in Viking graves are probably of the latter kind. On the other hand, we also find long slender points . . . so the theory might be wrong.'

'How were the spear blades shaped?' Culpeper asked, scratching at his chin thoughtfully.

'My dear man, as I said, it's not my subject, but I believe they varied considerably. Some were merely sharpened points, some had broad blades, some blades were leaf-shaped.'

'The Viking is usually depicted carrying an axe,' Arnold offered.

Dennis nodded. 'That was the other chief weapon of offence—in some ways it was the most emotive of all Viking

weapons. We find them often in Viking and Norse graves.'
Dennis glanced in Jane's direction. 'Is this of any use to
you?'

'Good background,' Jane replied. 'Many of these weapons were, of course, carried through into the Norman
period.'

'Oh, to be certain. And so was the organization, albeit
under a different name. But I've been remiss. I've not
offered you coffee. Three? Milk? Sugar?' He walked across
to a low table in the corner of the room and plugged in a
kettle. 'No service here, in the poverty-stricken academic
world. We have to make our own coffee.'

Jane sat tight with a feminist smile.

Arnold glanced at Culpeper: the man was sunk in
thought, his hands clenched together. There was a deep
frown on his brow and his mouth was tight. Dennis stood
over the kettle, leaning with one hand against the wall. 'It's
interesting to consider how many of our words come from
old Norse,' he mused. 'These warriors wore shirts of mail
—as did the Normans. The Vikings called them *hringskyrta*,
or "ring-shirts". Descriptive, isn't it? Then when there was
a blood-feud, the two antagonists often went to an island
to fight in isolation—it was called *holmganga*—or "island-
going". We've got Steepholm and Flatholm islands in the
Bristol Channel, while here in the north, Geordies still
"gang" to the races. These words have been with us a
thousand years. Like *Logmann*—the origin for our word
"lawman" or "lawyer".'

'Penalties,' Culpeper said gruffly.

'I beg your pardon?'

'What about penalties? You told us about the *Godar*—
how he could be an executioner. What were the penalties
he might impose?'

Dennis shrugged, and looked down at the kettle which
was beginning to rumble. 'They varied, really. Atonement
in cash was the common sanction. Outlawry—but that also
could be compounded by payment of an atonement. And

then there were physical punishments—whipping, mutilation—'

'When was mutilation used?' Culpeper asked sharply.

Dennis was slightly taken aback by the swiftness of the question. He shrugged diffidently. 'Only on slaves, never on free men, and for minor offences in the main. Beheading was counted as a decent mode of execution for the freeman, if the offence was heinous.'

'The *Godar* would do that?'

Dennis unscrewed a coffee jar and put some instant coffee in the cups. 'Ah well, the execution of criminals was properly the duty of those who had prosecuted them, providing proper publicity was given.' He switched off the kettle and began to pour the hot water into the cups. 'The function could on occasion be taken over by the *Godar*, if it was necessary. But normally, execution as a penalty was family against family, man against man: it was a private matter.'

He leaned over to pick up the cups. As Arnold began to get to his feet to render assistance Jane relented and rose to help Dennis hand the cups around the small group.

'Oddly enough,' Dennis continued, 'when it was in private hands the execution would not necessarily be of the culprit himself. It might be of a more prominent member of his family—a sort of blood-count went on, and it was deemed more honourable to take the life of the head of the family than of the individual who'd caused the trouble. Though he'd probably be executed too.'

Culpeper sipped his coffee slowly, and nodded. He put the cup down on the desk edge. The cup rattled as he did so: his hand was trembling slightly. 'Tell me, Professor,' he asked, some of his cloaked authority creeping back into his tone, 'have you come across the word *dreng* being used as a person's name.'

'Oh no, no—it's just a description. It's not a proper name.'

Culpeper was silent for a few seconds, thinking. 'So if you came across a name like, for instance, Dreng Crocker, it would be meaningless.'

'Dreng Crocker?' Dennis sipped at his coffee and shook

his head. 'Quite meaningless. Unless you use *dreng* adverbially, of course . . .' He wrinkled his brow in thought. 'How do you spell the second name?'

Slowly Culpeper spelled it out.

'Curious, I thought for a moment . . . You see, if you pronounce the word a little differently it sounds like the Norse *krokr*.'

'What does that mean?'

'Arrowhead.'

The room was silent as Culpeper stared at the Professor. The silence grew around them.

Arnold glanced at Culpeper: a vein beat steadily in the policeman's temple and he seemed to have difficulty breathing. As Arnold watched he saw that a slow flush was gradually staining the man's neck. He was struggling to contain a growing tension as he said, gratingly, 'What if the name was Dreng Hagger?'

Dennis shrugged, unaware of Culpeper's rising excitement. 'As I said, using *dreng* as a name is meaningless, except in an adverbial or adjectival sense, I suppose . . . As for Hagger—I don't know where you're dreaming up these names, Mr Culpeper—are they in some way ancestral names in your family?'

'You could say that. What does Hagger mean?'

Dennis pursed his lips. 'It derives from the old Norse word *hagr*.'

'And its meaning?' Culpeper almost growled.

'Skilful, dexterous.' Dennis hesitated. 'It was sometimes used as a nickname also and applied in various ways—but used in common parlance among war parties, it meant a "destroyer" because of the man's skill with the weapon used.'

'Destroyer,' Culpeper muttered, almost to himself. He sat silently for a few moments, considering. 'What if the name Hirder was used with Dreng?'

Dennis smiled. 'You seem to have an inexhaustible supply of these names in your family, Mr Culpeper. Are you sure they're not mythical? Hirder is spelled . . . ?'

Culpeper told him.

'I've not come across the name personally,' Dennis said. 'But I suppose you could regard it as a derivative from the *hird*—as I've already mentioned, the group to which *drengs* might belong. But linguistically speaking, I don't think *dreng hirder* makes a lot of sense.'

Culpeper clearly thought otherwise. He heaved a long sigh. It relieved some of the tension in his features. Dennis watched him curiously as he took a sip of his coffee. He waited, an odd light in his eyes.

Culpeper looked up. 'That leaves Baillehache,' he asked.

'What was that?' Dennis asked.

'Baillehache,' Culpeper repeated.

'That's not a Norse word,' Dennis said. He looked around, smiling, as though he were in the lecture theatre with his students. 'Any offers?'

'It's French,' Arnold said.

'Norman French,' Jane added. 'It means "Carry-Axe".'

Culpeper's hand was trembling slightly as he reached for his coffee cup again. Dennis watched him, a sardonic smile on his lips, amused but somewhat puzzled by the thrust of the questions and the effect the answers seemed to have had on his guest. 'Do you find all this helpful, Mr Culpeper? I don't understand how it works in with your . . . ah . . . family history, or with tracing the branches of a family tree, but—'

'It's most helpful,' Culpeper interrupted brusquely. 'But can I go back to a couple of things you've mentioned already? First, you said something about public executions.'

'Publicity,' Dennis corrected. 'The blood-feud meant that it was man for man, but the honourable thing to do was to name your victim, publicize the fact that you were going to exact vengeance. It was a sensible enough arrangement if you think about it: if you didn't announce in advance that you were going to kill your enemy, all sorts of deaths could occur and be unaccounted for. Secret slayings could cause all sorts of problems. It could lead to anarchy.'

'Talk to me again about the mutilation thing for a

moment. You say free men were not mutilated, only slaves.'

'This is beginning to sound like a cross-examination.'
Dennis smiled, seating himself behind his desk again. He
leaned back in his chair, and folded his arms. 'Yes, that's
the general picture.'

'There were exceptions?'

'Exceptional situations, yes.'

'Such as?'

Dennis looked at the ceiling. He was silent for a little
while, thinking, recalling. 'As far as I remember,' he said
slowly, 'the Vikings drew a distinction between enemies
who had behaved like honourable men and those who had
not. The Sagas are full of such stories—the concept of
drengila, men who had behaved after the fashion of a *dreng*
—an interesting abstraction in fact, that we find in scaldic
poetry and runic inscriptions at a very early date. Such men
would have to be killed honourably, but the same did not
apply to the *nidingr*.'

'What was that?'

'The *nidingr*,' Dennis replied, 'was the lowest of men, one
who was the object of hate or scorn. In assessing the con-
duct of men the Vikings held those two extremes: the *godar
drengr* and the *nidingr*—the honourable man and the
outcast.'

'What would cause a man to be so branded?' Arnold
asked curiously.

'The classical cause for being regarded as a *nidingr* was
wilfully failing those who had reason to trust you; the worst
was treachery towards a friend, betrayal of a comrade.'

'And such a man could be mutilated?' Culpeper persisted.

'I detect a certain persistent bloodthirstiness about you,
my friend,' Dennis said, smiling thinly. 'Yes, but it was
more often a case of burying the man in a valueless field,
and erecting a *nidstong*, a "shame-pole" above his grave.'

'But tell me, Professor Dennis,' Jane interrupted, 'didn't
Christianity affect all this? I mean, the Norsemen accepted
the Christian faith in the ninth century!'

'True, but you have to remember, in the Viking world there was a strong undercurrent of conflict and violence. *Ragnarok*—world end—was looming over gods and men, and all things would be consumed by fire and water in a battle against the dark forces, led by Loki.'

'And Christianity had no impact?'

Dennis shrugged. 'The hand of Christianity lay lightly on these men. They might lay claim to a belief in Christ—but they'd still make vows to Thor for sea voyages, or when they found themselves in tight corners.'

'And were they as ferocious as the Sagas would have us believe?' Arnold asked.

'They could be ferociously cruel,' Dennis admitted. 'They were subject to a murder-spirit which descended upon them in battle. The texts show that men so possessed —the *berserkr*—had an aura of mystery and horror. They were regarded almost as supernatural in their fighting skills. There's a famous passage in *Snorr* . . .'

Dennis rose abruptly and walked across to the book-shelves that lined the far wall. He ran a finger along the titles, pulled out a volume and checked in the index. Culpeper sat impassively, watching his every movement like a thirsty man watching a bottle being opened.

'Here it is,' Dennis exclaimed. 'I quote: "*They advanced without mailcoats and were as frenzied as dogs or wolves; they bit their shields; they were as strong as bears or boars; they struck men down but neither fire nor steel could mark them. This was called the Berserk Rage.*" '

As he closed the book with a snap and returned it to its place on the shelf, Jane shuffled uneasily in her seat. 'So what does "berserk" actually mean?'

Dennis returned to his desk and sat down. 'Bear shirt. When they wore their animal skins they took on the attributes of the animal—they became wild beasts . . . were-wolves. It may well be the origin of the concept of mediæval legends about the conversion of man into beast.'

'This didn't apply to all Viking warriors, surely?' Arnold suggested. 'They all weren't overtaken by the berserk rage.'

'Oh no, only those who were . . . inspired, shall we say? Overcome by blood lust. They were men who were feared —and revered—by their own kind, for they were regarded as having almost magical properties, capable of turning away sword and spear. And in this rage, the berserk rage, when they killed their enemy, they would cut a bloodeagle.'

Culpeper coughed. He stared at Professor Dennis. 'What do you mean, bloodeagle?'

'It was the signature of the berserker. Think of a chicken, carved for the table. The berserker would treat a dead enemy like that. After killing his enemy, he would tear the chest cavity apart with a sword or axe, and splay out the ribcages, alongside the arms.'

'Gruesome,' Jane muttered.

Dennis smiled, pleased with the impression he had made. 'I've no doubt. But that was the recognized technique—a sort of signature. That was the acknowledged handiwork of the berserker.' He sipped his coffee, pleased with himself. 'Cutting the bloodeagle.'

3

Culpeper left Professor Dennis's room at the same time as Arnold and Jane but he barely spoke, other than to say a brief, gruff goodbye. Arnold watched him walk away to his car, get in and drive out of the narrow street back towards the city centre.

'If I were to hazard a guess,' Arnold said, 'I'd suggest Mr Culpeper has something on his mind.'

Jane nodded. 'What was it all about?' she asked. 'I mean, all that talk about Baillehache and Hagger and so on?'

'I haven't the slightest idea.' Arnold thought back to the Professor's words in the room above, and the impact they had had upon Culpeper. The subdued excitement in the policeman's bearing and the intensity of his expression had grown significantly as Dennis spoke. Arnold had no idea what lay behind the questions Culpeper had fired at the mediævalist, but it was clear the answers had great significance for him.

'Do you think it will be some case he's involved in?' Jane asked as they strolled up the hill towards Castle Green.

'I'm certain of it. When I met Culpeper up at Birley Thore he asked me about *drengs* but made out it was just a matter of personal interest. After his questioning of Dennis it was so patently nothing of the kind that it must be a police matter. Anyway,' Arnold concluded, 'it's nothing to do with us. When are you going to come up to take a look at the Birley Thore site?'

'Whenever you say it's worth while.'

Arnold considered for a moment. 'Leave it with me. Work on the bridge is getting on apace, but I'll go up to the field site and see what's happening. Colin Marshall did tell me that Mike Swindon—he's the mediæval pottery specialist—is getting impatient to open up the pit they've got up there so it might be a good time to come along after that. I don't know what there'll be to see, of course,' he warned.

'You give me a date, and I'll come along.'

'Fine. Well, you'd better leave it with me for a few days, until I get back to you.'

For the first few days of the following week Arnold was busy at the bridge. The cofferdams had been completed and were being pumped dry; on the Tuesday he was allowed to get down into the first cofferdam and inspect the area carefully. He came out muddied and empty-handed: he had been unable to find any trace of the preceding bridge structure—neither wooden nor stone remains were present.

A close inspection of the bed of the cofferdam demonstrated no evidence of a paved or metalled ford, either. When he clambered out Arnold thought he might make another check and take a closer look at the piers themselves. He climbed down the scaffolding and dropped down into the shallows at the foot of the pier, but he could see there had been a heavy build-up of humic soil against the heavy stone. When he climbed back up to the bridge, some questions of the engineers elicited that the soil seemed to overlay a gravel subsoil.

The conclusion was inescapable. As far as Arnold could make out from this first investigation, the existing bridge, now being widened, had not been built over the older construction.

He discussed his findings later in the week with Frank Lindley and Mike Swindon. He joined them in the hut on the field site and over a cup of coffee gave them the results of his clambering in the mud. It was not an easy discussion because there was a palpable tension in the room: no explanation was offered to Arnold but the two men were clearly out of sorts with each other. Arnold could guess it would be something to do with Mike Swindon's ungovernable temper. But clearly, all was not well with the site team at Birley Thore.

'So what do you conclude?' Lindley asked, drawing on his pipe.

Arnold shrugged. 'You'll remember Gilbert Stoneleigh's survey of the bridge rebuilding in 1834 was rather less than satisfactory. He left pertinent details unrecorded.'

Mike Swindon hunched forward, glowering. 'Such as?'

'Well, to be honest, from his account it's not clear whether the old bridge—the one where they found the artefacts cemented into the pier—was actually completely destroyed, or whether its remains were used to found the 1834 bridge.'

'You mean we don't know how the new bridge was positioned?'

'It's not clear from Stoneleigh's account. He wrote that the old bridge was "ill-placed" but he did not elaborate upon that. Consequently, we don't know whether he meant it was badly placed in relation to the road, or as an actual crossing point for the river.'

'What about the artefacts?' Swindon asked.

Arnold was aware of Frank Lindley staring at Swindon with a frown of annoyance.

'None have come to light on this occasion, in the coffer-dam or on the bed of the stream,' Arnold said. 'And we don't even know whether all the artefacts were recovered from the excavations in Stoneleigh's time. But from my investigation at the first cofferdam, I would guess that the 1834 bridge was constructed at some small distance from the older structure—which means that the old bridge was indeed totally destroyed.'

Frank Lindley nodded thoughtfully. 'And you've found nothing to suggest another, older paved ford?'

'Not at that point. We have to accept, of course, that the river will have changed its course more than once since Roman times, but if we're going to find any Roman or earlier remains, it will be upstream, I would guess—not under the Birley Thore bridge as it presently stands.'

Mike Swindon bared his teeth in an unpleasant grimace. 'Which means your presence at the bridge site has been a waste of time.'

'Hardly that,' Frank Lindley demurred coldly, glaring at Swindon. 'The evidence Arnold raises may be negative, but it tells us something about the 1834 survey and the site itself. So . . . you say you've inspected one cofferdam, Arnold. What about the second?'

'Tomorrow. Clearly, something might turn up there but I doubt it. My guess is it will be a repeat of the first coffer-dam: I'm now quite convinced that we'll find nothing there either. The old bridge was at some distance upstream—and if we want to look for traces, that's where we should look.'

Mike Swindon heaved himself to his feet and stepped away from the table in the hut. He grunted sourly. 'That's hardly where we should be concentrating effort—we don't even know where the earlier bridges were sited. And we have a much more important task to finish here—before the bloody developers come flooding in. I don't see any further point in sitting here listening to a tale of failure. I've better things to do with my time. I'll see you later, Frank.'

There was an oddly menacing tone to his last words.

Lindley nodded. 'I'm still not happy, Mike, about the explanation you gave.'

'That's as may be,' Swindon growled. 'But I've none other. Later, then.' He stumped his way out of the hut. He paid no regard to Arnold.

Frank Lindley caught Arnold's glance, and grimaced ruefully. 'Don't worry about it,' he remarked as Swindon closed the door behind him. 'He's a surly character, with an unpredictable temper, but he's a good mediævalist— and you can forgive a lot for that.'

'How's the project coming along?' Arnold asked.

'Work? Or personnel relations? Huh, you'll have gathered Mike and I aren't seeing eye to eye at the moment. As for the work, I'd resisted opening the pit until we got some more mature labour in, but I intended in any case making a start this week. I was away a couple of days, unfortunately . . .'

'So?'

Frank Lindley squinted at Arnold through a screen of smoke. He frowned. 'Mike's a bit impetuous. He decided to make a start on the pit, and he cleared the first six inches or so overall and sank a shaft. When I returned I put a stop to it until Dr Ormond got back . . . I got the impression Mike wanted to boast to us of some finds he'd made when we were both absent at a committee meeting in Carlisle. So we had a few words.'

If it was Mike Swindon involved, Arnold thought, it would be a shouting match.

'But it wasn't just that, I have to admit. There have been some other problems,' Lindley continued. 'There's something odd in the air . . . I've talked it over with Colin Marshall, but he says he can't detect it. And Jill Ormond . . . well, she tends to get preoccupied with her own interests and is maybe insensitive to what I'm talking about. But then, my thoughts are vague anyway.'

'So what's the problem?' Arnold asked.

Lindley shrugged. 'Maybe I'm getting old. And fanciful. It's just that . . . I don't know. Once or twice, late in the day, perhaps when I've been here alone after the others have gone, I've had the feeling someone's watching the site —you know what I mean?'

'Frustrated developers?'

Lindley laughed. 'Perish the thought. No, it's as though someone is prowling around the perimeter, when most people have left the site—it's as though someone is watching and waiting . . . but for what? Apart from that . . .'

'Yes?'

Lindley shrugged. 'Oh, I don't know . . . A couple of things seem to have gone missing. At least, Dr Ormond says so. Mike Swindon had an argument with her about some mediæval shards—she said they'd gone missing, but he said Colin Marshall had no record of them in the log, and he'd never even seen them anyway. And when two experts get to arguing, Arnold, you can imagine how bitterly it develops!'

'I can imagine. But doesn't young Marshall have the responsibility for managing the site? How does it happen that Dr Ormond and Mike Swindon are arguing about such things?'

Frank Lindley shuffled uneasily in his chair, aware of the implied criticism regarding his protégé. 'Well, yes, in a manner of speaking. I mean, it would normally be Colin's job to keep a check on all items found, but you've got to remember he's inexperienced, and he's dealing with two strong characters. Swindon in particular doesn't like what he sees as interference . . . I'm worried, though, about some of these other things . . .'

Arnold waited, but Frank Lindley said no more, merely drawing on his pipe reflectively. It was none of Arnold's business, anyway. He finished the cup of coffee he had been given and stood up. 'Well, I'd better make my way back to Morpeth. I'll take a look at the other cofferdam tomorrow.'

Lindley rose with him, and came to the door. They both stood there for a little while, looking out over the activity at the site. Lindley hesitated. 'That pit we were talking about . . . we found some scattered bones there, and evidence of burning. Or rather, Mike Swindon did when he did his preliminary excavation. I stopped it when I got back until we could gear ourselves up properly, and not go half-cock at it. But it occurs to me . . . if this bridge project is going to be a waste of time, do you have to go back to the office for the next few weeks?'

Arnold considered the matter for a moment. He shrugged. 'Brent-Ellis won't be looking for me. As far as he's concerned, I'm on a secondment. He won't inquire what I'm working on, as long as no complaints are made.'

'Who's to complain?' Lindley eyed him thoughtfully. 'You know what I'm suggesting?'

'I guess so. You believe I could be better employed here at the site.'

'What do you think?'

'I think you're right. But how would Mike Swindon and Dr Ormond respond to such a suggestion?'

'They're both professional enough to accept that an extra pair of eyes and hands would be useful.' He frowned again. 'And maybe in more ways than one, Arnold. So if you agree, I'd like you to join us for a while, once you're satisfied there really is nothing more to investigate at the bridge.'

'I'll be happy to go along with that. And the excavation at the pit . . . ?'

'We'll be starting Friday. And I think we'll make interesting finds almost immediately. Dr Ormond and Mike Swindon are of the same view as me: we think it's a burial pit, not a refuse pit. And that means we could find a considerable number of artefacts. When Swindon did his preliminary shaft he found the bones, some carbonized materials, and a few small artefacts—military stuff, mainly. Moreover, Mike Swindon thinks . . .'

He hesitated, cogitating. Arnold waited.

'Swindon thinks the pit is larger than we've calculated. Considerably larger. And that could lead to all sorts of interesting possibilities . . .'

*

'Such as?' Jane Wilson asked Arnold on Saturday morning.

Arnold shrugged. 'Who's to tell? But if it is a burial pit, and a large one at that, we could find several layers of usage. Megalithic, Roman, mediæval . . . we'll have to wait and see.'

'So when can I come to have a look?'

They had met in Alnwick. Jane had rung from the cottage she had rented in Northumberland, where she had been undertaking her book research, and suggested that for once they could meet north of the Tyne, since she was in his area. Though she had not said so, Arnold guessed the meeting was designed to stress that she really would like to take up his half-invitation to the Birley Thore field site as soon as possible.

'I'd suggest leaving it for a few days. Maybe towards the end of next week. By then they'll have enlarged the shaft and a more sensible assessment of the pit can be made. Mike Swindon is extending the topsoil removal over a rather wider area now, but the conclusions are hazy. By the end of the next week—'

'Saturday?'

'Or Sunday. There should be no one at the site then. I think that would be just about the best time,' Arnold agreed.

Arnold had inspected the second cofferdam at the bridge, and as he had warned Frank Lindley, there had been no trace of wooden or stone constructions of an earlier date than 1834. Stoneleigh's account had been somewhat of a red herring and time had been largely wasted in checking the site of the road-widening scheme. There was a third cofferdam being constructed which he would be able to investigate as a final check, but it really meant his time would now be better spent lending a hand at the field site.

'I was up there over the last few days. Mike Swindon had removed quite a bit of the topsoil since I was last there and I had a look in his shaft.'

'What has he exposed?' Jane asked.

Arnold shrugged. 'It's early days yet, but apart from

the shaft findings, he has identified a number of U-shaped gullies, V-shaped ditches and a small number of shallows, which suggests use as land divisions and stock enclosures.'

'You mean since the bones were buried there?'

'Not sure. Probably contemporaneous.'

'Farming and gravedigging in the same place?' Jane asked, puzzled. 'Are they sure about this?'

Arnold nodded. 'On the western side of the pit area there were some carbonized plant remains present in the soil samples.'

'Have they been analysed?'

'Dr Ormond had them analysed and was able to confirm that they were cereal crops, predominantly barley and oats, but no species specific to the Roman period. So they were twelfth- to fourteenth-century, that's the educated guess.'

'Any pottery specific to that period?'

Arnold nodded. 'And some other stuff as well.'

'What stuff?'

'Mike Swindon got excited over some shcrds which Jill Ormond identified as fourth-century, but it was in her area that a second set of bones was discovered.'

'So is the damn place a graveyard?'

'It looks that way, though the scattering would suggest a rather disorganized one. And really, they're already beginning to revise their opinions as a result of the mixture of scattered bones, implements, arrowheads and bone handles that have begun to appear. It means that the site is an important one.

'In what sense, important?' Jane asked, waving to the waitress in the coffee shop, so she would bring the bill.

'Important in the sense of it maybe amounting to a military cemetery, or . . . something else.'

Jane Wilson watched him carefully for a moment. 'A military graveyard. In a field previously used for cereal growing. I'm going to jump to no conclusions,' she said slowly.

'It's as well.'

'But a scattering of bones and military implements, traces

of carbon, a field used for food production . . . I would be thinking not so much of a military cemetery as . . . a hasty burying of men after a battle . . .'

'You said no conclusions,' Arnold remarked gravely.

'What time do we meet on Sunday?'

It was a fine morning. They met as arranged at the statue of the stiff-tailed Percy lion in Alnwick, on the outskirts of the town. They agreed that Arnold should drive, and they would pick up Jane's car on the return journey.

'There'll be no one at the site except maybe Colin Marshall or a watchman, unless Frank Lindley himself is up there this morning.'

They drove through the summer Northumberland countryside. The hedgerows were green and heavy, thick with summer flowers and the sun beat warmly through the sun roof. Jane said very little: it was one of the reasons why Arnold liked her and found her easy company: she did not chatter like some women, or find it necessary to speak on a journey. The silence was companionable.

When they finally reached Birley Thore Arnold hesitated, wondering whether to take her down to the bridge to show her where he thought the ancient fords might have been. Instead, he decided to go up to the field site first— they could make their way back to the bridge later, and maybe stop for a light lunch in the local pub.

He parked at the gateway to the field. Wooden screens had been erected just inside the fences, but no attempt had been made to protect the site overmuch, on the assumption that determined vandals would be able to get in anyway, and strong defences might prove too tempting for local youngsters. The site Mike Swindon had started to excavate in Lindley's absence was fenced off with a locked gate, but Arnold had a key: Frank Lindley had provided him with one when told that Jane was coming to look at the site.

They entered the site and Arnold pointed out the shaft where the first bones had been found.

'It seems they've picked up quite a bit of stuff now. As

you can see, the excavations in the corner there are now down to about a metre. You can see the soil gradations there—Swindon reckons the sherds found in that section are thirteenth-century, so we're talking about a site which is bang in the middle of the period you're interested in.'

Jane shivered slightly. 'It's a gloomy place.'

Arnold looked about him. 'I can't say I've thought about it. What has come to mind is the fact that this slope would have been tree-covered at the northern end, and if this was a cereal field the roadway would probably have passed down to the south-west, there.' He pointed, extending his arm. 'So it's not too difficult to imagine an ambush being laid in this area, men concealed in the woods, rushing out to the cross-roads that may have been down there leading into Birley Thore, and then fighting, crashing out into the field itself.'

'So you think it was a battle?'

'A skirmish, rather.' Arnold hesitated. 'They've found the remains of about four men so far. All bear signs of injury—crushed skull, broken arms and legs. And there's more fire signs.'

'But no watchman,' Jane said absently, glancing around the field. 'I was hoping to meet Mr Lindley.' She leaned forward to gaze down into the pit. 'I still think it's a bit shivery. I mean, here we are on a warm summer afternoon, but there's a feel about this place, a bad feel, as though men died unrequited lives here, and the unhappiness has lain here ever since.'

She could be fanciful, Arnold thought, once she started romanticizing about a place, losing grip of the bridge that lay between reality and her fiction, toppling over into the moat of make-believe. He clucked his tongue: he was getting fanciful himself. He looked around the site. There was no one about. No watchman. No Frank Lindley. No Colin Marshall, or Mike Swindon.

No vandals.

Perhaps the lack of a watchman didn't matter too much if there was no one to damage the site. But he thought

Frank always arranged for someone to check the site weekends, keep an eye on the place.

The thought remained at the back of his mind for the
next hour or so as Jane pottered around the site, and he
showed her where the bones had lain, where they expected
others to be unearthed, where the arrowheads and amulets
had been found, and the leather belt and decayed shoes.

'And were they military?'

'There was no chainmail if that's what you mean,' Arnold
replied. 'But they wouldn't leave that anyway, would they?
Too valuable to be buried with the dead.'

'No *hringskyrta*,' she murmured absently.

'And no weapons—which is what one would have expected if it had been a ceremonial site.'

'Have there been no finds of any value at the site?' she
asked.

'You mean jewellery?' Arnold shook his head. 'Why do
you ask?'

'I don't know . . . it's just something that Annette
Dominick said to me the other day. I don't suppose you'd
expect to find jewellery dug up out of a battle place.'

'I wouldn't discount it. Things get lost . . .'

They wandered over the site for a little while longer and
then Arnold suggested they should make their way down
to the village, he'd show her the bridge, and then they could
have a sandwich and a drink in the local pub. There was
still no sign of the watchman when they left the site.

He left the car in the pub parking area and they strolled
across to the bridge. Normally, people would have been
sitting out in the sunshine close to the bridge but the road-
widening scheme had scarred the surface of the banks and
the road itself was still taped off, so apart from a few children throwing stones at the ducks in the lower reaches of
the stream there was no one near the bridge.

Arnold ducked under the fluttering tape. 'I'll show you
the cofferdam.'

They walked across the bridge, and leaned over the parapet to look into the cofferdam. 'You see, they erected these

sheet pile supports, drained the dam and then the idea is
they can construct new foundations. See, if you just lean
out a bit further . . . grab the scaffolding there . . . you can
just make out—'

He stopped, staring, and slowly his face paled.

'Arnold—what's the matter?'

Next moment, leaning out herself, she caught sight of
what Arnold had seen, lying in the bottom of the dry
cofferdam.

It had been a man. His torso was a bloody mess. He
was flat on his back, his arms flung wide, his face staring
sightlessly at the sky. His features were virtually untouched
and Arnold recognized him. He now knew why Frank Lindley had not been at the site.

But as he stared, horrified, down into the cofferdam, it was
something else that was dinning into his skull, something
that Professor Dennis had said in his rooms in Durham.

Bloodeagle.

CHAPTER 4

1

It was the second time that John Culpeper had been caught
out at Seahouses. He had not been able to take a break for
three weeks and he and his wife had decided to get away
for the Saturday night. The call had come through while
they were still trying to relax; his wife had sighed in resignation at the news there was another death to investigate,
so it was in no pleasurable mood that Culpeper returned to
his desk on Tuesday morning after a long day at Birley
Thore. His mood was not alleviated when he received a
summons from the Chief Constable.

The Old Man was not given to towering rages. When he
was angry he became ice-cold, his eyes glittered in their

sagging pouches, and his mouth became like a piece of bent iron. Culpeper knew as soon as he walked into the Chief Constable's office that it was going to be one of those days.

The Chief Constable was standing with his back to the door, staring out of the window with his hands locked behind him, spine ramrod-stiff. As Culpeper entered he turned around slowly and stared at him. There was no hint of welcome in his glance.

'Are you happy with the control of your people?' he asked, without preliminaries.

'Yes, sir,' Culpeper said in surprise.

'Well, I'm not.'

'Sir?'

'The killing at South Middleton,' the Chief Constable said in a voice like ground glass. 'You had instructions to keep the details under wraps.'

'Yes, sir. No details were released to the Press, in spite of a lot of harassment—'

'And now this killing at Birley Thore. The handwork is much the same—'

Culpeper ducked his head awkwardly. 'At first sight it looks as though we've got a repeat, sir, yes, and—'

'So who authorized a release of the Birley Thore details?'

There was a short silence. Culpeper stared at the Chief Constable's mouth: it was set grimly, unforgiving. 'I . . . don't understand what you mean, sir.'

'You've been too busy, not had time to read the morning paper?' the Chief Constable asked in a tone stained with sarcasm. 'You'd better have a look at the copy on my desk, Culpeper.'

Culpeper stepped forward and picked up the newspaper. It had been folded to give prominence to the front page story. His hand trembled slightly as he held it: he did not care for confrontations with the Chief Constable.

At first his eyes barely took in the words in front of him.

WHAT MANIAC DID THIS?

The body discovered in the cofferdam at the road-widening scheme at Birley Thore has been identified as Frank Lindley, 58, the project leader at the dig some two miles from the scene of the murder. It is the second murder in the county in a matter of weeks and there are strong similarities between the two killings, enough to lead to the belief that the murders were committed by the same person.

Police are working on the theory that there is a link between the deaths of James Lloyd at South Middleton and Frank Lindley at Birley Thore.

The discovery of the second body by two passers-by has caused a wave of horror to sweep through the village at the thought of the maniac who is loose in the area. The mutilations on the bodies are said to be of the most horrific kind, with the chest torn open in each case as though by a wild animal, with a deliberate smashing of the ribcage.

We are reliably informed that the police are treating seriously the scrawled signature that was discovered at the scene, as evidence of a further link with the death of James Lloyd . . .'

Culpeper looked up at the glowering Chief Constable. 'Where did this come from?'

'I thought *you* were going to tell *me*! Weren't the Press kept away from the site?'

'Yes, sir, they were! We had it tied up better than at South Middleton—once the call came in we kept everyone away, and it was easier anyway since the bridge had already been taped off. As for the signature, that wasn't even discovered until we went looking seriously for it. I can't imagine how anyone, the workmen, or just anyone—'

'Spare me the details,' the Chief Constable interrupted scornfully. 'I just want to know how this story got out.'

'Not from us, sir. Farnsby was there and I can guarantee—'

'Guarantee what, Culpeper? We've been instructed to keep this sort of thing under wraps and now every paper in the area will be screaming at us for further details. A maniac loose in Northumberland! For God's sake, that's the last kind of headline we want! You know what sensations they'll screw out of this—particularly now they scent a link between South Middleton and Birley Thore. It doesn't seem to me you can guarantee anything right now.'

Culpeper fumbled for the right placatory words. 'I've had a warning out, sir, and I can't understand—'

'I want this leak sorted out, Culpeper! Find out who is responsible, and throw the book at him!'

'It won't be any of the scene-of-crime unit, sir.'

'Well, then?'

Culpeper gritted his teeth and thought for a moment. A slow anger burned in his chest. 'I can think of one possibility, sir.'

The Chief Constable stared at him for a little while, saying nothing, his eyes boring into Culpeper's unhappy face. At last he nodded and sat down behind his desk. 'All right. I think you know how I feel about this. I'll take the flak—this time. And I won't even want to know how you plug this leak. But let's be clear. You are going to plug it, watertight!'

'Yes, sir,' Culpeper ground out.

The Chief Constable leaned back in his chair and put his fingertips together. 'All right, tell me what you've got. To start with, where are we on the South Middleton killing?'

Culpeper took a deep breath. 'I've been in touch with DCI Castle again, sir, and I can confirm there are a number of similarities present, with regard to the Dunwich and South Middleton murders. Both men were wrist-bound when they were shot. Both were mutilated, possibly by a heavy, sharp-edged weapon such as a sword—'

'Good God, a nutcase!' the Chief Constable muttered.

'Both men had some sort of spear or arrowhead driven through their throats. At both sites the word "Godar" was found, and in local hotels we think the killer signed himself in with the name Dreng. These details are consistent with information received from Basle and Saumur also.'

'And this Dreng thing . . . why the hell should he give himself away like that, stick a signature in an hotel register?'

'We're still working on that. I've told DCI Castle I've discovered what the word *dreng* means—and also the surnames used with the word. I don't know why they were used, but they're words of Norse origin, and they sort of tie in with a military organization of some kind. We're looking at the military connection. James Lloyd—the man murdered at South Middleton—was in the Navy before he retired to Northumberland. DCI Castle is checking in Saumur and Basle, but the pattern isn't really established yet, since the man killed in Dunwich had no service record. He was a solicitor and local politician of sorts. So the pattern—if there is one—is still hazy.'

'What about the Birley Thore killing? What fit have you got there—since I'm told by the newspaper that police *have* made the link!'

Culpeper shrugged and shifted uneasily from one foot to another. 'It's too early to say yet, sir. The forensic report isn't in, but I did take a look myself for the signs that they may be linked killings. At this stage I have a feeling they are, but, well, I could see no signs of the wrists being bound, Lindley wasn't shot in the head like the others—'

'How did he die?'

'I think forensic will confirm it was a heavy blow to the back of the head.'

'Did Lindley have a service record?'

'Only National Service in the 'fifties. He was based on Salisbury Plain—but seemed to have spent much of his time doing survey work in Amesbury and Stonehenge. He was released just before the Suez crisis in 1954.'

'Hmmm. Hardly classifies much as a service record,' the Chief Constable grunted. 'And the mutilations?'

'The chest was carved open as before, perhaps more bloodily, more crudely, but with the same intent, it seems to me. There was no short spear through the throat, but there was a piece of rough iron—one view is it might be a mediæval crossbow bolt—in the cofferdam, lying across the body as though it had been thrown down there. But not driven through the throat.'

'And this word . . .'

'"Godar"? Yes, sir, we've found a trace of the word scrawled on the bridge pier, but hurriedly, almost inde-cipherable. Written with a piece of chalky stone, it seems.'

'So it looks like it's the same killer?'

Culpeper pursed his lips. 'Bound to be. The carving of the chest, the use of the word "Godar" . . . who else would know about such details?'

'Most people in the north of England, it seems to me, after this newspaper fiasco,' the Chief Constable replied grimly.

Culpeper swallowed. 'Yes, sir. But I do think we're deal-ing with one killer here—the details match those from Dun-wich, Saumur, Basle and South Middleton.'

'But not entirely, it seems. You have a theory at this stage?'

'I think the man was disturbed at Birley Thore. Didn't have time to complete the operation. Maybe he was hur-ried, couldn't use his pistol, couldn't drive in the spear thrust . . . I'm not sure, sir, but I think all the signs are we're dealing with one killer. Farnsby is now doing a check of hotel registers.'

'For this Dreng thing?'

'Yes, sir.'

'And what then?'

Culpeper hesitated. 'I've been in touch with DCI Castle. I've suggested we get together on this one, sir.' He waited, breathing lightly.

The Chief Constable shifted heavily in his chair. He was proud of his patch. He was notoriously unwilling to admit that outside assistance was necessary in the policing of his area. He sat there now, glowering at Culpeper, clearly un-happy at the thought that his own men couldn't handle two murder inquiries at the same time.

'You feel we're overstretched, Culpeper?'

'Not exactly, sir. It's just that I think two heads are better than one, as far as these cases are concerned. And DCI Castle has been involved longer than I have—with the overseas killings. He's also got direct access to computer facilities—and a link with Interpol. So I think a preliminary discussion up here would be useful. And there are some thoughts I want to test out on him—see if they gel for him.'

The Chief Constable drummed his fingers nervously on the desk. He inspected Culpeper with a critical eye for a few minutes, then slowly nodded. 'All right. Get him up here. But let's make it clear, while we're doing that, just what we're about. This is a collaborative and cooperative attitude we're showing—but that's all. Castle takes no part in our investigations up here—he's drafted in just to discuss similarities, not offer advice. That's clear?'

'Yes, sir.'

'And if his visit gets to the Press, you'll make sure it's clear to them too, won't you, Culpeper? I have every confidence in your relationship with those gentlemen,' he added drily, 'so you can get any stories you want published. It's nice to know we have such close links with the media.'

Culpeper wanted to make an angry rejoinder, but kept his mouth shut. Nevertheless, once he was dismissed he returned to his own office in a foul mood. Deliberately, he had a cup of coffee before he called in Vic Farnsby: it gave him time to cool down.

'You seen the papers this morning?'

Farnsby nodded. His face was pale, and his eyes were dark, as though he had been sleeping badly.

'So?'

'Sir?'

'So do you have any explanation?' Culpeper snapped angrily. 'Who the hell do you think will have supplied those details to the Press?'

'It's not one of the unit, sir, I vouch for that.'

'Come on, I know about canteen gossip—'

'Sir, there's been a strict injunction, and no contacts have been made with the Press.'

'Well, someone talked, Farnsby. Someone gave an interview. Someone spilled his guts about the mutilations and "Godar" and the link with the Lloyd killing! I want you to find out. Check with the newspapers. They'll probably give you a lot of guff about protecting their sources, but impress upon them that this is serious stuff.'

'I'll do that straight away, sir.' Farnsby hesitated. 'There is one thought . . .'

'Yes?'

'The two people who found the body in the cofferdam. Maybe it was one of those who got in touch with the newspapers.'

'I've already thought of that.' Culpeper grimaced unpleasantly. 'But you get on with talking to the newspaper editors. You can leave Landon and Miss Wilson to me.'

He motioned Farnsby to a chair and for the next hour or so they went over the details of the scene-of-crime-unit report on the killing at Birley Thore bridge. Farnsby was able to report that they had swept the area clean, and it was clear that, as in the case of the murder of James Lloyd, the killing had taken place away from the bridge itself.

'What about the site where Lindley had been working?'

'Swept clean also, sir. Not a thing—no signs of struggle or blood, or anything else.' Farnsby hesitated. "The odd thing is, he should have been up there that night. According to the statement DC Jenks took from the site manager, and from Michael Swindon, one of the archæologists, the site had been unworked the night before the body was found and Lindley had agreed to spend some hours up there as watchman.'

'Time of death?'

'Indeterminate as yet, sir, but first guesses are around about ten-thirty at night. By which time he would, presumably, have left the site anyway. In normal circumstances, he would leave about nine-thirty, as dusk was falling. But where he went from the site—if he was up there at all—or where he died, we can't tell yet.'

'No sightings?' Culpeper asked.

'None.'

Culpeper sighed. 'All right. The main thing now is to keep our heads down, get on with the basic stuff. We've got the chest slashing, the "Godar" signature, but we don't have the bullet in the head and the spear through the throat. Are you still with me in thinking the killer must have been disturbed?'

Farnsby nodded. 'I guess so. He didn't have time to complete the job.'

'Why the cofferdam, though?'

'How do you mean, sir?'

'The other sites have been fairly open . . . with mediæval connections.'

'There's supposed to have been an old bridge under the one being worked on. Mr Landon said that's why he's been observing there recently—'

'Yes, but setting aside the possible mediæval connection, if our guy wanted to use the same techniques as previously, he was making it bloody difficult for himself, wasn't he? I mean, throwing the body down into the cofferdam . . . he would have to climb down and drive the bolt in down there. He didn't do it—he tossed the thing down on top of the corpse.'

'As we say, sir—maybe he was disturbed.'

'He still had time to scrawl "Godar" on the bridge pier.' Culpeper shook his head doubtfully. 'No, something isn't ringing true here. And if he was disturbed, it's got to have to have been at the bridge, I would think. In which case, what disturbed him there? A passing car? Nothing was going over the bridge because of the roadworks. Strolling lovers? I don't think the scene there is very romantic at the moment with all the heavy machinery lying around. Legwork, I'm afraid, Farnsby—we've got legwork to do. Or rather, you have.' He scowled. 'I've got to have some sessions with DCI Castle, and get all the bloody paperwork done.'

'Yes, sir.'

There was a miserable tone in Farnsby's voice and Culpeper looked up. Farnsby was looking down at his hands and his eyes were hooded but the droop of his shoulders was expressive. Culpeper leaned back in his chair and wondered whether he'd been too hard on the Detective-Inspector: he himself had had two weekends ruined, and the prospect of running two murder inquiries at the same time alarmed him. It could well be even more tough for the younger man, because it was on his shoulders that Culpeper would be pressing heavily, delegating the hard slogging tasks that had to be done in any such inquiry. And Farnsby, for all his previous reputation, seemed to be flagging.

'You all right, Farnsby?'

The man's head came up slowly: his eyes were vague. 'Sir?'

'I . . . I've had the impression you're under a bit of pressure. You sleeping all right?'

Farnsby hesitated. 'Well enough.'

Culpeper had had a few dreams himself, tossing in a half-awake state as he saw again the devastated chest cavity of James Lloyd, and the ripped open corpse of Frank Lindley. 'It's part of the job, lad—this mucky stuff. I had more of my share of it as a young copper—heads burst open on railway lines—you just have to get over it. You never do, not entirely, but you have to thicken your skin, build a shield, not let it affect your life—'

'Easier said than done!' Farnsby said sharply.

Culpeper's eyes widened. He stared at Farnsby reflectively. 'I never said it was easy. But get the walls built; don't get involved.'

Farnsby shook his head. 'It's not that, anyway.'

There was a short pause. 'So what is it, then?' Culpeper asked quietly, aware that the Detective-Inspector needed to talk.

'You're married, sir?'

'A long time.'

'I've been married four years. My wife . . . she's a child psychologist. Good job.'

'I believe it.'

The silence grew around them again. Farnsby shuffled

uneasily in his seat. 'The fact is, she thinks I'm . . . uncommunicative.'

Culpeper sighed. 'There are some things you can't talk about.'

'Yes, but I've tried. At first, it was OK and we got along well enough, but then she started coming out with some of her psychobabble about how she felt we weren't being close enough, not communicating, drifting apart, all that sort of rubbish.'

'Maybe not rubbish . . . all marriages go through sticky patches from time to time. It'll blow over, I'm sure—'

'Well, I'm not. Sure, that is . . . She's seeing someone else.'

Culpeper grimaced, and said nothing. He waited.

'I don't know who he is, but I've had suspicions for some time. The way she acts. The way she talks sometimes. Short-tempered. Daydreaming. All the signs, you know? Signs that in her mind she's elsewhere, not with me. And things have been busy this last year . . . even busier these last few weeks. There've been rows . . .'

'But these are only suspicions, Farnsby. Could be other reasons. Maybe she's upset because she sees so little of you. Maybe . . . well, you know, maybe it's simply she wants a child—'

'It's not just suspicion,' Farnsby interrupted sullenly.

Culpeper cleared his throat nervously. He had a quick image of his wife, the problems they had faced years ago— all over now, in their settled, mature, reasoned existence together. 'You *know* she's involved with someone else?'

'I've seen them together.'

'A chance meeting—'

'No,' Farnsby interrupted sharply. 'I saw them. I was in the car—coming back from South Middleton. I saw her getting on a bus just outside Morpeth. He was kissing her. Then I checked at her office. She's been working flexitime: she's been taking a half day off each week for some time. To shop.'

'Yes, but—'

'Wednesday's not a good shopping day,' Farnsby said sullenly.

Culpeper hesitated. 'And you don't know who this . . . friend is?'

Farnsby shook his head. 'I got a good look at him, but I don't know him. And I thought it best not to bring the matter up. I've a marriage to save as well as a job to do, so I thought it best to try to . . . smooth things over. Talk, get closer to her, make her understand how important this job is to me. She certainly can't complain of my being un-communicative of late . . .'

'A lot of us have hit rocky patches—the job and mar-riage, they're difficult to reconcile at times.'

Farnsby nodded. He straightened up in his chair. 'And it's my problem, not yours. I'm sorry I even brought it up. But you asked . . .'

Uneasily Culpeper nodded. He did not have the right words; he didn't know how to help. Gruffly he said, 'Well, if there's anything you need, or if you feel . . .'

'I've got a job to do, sir, I'll get on with it. My marriage is my business.' The resentment in his tone was directed at Culpeper, as though the DCI was responsible in some way for the shaky status of the marriage.

'Yes,' Culpeper said shortly. 'Well, you've enough to get on with. I'll need a report as soon as you come across another registered *dreng*—if you do. Meanwhile, I'm going to chase up the Ministry of Defence—see if I can find any military connection . . .'

After Farnsby left the room Culpeper remained sunk in thought. He felt uneasy and disorientated. He wondered whether he had been too hard on Farnsby, as the Chief Constable had suggested; but the Chief Constable did not know about Farnsby's marital problems.

And John Culpeper didn't want to know—not in the middle of an investigation.

He stood up and paced about the office. He was looking forward to DCI Castle's visit. The man was immersed in the killings, had spent a lot of time on them, and it could be that if they got their heads together some pattern would emerge.

Pattern . . . He had contacted Castle after his visit to see Professor Dennis. They had discussed the significance of the names, and the possible motivations behind their use, but had come to no conclusions. The military, Viking connection seemed to have little relevance to the modern world, but Lloyd had been a serviceman and it was just possible there was a pattern there . . . if only they could find it.

And then there was the matter of the mediæval sites. Birley Thore bridge was a bit thin, as a mediæval connection. From what Arnold Landon had told him, the bridge dated back to 1834, not before. Whereas the site up at the field, that went back a thousand years . . .

Thoughtfully, Culpeper picked up the desk phone and called Farnsby's number. The Detective-Inspector was quickly on the line.

'You say we found nothing at the field site in Birley Thore?'

'That's right, sir. I wasn't up there myself, the work was done by Jenks, he did the interviews and took the statements, while I concentrated on the bridge site. Is there a problem?'

'No, no, but I gather a Mr Swindon has been pressing that we allow work to continue on the site. They have time problems. There's no reason why we shouldn't allow them to get on, is there?'

'Not that I can see.'

'Fine.'

Let them carry on, thought Culpeper: it wouldn't hamper the investigation. But perhaps a pair of eyes . . . With two murder investigations in train, they were very tight on manpower. And would it be worthwhile to put someone in there, under cover maybe, to keep an eye on what was going on? The Chief Constable, no doubt, would veto it as a waste of time, but if Culpeper could find the manpower, it might be worth doing. He had an odd feeling about Birley Thore.

A pair of eyes, at the Birley Thore field site.

If he could spare the manpower.

2

He stood out like a sore thumb.

Arnold still felt the occasional slow surge of anger more than a week after the event. It was not simply the humiliating manner in which he and Jane had been summoned to Culpeper's presence at headquarters in Morpeth, nor even the upbraiding tone that Culpeper had used with them both. It was all made worse by the fact that Culpeper clearly did not believe them.

'I don't know what I've got to say to persuade you that you're barking up the wrong tree,' Arnold had expostulated angrily. 'We've cooperated completely with you—we waited at the bridge, made statements then, and completed full statements later—'

'We rang you as soon as we saw Mr Lindley's body in the cofferdam—' Jane interposed.

'And rang the newspapers at the same time, I presume,' Culpeper sneered.

'Why on earth should we want to do that?' Arnold asked in amazement. 'I was completely shaken by what I saw— I knew Frank Lindley, after all—and Jane was in worse case than I was. The state of the body—'

'Which you saw, and the scene-of-crime unit saw, but who else was there to see just what had been done? Who else saw the mutilation, and the scrawled word on the pier?'

'Neither of us saw anything on the pier, or we'd have said so in our statements. All we saw was Lindley's body—'

Culpeper snorted in disbelief. 'According to your statement, once you saw the body you called us from the phone-box. Then you sat on the bridge—shaken, I think you said —waiting for us to arrive.'

'And the ambulance,' Arnold corrected him. 'We rang for an ambulance.'

'Fat lot of good that was.'

'We didn't know whether he was still alive.' As soon as he said it, Arnold felt foolish. The state of the body had showed quite clearly that Lindley was dead. But he had been overcome, not thinking straight. 'Maybe it was one of the ambulance crew.'

'No,' Culpeper said firmly. 'They never got to look into the cofferdam—if you remember, we arrived first and took over, kept the ambulance crew away.'

'But there were plenty of people—'

'*Our* people,' Culpeper interrupted, 'who know the score.'

'So what was so important about not telling the papers anyway?' Jane protested. 'They'd have found out soon enough—you'd have had to issue a statement. You couldn't have kept it quiet.'

'We wouldn't have kept the fact of the murder quiet. It's the manner of the killing we wanted to keep under wraps.'

Arnold had stared at him. A slow realization crept into his brain. His lips were suddenly dry. 'This isn't the first time.'

Culpeper stared at him impassively.

'What do you mean?' Jane asked.

'This isn't the first time someone's been killed like this.'

'I didn't say that,' Culpeper replied heavily.

'No, but it's pretty obvious. You're upset because the details have been released . . . details you've managed to keep out of the papers when it's happened before.' Arnold frowned. He was about to ask another question, but thought better of it. But Jane was puzzled.

'Why would you place such emphasis on keeping details quiet?'

Culpeper hesitated. Cautiously he said, 'Where a crime has . . . odd or peculiar characteristics it's best to keep some details back from the public. If they're gruesome, for instance . . . and also it helps to . . . ah . . . eliminate people where other crimes occur. Similarities can be checked, of course—'

'And there's the possibility of a copycat,' Arnold said in a subdued tone.

Culpeper glanced at him, and nodded. 'That's right. If

we release details, there's often the chance that some nut-case will try to emulate the method, the system, the details that have become public knowledge. It can play havoc with an investigation—really mess up an inquiry. When I tell you that previously we've successfully kept under wraps some of the details that you've now exposed—'

'*We* didn't expose them,' Arnold interrupted wearily.

'Well, who the hell else did?' Culpeper exploded, losing his temper. 'All I can say is it was a damn fine day's work on your part, and for what? For the glow of instant fame? For cheap excitement . . . a feeling of momentary power? Telling secrets to the newspaper? For God's sake!'

'Damn it, all you have to do is check with the news-papers!' Arnold almost shouted in return. 'They'll tell you it wasn't either of us who phoned them!'

'We *have* checked! And we've been given the runaround, of course! An anonymous telephone call, they say. I've heard that guff before—they're just covering up. Well, there's not much I can do about it now, but I tell you this. I've had my backside in a sling over this business, and I'm not taking any more of it. I know one of you two made that phone call—and I don't give a damn now about which one it was. But I'm warning you—keep your heads down. We've got big problems here and we want to catch the bastard who did this. It doesn't help if there are loose mouths around, like yours.'

He would not be convinced. Jane rose to her feet with studied dignity and asked, 'Is that all, Mr Culpeper?'

He was breathing angrily. 'For now,' he grated. 'But remember—I'm keeping my eye on you. I don't forget or forgive easily . . . and I'll be watching you.'

And the watcher stuck out like a sore thumb.

He had been recruited by Colin Marshall shortly after Arnold's discussion with Culpeper, and he worked quietly and well in Dr Ormond's group. But he had a breezy self-confidence and an assurance that set him apart from the others who had joined the dig: he was older, to begin with,

probably in his mid to late thirties. Arnold calculated he
was about five feet ten in height; he had an easy-going air
about him, sharp blue eyes and good-looking features, with
an irregularity about his mouth that would be attractive to
women. It was certainly attractive to Dr Ormond: she
began to lighten her attitudes considerably in his presence
and when they worked together it was obvious she enjoyed
talking to the man.

He was called John Vincent; dark-haired, physically
strong and muscular, he had an extrovert personality and
a deep, booming laugh that tended to make others smile.
His good humour was infectious, but Arnold noted how he
displayed a certain curiosity, keen to know what was going
on all over the site, and several times while Arnold himself
had been working there he had caught Vincent watching
him.

But he was obvious to Arnold: the man bore himself like a
policeman, accustomed to discipline for all his stained sweatshirt and ragged jeans, and Arnold resented his presence.
Culpeper had not believed him or Jane; he had threatened
to keep an eye on him; and now this policeman was pretending an interest in working the site. The resentment
churned inside Arnold and robbed him of much of the pleasure he would otherwise have taken in the dig.

Mike Swindon had approached him as soon as the police
had given them permission to continue the work at the field
site. Swindon had said little about Lindley's death: he had
simply told Arnold that it had been agreed that he, Swindon, would take over leadership of the project and he understood Lindley had made an approach to Arnold before his
death. He expressed no personal regret at Lindley's death,
but that was like the man. It was with a degree of reluctance
that Arnold said he would work on the site for a few weeks:
the prospect of working under Swindon was less pleasant
than that of working under Lindley, but he felt in a sense
he owed it to the dead man—Lindley had been enthusiastic
about Birley Thore, and it seemed wrong now to back out.

Colin Marshall had asked him about it, two days after he joined the site team.

'I gather you and Frank spoke about your joining us.' Marshall stood half facing away from Arnold, looking down across the rest of the site, one hand shading his eyes against the sun.

'Tne work at the bridge was getting pointless, and anyway the police have closed it down for the time being.'

'At least they've left us alone up here,' Marshall said. He hesitated. 'Did you and Frank have a long chat?'

'How do you mean?'

Marshall shrugged. 'I don't know. I wonder if he told you . . . about his disagreement with Mike Swindon.'

Arnold shook his head. 'I could see they'd been having some sort of argument but I didn't get any details. It wasn't particularly serious, though, was it? I mean, they were still working together.'

'Mike can get a bit violent when he's roused,' Marshall said carefully. 'I just wondered . . .' He was silent for a little while. 'Frank was a good friend to me.'

'So I gather.'

'I can't think why anyone should want to kill him.'

'Nor I.'

Marshall glanced sideways at Arnold: his eyes seemed to be weighing him up. 'You've not got any theory about it? I mean, you've heard nothing . . . ?'

Arnold shrugged: he found the conversation peculiar and unsettling, and the resentment at his treatment by Culpeper still burned in his chest. He wondered whether Marshall had heard about it. 'No,' he replied abruptly. 'I liked Frank, and I found him an equable fellow. I can't imagine he had any enemies—and as for the quarrel with Swindon, well, I imagine Swindon quarrels with most people from time to time.'

'That's true enough.'

Arnold looked down the field. 'Where did you find that chap Vincent?'

'Eh? Oh, he came up in the general trawl. Once we lost

the students I had to organize a field force, so I advertised locally in the Press. He turned up. Friendly guy, but doesn't really say much, you know? I had a session with him the other evening, though: he's a great one for drinking and for the girls too, it seems.' Marshall laughed suddenly. 'I think Jill Ormond has taken a shine to him, and that's a turn-up for the books.'

Grinning, Marshall turned to face Arnold. Something in the older man's face gave him pause and the smile vanished. He stared at Arnold for a few seconds. 'You must think we're a bit . . . odd up here on the site. Mike Swindon didn't get on with Frank, so it's obvious he wouldn't mourn. Jill Ormond, well, I think she was badly shaken, and maybe that's why she's getting so friendly with Vincent—a sort of reaction, trying to get away from thoughts of Frank. As for me . . . I don't wear my grief on my sleeve, Mr Landon.'

Arnold shrugged. 'You were close to Frank Lindley.'

'That's right. I owed him a great deal. And I don't forget. But life has to be lived, and what mourning I do, I do in private.'

'Why tell me this?'

Marshall shrugged. 'I suppose I just wanted you to understand . . .'

And perhaps Arnold did. Marshall was a young man who had enjoyed an erratic career: he had been helped considerably by Frank Lindley but that was no reason for him to parade his grief at the site, now Frank was gone. Marshall clearly had settled after a wild youth—even to the extent of being prepared to work with someone he clearly disliked, like Mike Swindon. Even so, Arnold felt there was a certain insincerity in what he said and he wondered just how deep the man's feelings went. Some people could forget a helping hand quickly; some could even resent it.

Work proceeded at the site slowly for several days and then, as the pit was opened further, in two sections superintended by Swindon and Dr Ormond, an element of competitiveness began to creep in as more discoveries were made. Three more scattered skeletons were unearthed at

the Ormond dig, but these were matched by a pile of artefacts in Swindon's area. They consisted of arrowheads,
some pottery sherds and the bone handle of an axe. Consultations became frequent: Colin Marshall organized the col-
lection of the finds and grouped them on the table in the
little hut, cataloguing and marking them. He himself had
become enthusiastic about working at the site in the south-
west corner, and he was present at the consultations in the
evening, listening with interest as Ormond and Swindon
discussed the progress. Arnold attended the sessions, and
after the first few days, so did John Vincent.

There was no real reason why he should not, since they
were regarded as open sessions where anyone who wished
to make a comment could do so, but Vincent said nothing,
merely listened. Arnold was aware of his presence, however,
with a bristling of hairs at the back of his neck and a sullen
resentment at being observed at close quarters in this
manner.

Towards the end of the second week it was clear they
were unearthing what had been a hastily constructed grave
mound for perhaps twenty men or more. All bore the marks
of hasty burial, and of wounds that had hastened them to
their grave. The general consensus was that a skirmish had
been fought here, and that the burials had been quick. Little
attempt seemed to have been made to remove valuable
items such as rings, a cloak clasp and bronze bangles: Marshall was beginning to catalogue a number of items such as
buckles and sword pommels, clasps of iron and bronze, and
a scattering of coins. They were identified by Swindon as
thirteenth-century and the coins had been minted by Henry
II, apart from a few which had been Scottish in origin—
hardly surprising in view of the extent of movement between the two countries in the Borders area.

There was some intrusion by local reporters as news of
the finds leaked out, but the questions soon deteriorated
into speculations about the death of Frank Lindley, for in
spite of the excitement that had been generated by the
mediæval finds a feeling of restraint still hung over the field,

to surface from time to time as a palpable gloom. When the reporters began to switch the topic, however, Mike Swindon called a swift halt to the proceedings: the scowl on his face made it clear he was unwilling to brook discussion other than concerning the dig itself.

Nevertheless, Arnold enjoyed the work, the slow, meticulous patience demanded was close to his heart, and he found personal delight in identifying some of the stone foundations, when called to the Ormond site, as having been eleventh-century, probably a wayside hostelry. It would have been burned perhaps in William the Conqueror's harrying of the north, and built over later, only to decay again as the area was turned over to agriculture. John Vincent was watching him curiously as he expounded his views, and the observation irritated Arnold.

That particular find kept him late at the site one evening, and it was getting dusk before he left. He was hungry, so decided to call in at the pub in Birley Thore to have a meal before he essayed the drive back to Morpeth.

When he entered the pub he was surprised to see John Vincent there. He was seated in the corner, leaning forward on his elbows, smiling and talking to Dr Jill Ormond. Her face was flushed, her eyes animated, and she had one hand touching his arm, laughing about something Vincent had said.

Arnold recalled that when he had first met her he considered she could be an attractive woman: he now revised the opinion—she *was* an attractive woman, her face lit up, responding, enjoying the presence of the man across the table from her. It was a situation in which Arnold had no wish to intrude: he made his way to the bar, ordered some sausage and chips and a half of lager, and went back to his seat.

He kept his back to the couple while he sipped his lager: when his meal arrived a little while later he ate in silence. He finished the meal and it was cleared away, but he stayed, brooding over thoughts of Frank Lindley and Culpeper's haranguing when a voice behind his left shoulder made him jump.

'Mr Landon? Would you like a drink?'

John Vincent was standing just behind him, smiling, an empty beer glass in his hand. Arnold glanced back towards the seat Vincent had occupied. Dr Ormond was no longer there.

'She's away off home,' Vincent explained. 'And I saw you sitting here by yourself—'

'I don't want a drink, thank you. I've a drive to make back to Morpeth.'

'That's where you live, is it?' Vincent said conversationally.

As if you didn't know, Arnold thought to himself.

Vincent hesitated, staring at Arnold thoughtfully, then walked away to the bar. Arnold watched him as he bought a half pint of Newcastle Brown, then to his consternation Vincent came back and slid into the seat opposite him. 'Might as well keep you company till you leave. I'm in no hurry myself.'

Arnold scowled. 'You far to go?'

'Far enough.' Vincent eyed him over the rim of his beer glass and was silent for a little while. The silence was marked by a certain tension on Arnold's part: he resented Vincent's presence.

After a while Vincent said easily, 'There's something bugging you, Mr Landon. I can tell. You give me the impression you don't like me.'

'I don't know you.'

'Exactly.'

'But I know what you are.'

Vincent stiffened momentarily. 'Indeed?'

'And I know what you're doing here at the site.'

Something burned in John Vincent's eyes for a moment, and the irregularity of his mouth became more marked. He was gripping his glass tightly as he searched Arnold's features with an odd intensity. 'Now is that so?'

His tone was gritty. Still angry, Arnold nodded. 'I knew

you were from Morpeth as soon as you set foot on the site.'

For a moment Vincent seemed to be about to say something, then he stopped, remained silent, staring at Arnold. Then, slowly, he relaxed and a slight smile came to his face. 'So there's no more need for me to . . . dissemble, then.'

'Don't play games with me,' Arnold said shortly. 'Your boss, Detective Chief Inspector Culpeper, made it clear that he intends keeping an eye on me, as he says, to make sure I behave myself. But I'll tell you, as I told him, neither I nor Jane Wilson phoned the Press about Lindley's death.'

Vincent was silent for a little while, his eyes hooded as he contemplated his glass. Then he raised his head: he had intelligent, quick eyes that held a hint of calculation. 'But it *was* you who found the body,' he demurred.

'And that's all there was to it.' Arnold finished his drink. 'So as far as I'm concerned you're wasting your time, working on the site just to keep an eye on me. Your cover, as they say in your business, is blown!'

John Vincent frowned. He seemed to be thinking something over for a moment and then his brow cleared, he shrugged and chuckled. 'You are a perceptive man. It doesn't please me to realize you picked me out so quickly —I thought I was better than that. But I also think you have a peculiar idea about . . . police work, Mr Landon.'

'How do you mean?'

Vincent leaned back in his seat and observed Arnold gravely. He appeared to have made a decision. 'You don't really think a police officer would be assigned to this site just to make sure you didn't get into any mischief, do you? We've better things to do with our time. All right, it might have started that way . . . it might have been the original reason, but . . .'

'What are you getting at?' Arnold asked suspiciously.

'Frank Lindley was murdered and his body found at the bridge, but he worked up here,' Vincent said quietly. 'Just what exactly did you see down at the bridge?'

'It's all in my statement—the mutilated body, that's all.'

'Nothing else? Not the . . . signature? Or a . . . Nothing else?'

Arnold shook his head. 'Nothing. And I can't imagine what you would expect to find up here at the field site.'

Vincent's eyes were calculating. He hesitated, then said, 'Lindley worked up here. And I gather things weren't too happy. Dr Ormond tells me Lindley and Swindon were at daggers drawn.'

So that was why Vincent had been spending so much time with Jill Ormond: he'd been weaseling his way into her confidence and perhaps affection in order to get information . . . Something of Arnold's disapproval must have shown in his face, for Vincent smiled gently. 'She's an attractive woman, Mr Landon. And I've always liked attractive women.'

'As part of the job?'

Vincent shook his head slowly, his eyes boring into Arnold's. For a moment there was something hard in his eyes, hard, committed and ruthless. It was gone in a moment as Vincent said, 'Let me tell you something, Mr Landon. I've done many things in my time—salesman, office clerk, warehouse supervisor—and I've known a lot of women. I enjoy women. But I've never married. You see, it's a path I've never wanted to tread. And for some years now . . . well, you know how it is . . . in the police, I mean. There's no time for the soft things of life. There's duty . . . and obligations.' He paused. 'You're not married either, I guess.'

'That's right.' Arnold hesitated, curious in spite of himself. 'So you've been talking to Dr Ormond, maybe seeking her company, for a reason.'

'I didn't say that,' Vincent objected. 'She's a fine-looking woman.'

'And she's attracted to you,' Arnold said impatiently. 'But you do have a reason. What is it? You surely don't think anyone up here at the site has any connection with Frank Lindley's death?'

'Most murders are committed by people well known to their victims.'

'But surely not in this case. It's not the first time this kind of killing's taken place.'

Vincent was silent for a moment, his glance fixed on Arnold, hard and bright. 'So you know about that . . .' He paused, and his glance swept around the bar. 'All right, but we have to check on everything. And it's a funny thing, in police work. I mean—I'm set up to keep an eye on you and make discreet inquiries around the site as well, sort of under cover—even if you spotted me a mile off! And then, well, other bits of information sort of start trickling in.'

'What kind of information?' Arnold asked suspiciously.

Vincent smiled. 'What have *you* heard?'

'I don't know what you mean.'

'What about the quarrel between Swindon and Lindley?'

Arnold shrugged. 'I don't know the reason for it. Frank Lindley led me to believe it was partly to do with the fact that Swindon opened up the pit in the absence of Lindley and Dr Ormond.'

'Jill Ormond verified that.' Vincent nodded smoothly. 'Anything else?'

Arnold frowned and shook his head. 'Nothing specific. He said there'd been some problems with unlisted artefacts or something like that, but I wasn't very clear what it was all about.'

'Neither was Jill Ormond. Still . . .' Vincent was silent for a little while, then he sipped at his glass. He rose suddenly and ordered Arnold to stay where he was. 'Whether you like it or not, I'm buying you a drink.'

Ignoring Arnold's protest, he walked to the bar and ordered Arnold a Scotch. 'Now, then,' he said as he returned with the glass in his hand, 'I think it's time we made a new start, hey?'

'I don't see—'

'You're not flavour of the month at headquarters.'

'I can't help it if Culpeper sees fit to disbelieve me,' Arnold replied sullenly.

'Be that as it may. I've been set to keep an eye on you, but I've got some funny feelings about this site, and its connection with Frank Lindley's death. My boss—DCI Culpeper—he might not agree with me. But he's not always right. Who is, for that matter?'

'I think Culpeper has a different view.'

Vincent smiled confidently. 'That's Culpeper for you. But I have a proposition. I think I can . . . trust you. And I'm impressed by your . . . perceptiveness. You notice things. You keep your head down and your eyes and ears open, right? I'll not waste time watching what you're up to—and maybe if either of us come across anything . . . interesting, we could get together. Sort of compare notes. Is it a deal?'

'I don't know what you think I should be looking for.'

'Neither do I, at this stage,' Vincent replied. 'But I'm going to keep tapping Jill Ormond, and who knows what might turn up when people relax? But as I said—do we have a deal? You keep well away from Morpeth head-quarters and my boss, and I'll not dog your footsteps. And then we trade information if we get any. Are you on?'

He had raised his glass.

Reluctantly, confused, Arnold raised the glass of whisky in a return salute. 'All right, it's a deal.'

He had the feeling, nevertheless, that he might have cause to regret his arrangement if it ever came to the ears of Detective Chief Inspector Culpeper.

3

Detective Chief Inspector Castle's second visit to Morpeth was a surprise.

Out of the blue, Culpeper received a phone call to the effect that Castle was on the way. Since nothing more than that was said, Culpeper was puzzled, but a feeling of antici-pation soon crept into his chest. If it was important enough to bring Castle hot foot up to the North-East, it must mean he had something interesting to impart to Culpeper regarding the Dreng Murders, as he and Farnsby had now begun to refer to them.

At the first meeting with Castle at Morpeth Culpeper had communicated to his Suffolk colleague the details furnished by Professor Dennis regarding the names used by the killer. They had sat and discussed them for a long while and Castle had agreed to undertake the further checking of the backgrounds of the people killed at Saumur and Basle.

Castle had stayed overnight near the Newcastle racecourse and Culpeper had joined him for dinner: when Castle had commiserated with Culpeper over the breach of security in the newspapers the men had become friends . . . or perhaps it had been the effect of the wine.

'So have you stopped the chance of any further leaks?' Castle had asked.

'I've done all I can,' Culpeper replied.

In the meanwhile Culpeper had finally managed to get information out of the Ministry of Defence. It had taken a long time, but he had now developed a reasonable contact in one Commander Askwith, who had proved quite helpful over the phone. He had been able to trace for Culpeper the record of James Lloyd who, it seemed, had not just been 'Navy', but had actually spent some time in the Special Boat Service, had undertaken a number of missions for the service and had barely escaped with his life on one African occasion—after which he had left the SBS, and finally the service itself, to live in Northumberland, where he had died.

It did little to help the case investigation, but at least it fleshed out the man for Culpeper: he checked some of the details with Mrs Lloyd, but she was able to confirm very little. James Lloyd had been pretty tight-lipped about his naval service.

It had been left to Farnsby to look further into the activities of the businessman with whom Lloyd had had an appointment the day he died. He had come up with some interesting information—and some suspicions.

'It seems that James Lloyd was introduced to Clem

Stevens—the guy he was supposed to meet that day—by none other than Mrs Lloyd.'

'So?'

Farnsby shrugged. 'It seems Mrs Lloyd and Stevens were old acquaintances. She introduced her husband to Stevens and then Stevens tried to get Lloyd interested in this riding stable venture. But I get the feeling that Mrs Lloyd was perhaps pushing the deal a bit.'

'She told me Lloyd thought the business shaky,' Culpeper said.

'I think it probably was . . . but it seems she was pretty keen he should invest.' Farnsby hesitated. 'Maybe to help out an old boyfriend?'

Culpeper raised his eyebrows. It was making a large supposition . . . and then he recalled Farnsby's own situation at the moment, and wondered whether the Detective-Inspector was allowing his own condition to colour his judgement. Perhaps something of the thought showed in his face, for Farnsby ducked his head and set his mouth grimly.

Culpeper had suggested he kept digging at the matter to see if he could come up with something more positive, but it sounded a bit light to him, and he was now far more interested in what DCI Castle might have to say.

Castle bustled into the office at four in the afternoon. The two men shook hands warmly, and Culpeper ordered some tea to be brought in. They sat down, and Culpeper was immediately aware of a sense of subdued excitement in the man who sat facing him.

'You've got something,' Culpeper said flatly.

'It could be a breakthrough,' Castle said, and smiled. He was carrying a leather slipcase, and he unzipped it and removed some sheets of paper, placing them on Culpeper's desk. 'I think I've dug up the link between several of these killings. There is a pattern after all . . . and it's emerging.'

'Tell me,' Culpeper said, trying to keep the excitement out of his voice.

Castle took a deep breath. 'Well, I contacted Interpol and asked them to run several checks through their computers. While they were doing that I had a close look at the Dunwich killing . . . and ran another check on the man killed in Suffolk. You'll remember he was called Michael Jenkins —the solicitor and local politician. And something curious turned up. It wouldn't have come out earlier, of course, but after the South Middleton killing on your patch . . .'

'What was it?'

Castle leaned forward, his eyes glittering. 'Michael Jenkins was married, but his wife predeceased him. They had no children. Family was scarce, in fact. But Jenkins did have an older sister. She also predeceased him.'

'No other family?' Culpeper asked.

'Ah, that's the point.' Castle's voice had a self-satisfied note. 'Michael Jenkins's sister was called Jean. She married a man called Lloyd. Both Jean and her husband were killed in a car crash twenty years ago. Their son survived.'

Culpeper stared at the Suffolk policeman. 'Lloyd . . . James Lloyd? Are you telling me James Lloyd and Michael Jenkins were related?'

'Absolutely. Uncle and nephew.'

'And both killed in the same way?' Culpeper frowned. 'But you'd have thought Lloyd . . . when his uncle died . . .'

'James Lloyd and Michael Jenkins weren't close: they weren't even in touch. Lloyd may have known of his uncle's murder . . . but he certainly didn't go to the funeral. However, let's face the facts: they were related and both killed in the same manner.'

'So the link is *family!*' Culpeper burst out excitedly.

Castle raised a hand. 'Hold on a moment. I thought that too, initially—because it's a hell of a coincidence, two members of the same family dying the same way. So I contacted Interpol and asked them the question.'

'And?'

Castle shook his head. 'No family connection whatsoever between Lloyd and the men killed in Europe.'

Culpeper pursed his lips and thought for a moment. 'Was there a connection between the Saumur and Basle killings?'

'A family connection?' Castle shook his head. 'No. If you

remember, the Saumur, Basle and Dunwich killings had only two things in common: the men were all of an age group and were reasonably well-heeled. Everett Chesters was killed in Saumur: a seventy-year-old retired banker. Samuel Conor was killed in Basle: late sixties, a director of a travel agency. And there was Michael Jenkins, our lawyer-politician from Dunwich. James Lloyd was different —younger, service record—'

'Do the others have service records?'

'Chesters, no—he was in the United States during the 'forties. Conor served in the Royal Pay Corps during the Second World War. Jenkins never served: a heart condition, apparently.'

'And though there's a family connection between Lloyd and Jenkins, there's none between the others?'

'That's the size of it.'

Culpeper leaned back in his chair. 'And yet you're looking pleased with yourself.'

Castle smiled. The door opened and a young constable brought in a tray with a teapot, sugar bowl and two mugs. After he had left the room Castle said, 'You got them well trained.'

'If I had, they'd provide cups and saucers, not mugs. But you're showing me a very smug expression. What have you found out?'

Castle sipped at the hot tea and grimaced. He ladled some sugar into the mug. 'Well, you know how it is. Once you start asking a computer questions, it throws all sorts of information at you and that leads to other questions. It was a long haul, believe me, but some interesting things began to emerge when I started asking Interpol about family relationships. What they did eventually, of course, was give me a bloody list—family trees.'

'The Michael Jenkins list was pretty short.'

Castle nodded. 'Not like the others. And that caused a problem. But the next step was to look more closely at the families. I mean, once I knew that Jenkins was related to James Lloyd, the related questions were there in the air, weren't they?' He snorted. 'As I said, it took ages, but if Interpol isn't a sound information service I'd like to know what is. They did a hell of a search on this one, and suddenly, there it was.'

'A connection?'

'Absolutely. A tenuous one, maybe, but a connection—between all four killings. What I've done is to write it down on this sheet—sort of spell it out, so you can see.'

He took the sheet in front of him and turned it around so Culpeper could read it. It was brief.

Everett Chesters	Leo Chesters (son)
Sam Conors	F. J. Wicklow (son-in-law)
Michael Jenkins	James Lloyd (nephew)

Culpeper frowned. 'You haven't spelled out the connection.'

'You gave me the clue over the phone the other day when you told me that James Lloyd had a service record. Interpol finally told me Everett Chesters and Sam Conors had relatives with service records also, just like Michael Jenkins.'

Culpeper hesitated. 'In the Navy?'

'Better than that.' Castle grinned.

'Not SBS?'

'Absolutely.'

They were both silent for a while as Culpeper stared at the sheet of paper. Culpeper cleared his throat. 'I don't see what sense it makes. Three elderly men are murdered, and it turns out that each of them had a relative in the SBS.'

'Statistically, that's a hell of a coincidence,' Castle said warmly.

'I agree. And then, the fourth killing is of James Lloyd—'

'Who was actually in the SBS.'

Culpeper grimaced. 'That leaves these two . . . Leo Chesters and F. J. Wicklow.'

'You can forget Leo Chesters. He was killed in the Gulf War. It seems that, unlike James Lloyd, he couldn't settle in civilian life and went back into the services. He was drowned at sea. No suspicious circumstances: an accident on a training exercise, of all things.'

'And this F. J. Wicklow?'

'Left the SBS—and the Navy—some years ago.'

'Like James Lloyd.'

'That's right. Not been able to trace him since, but we're still looking.'

Culpeper sighed. 'I still don't see this is getting us anywhere. I don't know what it all means.'

'Aw, come on, John, at least we've got a link of sorts! Three elderly men killed, with relatives who were in the SBS. A fourth killing—one of the relatives. It gives us something to work on. And once we trace this Wicklow character . . .'

'Chesters,' Culpeper said reflectively. 'Leo Chesters . . . Just wait a minute.'

He rose and left the room, Castle waited, sipping his tea, staring at the sheet in front of him, thinking. Some ten minutes later Culpeper returned, with a file in his hand. He opened it, took out a photograph and handed it to Castle.

'What's this?'

Culpeper pointed to one of the three men, standing with their arms across each other's shoulders in the photograph. 'That's James Lloyd.'

'So?'

Culpeper pointed again. 'And that's Leo Chesters.'

'Hell's flames!'

'Exactly. This is a copy of a photograph given to me by James Lloyd's widow. Now talk to me of coincidences.'

'They served in the SBS and they knew each other!'

'From the evidence of the photograph, they were *friends*. And go back to the period before Lloyd's death and we have the coincidence that two men who served in the SBS had a relative murdered in the identical, horrific way.'

'Then Lloyd himself got killed the self-same way—'

'You sure the death of Leo Chesters was an accident?'

Castle nodded. 'I've seen the report—there was an inquiry. No doubt about it in the Navy mind.'

Culpeper sat down again heavily, and sighed in frustrated excitement. 'But even with all that, there's the problem of Frank Lindley. What's the connection there?'

'You've checked his background?'

Culpeper nodded. 'Most of his life working at archæological digs. He was with a Locating Regiment on Salisbury Plain for his National Service in the 'fifties, but after that took a degree in history and worked for various museum services before undertaking project work. A pretty level sort of unexciting life—if you discount the excitement of archæology, that is.'

'You'll need to start looking at his background again.'

Culpeper shrugged. 'I suppose so—but he doesn't seem to have had any family, though we'll have to check now on whether there's an SBS connection.'

Castle had turned around the sheet on Culpeper's desk again and was doodling on it. Culpeper watched him and saw what he had done.

Everett Chesters**	Leo Chesters*(son)
Sam Conor**	F. J. Wicklow (son-in-law)
Michael Jenkins**	James Lloyd**
Frank Lindley**	?

'What's that mean?' Culpeper asked.

'One asterisk for an accidental death. Two for murder. I was just thinking . . . it sort of makes it quite important, doesn't it? To fill in the blank where I've put a questionmark, before someone else does it for us.' Castle looked up, staring directly into Culpeper's eyes. 'And to find out the exact whereabouts of Mr F. J. Wicklow.'

Castle's return to Suffolk left Culpeper somewhat disorientated. He tried to clear the confusion in his mind by briefing Vic Farnsby, but though they both teased away at it, the confusion persisted. The fact was, a connection had been found—the SBS connection—but it seemed to lead nowhere, particularly when the Lindley killing seemed to have no obvious link.

On the other hand, the link between the other deaths had not been obvious. Culpeper decided to give Farnsby the task of checking further into the background of Frank Lindley, to determine whether there was even a remote SBS connection. He himself needed to pursue more closely the other issues, which he and Castle had only touched upon.

'I'm still defeated,' Castle had admitted, 'by this naming thing—*drengs* and *Godar*. And now you've told me you've got meanings for them—'

'And for Baillehache, Hagger and Crocker,' Culpeper added.

'Yes, but where does it take us? I still think this murderous bastard is playing a game with us.'

'But getting more careful,' Culpeper suggested, 'staying at Elsdon, a quiet out of the way place, before the South Middleton killing. And we've not found a hotel register entry for the Lindley killing yet. But it's as though he wants to give the matter publicity, but also is getting nervous that the publicity might reach us too soon.'

As he said it, something flitted into his mind, a half-forgotten statement, seemingly unimportant at the time, and yet with some possible significance to their present discussion. It was gone before he could grasp it and then Castle was shuffling to his feet.

'Well, if you have any further thoughts about it, get in touch. I'll have to get back today—the world doesn't stop for this investigation and I've plenty enough else to do back in Suffolk.'

'I'll keep in touch,' Culpeper said, irritated that the shadowy thought had gone.

But the SBS connection meant he should get in touch with his Navy contact again.

He phoned him the following morning. Commander Askwith was affable enough when he came on to the line and greeted Culpeper warmly. Culpeper explained that he now had need of information about James Lloyd in respect of his membership of the SBS. He also mentioned Wicklow's name, and that of Leo Chesters. Commander Askwith's tone was suddenly a little less confident.

'I'm not sure whether I can help you a great deal. Navy is one thing—service records are open enough. SBS . . . well, between you and me, old chap, they're a rum lot, the ones who go into the SAS and the SBS.'

'How do you mean?'

'Special is the word, hey? It demands particular kinds of commitment, you know, and a particular kind of . . . well, hardness. And the SBS people themselves, they play their hands close to their chests, naturally enough. Tight-lipped bunch. It's different from regular Navy—it's a bit like a closed society, if you know what I mean. So I'm not sure what I can do.'

With a degree of irritation, Culpeper reminded Askwith, 'This is a murder investigation, Commander.'

'Even so . . .' There was a short silence. Eventually Askwith said, somewhat nervously, 'I'll see what I can do, Chief Inspector, but I think in the end you may well have to come down here . . .'

The call came three days later, and Culpeper took the train to London.

Constructed in 1788 and restored in 1965, Admiralty House had been built by an architect who had eschewed the rather heavier Palladian style of the previous generation. Culpeper had never been there before and discovered that though the house had a façade to Whitehall there was no direct access to that thoroughfare. Instead, he approached the Ministry of Defence building through a courtyard, past Robert Adam's handsome stone screen adorned with carvings of ships and fabulous sea creatures. He was directed to the left of the Admiralty portico and was met there by a Civil Service-suited gentleman who led him past the windows of the ground floor, where, Culpeper was informed, Nelson's body had rested on the eve of his state funeral. The doorway in the left-hand corner was simple and discreet.

The inner hall was stone-paved; a grand staircase extended beyond the pillared archway and on the landing was a tablet with the names of past First Lords of the Admiralty. Everywhere was apparent a strong sense of tradition: a rostral columned chimney copying Roman commemoration of Carthaginian Wars, decorative prows, a Chippendale side table and Regency mirrors, an eighteenth-century Coromandel screen.

Culpeper was escorted into an elaborately carved drawing-room. There were two men standing there. The fresh-faced man in uniform advanced to introduce himself as Commander Askwith—the dark-suited, grey-haired, rather grim-visaged man with him was introduced as Mr Taylor. Askwith waved Culpeper to a seat and offered him coffee. While it was being served, in small, delicate, gilt-edged cups, Askwith beamed around in proprietary fashion.

'First time in Admiralty House? Splendid place, hey? Somewhat inappropriate chimneypiece,' he admitted, nodding to the fireplace, 'but it came from Sir Gregory Page's Palladian mansion at Blackheath. But the pictures are fine. I particularly like that one of Flinders's Australian expedition of 1801—'

'Perhaps Chief Inspector Culpeper is not a lover of art,' Taylor suggested in a cool tone.

'Don't see much of it in Morpeth HQ,' Culpeper admitted.

'And your time will be precious,' Taylor added, meaning that his certainly was.

'Ah yes,' Commander Askwith said, flushing slightly. 'I ... ah ... asked Mr Taylor to be present because ... well, anyway, you were asking about the SBS records. In particular, relating to three names: Chesters, Lloyd and Wicklow. I'm afraid we can't go into great detail, but we can confirm that all three did spend a period of service with the SBS.' He hesitated. 'None of them are with us now.'

'Not least because two of them are dead,' Culpeper observed.

The mysterious Mr Taylor smiled thinly.

Askwith coughed. 'Quite. As for F. J. Wicklow, we can give you his last known address, but he left the service four years ago and seems to have dropped out of sight. He took a job—administration, it seems—with an engineering firm in Hamburg, and we have a record of his being employed in security in Bruges, with some Portsmouth based company, and we've included the details here in this folder, but beyond that I'm afraid there's little we can do to assist.'

Culpeper took the proffered folder from Askwith. 'The death of Leo Chesters?'

'Certainly accidental.'

Culpeper raised his eyebrows. The Ministry of Defence had brought him to London to tell him only this? Askwith's fresh face flushed again, and he glanced uncertainly at the silent man seated to his left. 'Then there's this thing you asked about *drengs* . . .'

The room was silent for a little while. Culpeper was aware of the cold, cautious eyes of Taylor on him, but he waited stoically. At last Taylor spoke; his voice was soft, and sibilant.

'*Drengs* . . . and *hirds*. Do you know very much about service life, Chief Inspector?'

'Can't say I do,' Culpeper replied gruffly, a little nettled by the man's manner.

'Yes . . . It's a peculiar life in many ways. Different, very. And in special units like the SBS it can develop into what one might call a somewhat closed society. The men involved form a tightly knit group; strong senses of loyalty are developed; a group identity is established; the outside world comes to be regarded as slightly unreal. Only the group is real. Young men in such groups can begin to form bonds that are never dissolved . . . not even by death.'

'I understand what you mean.'

'I wonder if you do?' Taylor gave another of his thin smiles: he had very white teeth that gleamed with a vulpine shine. 'It's difficult really for a civilian to comprehend. The group becomes a living thing in itself—and that's important, operationally, I mean, because in situations of stress and extreme danger it becomes necessary to rely absolutely upon each member of the group, to have absolute faith in each man's capacity, commitment and support.'

Commander Askwith shuffled in his chair; he had not touched his tea, and he remained clearly nervous in the presence of Taylor.

'When you asked about SBS records,' Taylor continued, 'the matter was referred to me, naturally. And I was curious. Then Askwith told me about your investigations. How do you think the SBS comes into this?'

'I'm not certain it does,' Culpeper said doggedly. 'It's merely a line we're following, since James Lloyd was in the service.'

'Yes . . .' Taylor replied thoughtfully. 'But this *drengs* thing . . . You see, when young men form these groups, there's a tendency to become a bit . . . I think "gung-ho" is the expression in some circles. They play what might be seen as childish games. They adopt nicknames, that sort of thing. Set up their own identification. But it's actually quite an important part of the cementation of relationships within the group: the role-playing creates a distinct sense of identity. For that reason we quite . . . encourage the development of such . . . ah . . . identification.'

He glanced at Askwith for a moment, and nodded. 'Yes, the word *drengs* is familiar to us. It has been used in an SBS context. It's one of the . . . terms that demonstrates a togetherness, a group reality, a loyalty—'

'Comrades,' Culpeper said.

'Precisely.'

'And *Godar?*'

Taylor inclined a shoulder. 'I've not come across that one. But if it had a Norse connotation . . . well, these groups developed their identities and names in more detail than would be apparent to us at the centre.'

'The use of *drengs* was common?'

'Oh no, you don't get my point. There are numerous ways in which groups identify themselves. This was merely one. The group—the unit—in question was identified by them as a *hird*; they called themselves the *drengs*. That we knew. A Viking derivation I believe. Appropriate, some of us thought, for an SBS unit.'

'How many were in the unit?'

'Eight.'

'Their names?'

Taylor leaned forward smoothly. 'We wouldn't normally do this, of course, but none of these men is now with us, and we appreciate the nature and importance of your investigation. Of the eight, it seems only one is still alive. Now.'

'Now?'

'Five were killed in action while serving with the SBS. Their names are on this sheet.' He slipped a single sheet of paper across to Culpeper. 'One was killed after he left the SBS. In the Gulf War, on a naval vessel. The seventh— well, it seems he's the subject of your investigation: James Lloyd.'

Culpeper opened the folded sheet. He read the names printed there.

Alan Laurie

Philip Roberts

Edward John

George Peters

Samuel Elliott.

'These five were killed in action,' Culpeper said slowly. 'The others in the unit were Leo Chesters—'

'Killed in the Gulf.'

'James Lloyd, murdered, and F. J. Wicklow.'

Taylor inclined his head. 'And that, I'm afraid, is about all we can tell you, Chief Inspector Culpeper.'

It was not until Culpeper was in the train travelling north again that, staring at the list of names the mysterious Mr Taylor had given him, the significance of the list suddenly clicked in his brain. He put down his brandy and soda as he stared at the names, his pulse quickening.

He rang Vic Farnsby as soon as he reached Newcastle station, insisting they met in his office at Morpeth.

A somewhat irritated Farnsby arrived ten minutes after Culpeper did. He stared at the sheet Culpeper pushed under his nose.

'I don't follow you, sir.'

'Look at the surnames!' Culpeper hissed. 'Laurie, Roberts, John, Peters . . . Remember the *dreng* names in the hotel registers? *Robert* Dreng Baillehache; *John* Dreng Hagger; *Peter* Dreng Crocker!'

'But what's it mean?' Farnsby asked desperately.

'Damned if I know! But I've got a feeling there's someone who could tell us!'

'Who?'

'The last one left alive of the whole SBS group. F. J. Wicklow.'

'Ah.' Farnsby's mouth tightened and his eyes were clouded. 'We . . . DCI Castle rang this morning. He's managed to trace this character Wicklow.'

'Where?'

Farnsby licked his lips. 'Up here, sir. To our patch. Newcastle.'

'*What?*'

'We went straight around to his office this morning, sir, after the DCI's call. Wicklow's been working as security officer at a Wallsend firm. But it seems they haven't seen him for some time. Apparently—'

'Go on!'

'It seems Wicklow left his job suddenly. Two days after the story of the mutilations appeared in the newspapers.'

Culpeper grinned, but there was no humour in the grimace. 'I have a feeling,' he said, almost snarling, 'when we find our friend F. J. Wicklow, we'll get the answer to all our questions.'

'Sir?'

'When we find Wicklow, I think we'll have found Bloodeagle.'

CHAPTER 5

1

Arnold quickly found himself immersed in the work at the field site in Birley Thore. The splitting of responsibilities between Dr Ormond and Mike Swindon meant that work proceeded apace and Colin Marshall was kept busy with his cataloguing of the site finds and locations. He appeared to be in his element: keen, excited, busying himself about the site with the workers, and arranging the evening conferences which were attended by a growing number of the workers, who were themselves being caught up in the enthusiasm generated for the project.

The enthusiasm itself—and, Arnold suspected, the splitting of responsibilities—seemed to have removed much of the friction that had been present under Frank Lindley's leadership. It was a paradox, in a way, for Lindley had been universally liked, while Swindon did not rank high in the popularity stakes. Nevertheless, Arnold was forced to admit that Swindon seemed to be making a good job of the project and the work was going well.

John Vincent had been as good as his word. Arnold was no longer particularly conscious of the man's presence: certainly, he did not feel he was being watched. Vincent seemed to be getting on with the dig in a cheerful manner that clearly impressed Jill Ormond. She was never far from his side while they worked, as though she had taken no particular care about her appearance in the working environment, Arnold thought he detected a new shine in her eye. There was no doubt in his mind that she was smitten by the man Arnold knew to be a policeman. Arnold had seen her car down at the Birley Thore pub on a couple of occasions; it led him to believe she was being entertained by Vincent.

It was on the Thursday that the site received another police visitation. The man was not known to Arnold, though he had seen him at Morpeth when statements were being taken. He arrived in an unmarked car and when Mike Swindon was pointed out to him he spent some time talking to him. Most of the time Swindon seemed to be shaking his head, as though he felt he was unable to help the man. Thereafter the visitor approached Dr Ormond, who was having coffee in the hut, and then Arnold.

He introduced himself as Detective-Inspector Farnsby. He was making further inquiries about Frank Lindley—checking on the dead man's background.

Arnold shook his head. 'I'm afraid I can't help you on that. I barely knew Mr Lindley—the first time we met was when he recruited me to this project.'

Farnsby frowned. 'So who did know him best on this site?'

'I would suggest Colin Marshall—the organizer. He knew Lindley from way back. Lindley was a sort of benefactor—gave Marshall a leg up when he needed it. You should talk to him.'

Farnsby looked around. 'He's on site?'

Arnold shook his head. 'He left a little while ago in the Land-Rover. He should be back soon.' Arnold hesitated for a moment, then, mischievously, he added, 'John Vincent might be able to tell you when—they were talking just before Marshall left.'

Farnsby's cold eyes were fixed on Arnold. They gave nothing away. Slowly, Farnsby said, 'Which one is Vincent?'

With a mocking smile, Arnold gestured towards Dr Ormond's dig. 'That's him down there. He might be able to tell you where Marshall's gone and when he'll be back.'

Farnsby's features betrayed no hint of recognition as he stared across the field at Vincent. He nodded, thanked

Arnold, and then began to walk stiff-legged towards the Ormond excavation team.

Arnold told Jane Wilson all about it on the following Saturday morning, when he called in at the bookshop on the Quayside in Newcastle and had a coffee with her in the back room.

'It was really rather odd,' he said. 'I mean, I suppose I was being a bit malicious sending Farnsby over to Vincent—'

'That's the copper Culpeper's placed on site to watch you,' Jane said.

'That's right, but we've reached an agreement since—he seems to feel there's something else odd going on at the site, something to do with Swindon. Anyway . . .'

'Yes, you were saying . . .'

'Farnsby walked over to Vincent, pretending he didn't recognize him, and they had a short conversation. After a few minutes Colin Marshall came back, driving on to the site in the Land-Rover. He'd been to get some supplies, it seems. But the funny thing was that Farnsby didn't go across to speak to him.'

Jane shrugged. 'What's strange about that?'

'Well, it seemed odd to me. I mean, Farnsby came on site ostensibly to question people further about Frank Lindley. Colin Marshall must be the one person who knew Lindley well—they were quite close, in a sense. Lindley had rescued him from a life of young dissipation, so to speak.'

'Me, I never had the chance,' Jane regretted. 'To be dissipated, I mean.'

Arnold ignored the comment. 'So when Marshall returned, and Vincent pointed him out, Farnsby didn't go across to him and talk at all. I mean, he'd asked me and Vincent where he was, but when Marshall returned he avoided him.'

'How do you mean—"avoided"?'

'Just that. It was most peculiar,' Arnold replied. He paused for a moment, thoughtfully, struggling to explain what he had observed. 'He sort of stood there, staring at

Marshall as he got out of the Land-Rover, but made no attempt to go across to him. And when Marshall began to walk towards the excavation site organized by Dr Ormond, Farnsby sort of . . . fled.'

Jane Wilson smiled. 'A policeman, fleeing from a young archæologist?'

'He's not exactly an archæologist; just a site organizer, really. And maybe "fled" is overstating things a bit. But I got the distinct impression that Farnsby didn't want to talk to Marshall after all; he sort of back-pedalled out of the dig, marched across the field back to his car and then . . . well, he sort of sat in it for a while, with his head down. I wondered whether he was ill, and thought I ought to go across to see if he was all right.'

'And did you?'

Arnold shrugged. 'I started to. But when I got about twenty yards from the car he caught sight of me and turned on the ignition. His face was pretty pale. Could have been he was taken ill.'

'What about his colleague?'

'Vincent?' Arnold shook his head. 'He didn't make a move—he was talking to Jill Ormond and maybe didn't notice.'

'Hmmm.' Jane Wilson cocked her head to one side and regarded Arnold quizzically. 'They seem to be getting pretty thick, from what you say—Dr Ormond and this policeman.'

'Looks like,' Arnold paused. 'They go down to the pub most evenings. But he . . . he's not serious, so I hope she doesn't get hurt.'

'You think she might?' Jane asked curiously.

Arnold shrugged. 'Don't know. Not my business. But I saw them leave one evening: he left her in the car park, and she sort of stood there looking lost, staring after his Shogun —he's got a four-wheel-drive vehicle. It was as though she didn't want him to leave. Then she got into her car and sort of . . . well, drove off in the same direction.'

'Following him, you mean?'

Hastily Arnold said, 'I really can't say.'

'Maybe she's afraid he's married—and wants to check.'

'I really don't know about that sort of thing. All I said was that they seemed to be getting pretty friendly.'

'Do you think people say things like that about you and me?' Jane asked mischievously. 'After all, we meet pretty regularly.'

Arnold flushed. 'I shouldn't think so. I mean, it's different with us.'

Jane's features were expressionless: he could not be sure whether she was annoyed or not. She pursed her lips. 'Hmmm. Anyway, maybe you got it wrong. Whatever Farnsby said, perhaps he wasn't checking up on Lindley's background after all. Maybe he was checking on his colleague checking on you.'

Arnold laughed. 'That's a bit elaborate!'

'The circumlocutions of the police mentality.'

Arnold shook his head. 'No. As I said, Vincent is leaving me alone: he's got interested in something else, as far as I can make out. And I think he's cultivating Dr Ormond—possibly not for the reasons she might suppose . . .' He accepted another cup of coffee from Jane's percolator. 'Anyway, how's the research coming along?'

'All but complete. What you've told me about Birley Thore is useful, too. You know, Arnold, I'm all but convinced that the site was probably where the Fitzstephen skirmish could have taken place.'

'Could have—but it would be difficult to prove.'

'From what you've been telling me about the excavation it looks as though a battle of some kind was fought there; and it is on the main route north through the valley. Anyway, I don't have to *prove* it.'

'You can't go around making bald statements and saying things are fact when you don't have final evidence—'

Jane overruled his protest with a flick of her finger. 'I write fiction, not history. If it suits me to believe that Birley Thore was where William Fitzstephen narrowly escaped with his life, and then rode north to Berwick to warn Hugh le Puiset, that's good enough for me and my readers. All I'm really talking about is atmosphere—not essential reality. And the Birley Thore site gives me . . . a shivery feeling. Like it all happened there. That's good enough for me.'

'Humph.'

'That doesn't sound like approval,' Jane said primly.

'You know your own business best.'

'Exactly. Anyway, I am now about to start the writing itself, William Fitzstephen's ride to Berwick is an essential part of the plot—and he'll be riding from Birley Thore after a skirmish with the reivers. So there!'

The doorbell tinkled—after a moment there was a murmur of voices in the shop. Jane frowned. 'That might be Annette.'

'Who?'

'You remember Annette Dominick? You know, the young woman who made up the dinner-party at my place when Professor Dennis was there. You talked to her.'

'Because you weren't talking to me,' Arnold grumbled.

'She's coming in to see me this morning. No, don't go— you might find it interesting.' Jane paused for a moment. 'I did mention it to you the other day, in fact, but never got around to telling you. Do you recall Annette telling us about her involvement in the antiques business?'

'Vaguely.'

'Well, she says there's some interesting stuff floating around at the moment, and she wondered whether I would be interested in it.'

'I didn't know *you* were interested in antiques.'

'It depends, doesn't it? But what Annette tells me is that . . . Well, here she is, anyway. She can tell you herself.'

'Mr Landon! How nice to see you again!' Annette Dominick entered the room, smiling, holding out her hand. Awkwardly, Arnold took it. He remembered her clearly now: a slender young woman with a slight cast in her left eye. He recalled the way she had quickly tired of his conversation at the dinner-party, and turned her attention to the much more interesting university professor.

'Coffee, Annette?' Jane asked brightly. 'I was just telling Arnold about the whispers you've been hearing.'

Annette Dominick's features coloured. 'Jane! What I told you was confidential!'

'Arnold's an old friend,' Jane said complacently. 'He won't betray a confidence.'

Arnold wriggled uncomfortably in his chair, not understanding what was going on. Jane glanced at him, and smiled. 'Don't worry, Arnold, it's nothing salacious. Though probably a bit . . . under the counter.'

Annette Dominick took a hurried sip of the coffee Jane had given her. Her rather long face seemed to lengthen even further at Jane's comment. 'You know I wouldn't touch anything which I thought had been illegally obtained, Jane! And so far, all I've mentioned is that I have an interest in the items.'

'Henry II,' Jane said to Arnold.

'What?'

'Annette thinks she can get her hands on items dating to Henry's reign.'

'Really? What kinds of items?' Arnold asked, his curiosity becoming aroused.

'You'd better tell all, Annette,' Jane said.

Annette Dominick's brow clouded; she lowered her voice and her tone became serious. 'If you're sure it's all right . . . I mean . . . do you know very much about the operation of the world of antiques, Mr Landon?'

Arnold shook his head. 'Very little.'

Miss Dominick took a deep breath. 'Well, one could say there are two major sources of items. Those with provenance, and those without. The problem is distinguishing between the two in some cases.'

'I imagine it could make a tremendous difference as far as prices are concerned,' Arnold remarked helpfully.

'It certainly can! But very often it's really difficult to find out the truth. I mean, for instance, these days there's a huge market for stone statues—you know, the kind that grace the gardens of large country houses. A Georgian lion, for instance, can command a huge price.'

'I believe it.'

'And with so many houses selling up because of taxes . . . well, there's quite a brisk trade in that kind of artefact.'

'Do you stock such items?' Arnold asked.

'Oh no, certainly not! Size is one reason . . . and provenance is another. The point is, while a lot come on the market legitimately, one hears constant stories of raids on old houses by thieves who wouldn't turn from ripping up a statue even if it's cemented in. No, I stay well clear of that field. On the other hand . . .'

'On the other hand,' Jane said firmly, 'Annette keeps her ear to the ground.'

Annette Dominick preened a little, even though her mouth was serious. 'The fact is, Mr Landon, some sellers are . . . shy. One can understand it, of course: some sellers wish the sale to be . . . unobserved, for family reasons. Others genuinely wish to keep their names out of the public eye.'

'Some want to avoid tax,' Jane suggested.

'I don't think that kind of check is my responsibility,' Annette Dominick protested.

'I'm sure it isn't.' Arnold helped her from Jane's teasing. 'But how do . . . shy sellers reach the market?'

Annette Dominick threaded the fingers of her left hand between those of her right and seemed inordinately pleased at her skill in doing so. 'There's a sort of . . . underground system.'

'Romantic, isn't it?' Jane grinned.

'Not at all.' Annette bridled. 'It's simply sensible business. You see, what happens, Mr Landon, is that a large number of dealers receive information from time to time on a sort of unofficial network. Now it has to be handled very carefully, and for me, I only . . . tap into the network through people I can trust. Otherwise there's always the thought that one could be dealing in stolen goods and that wouldn't do at all.'

'It could put you out of business,' Arnold agreed gravely, 'if you were to be caught.'

'So I'm always very careful. And that's why, when I heard about these items coming on to the market, I was . . . wary, shall we say? The information came from a good friend of mine whom I trust personally—but his judgement is sometimes clouded with enthusiasm, you know what I mean? And there's been a certain vagueness about the description of the items. So although I mentioned it to Jane, I'm not sure I could even recommend . . . The fact that there's to be an auction makes it even more odd, I think.'

Arnold raised his eyebrows. 'Why should an auction worry you?'

Annette Dominick smiled. 'I didn't mean a sort of Sotheby's thing. No, a dealer's auction. It's a bit different from the public operation. I've been to several—they're often held in rather out of the way places. The last one I went to was on Holy Island.'

'Lindisfarne?' Arnold smiled. 'That is taking the privacy idea to great lengths.'

Annette Dominick frowned. 'Well, that's the point about these mediæval items. The seller wishes to remain anonymous . . . I understand that. Reserves have been put on the items—and that's understandable too. But the seller doesn't want more than three or four bidders. That's unusual. It leads me to believe he doesn't want the sale to be widely known—and that makes me feel the . . . secrecy is rather too emphatic.'

'And in your suspicious little mind,' Jane interposed, 'that would suggest the provenance of the items is suspect.'

Annette Dominick ducked her head in doubt and sipped her coffee. 'Well, I think so. Consequently, one is reluctant to recommend to a friend like you, Jane, that involvement as a possible purchaser would be wise. I had had it in mind, as you know, to represent you but on reflection . . . And there's the matter of price . . .'

'Expensive?'

'Very.'

'How much?'

'Thousands.'

'It must be of historical significance,' Arnold suggested.

'The one item I'm talking about in particular is a mediæval jewel. And yes, it does have historical significance,' Annette Dominick admitted.

'Don't be so damned mysterious!' Jane snapped. 'What is the item?'

Annette shook her head. 'I can't tell you, because I don't know. I've given you all the information I have. All I can say is that serious buyers are being sought, and they will be whittled down. My advice to you, Jane is: forget it. It all seems a bit . . . fishy to me.'

'How disappointing,' Jane replied. She glanced at Arnold. 'Wouldn't it be interesting to know more?'

'I suppose so . . . The likelihood is, of course, if the sale goes through the item could disappear for years.' Arnold stared at Annette Dominick for a few moments, thinking. 'This dealers' ring—'

'Auction group!' she corrected him sharply.

'All right.' He smiled, to mollify her. 'How would one make contact with them?'

'It can be done discreetly. Anyone who is familiar with people in the world of archæology, or indeed, who visits an antique shop and asks the right questions, could make contact and tap into the group. Why, do you have something to sell?'

Arnold shook his head. 'No. And I'm not a buyer, either. But with these mediæval items . . . do you have any information about whether they are . . . well, recently on the market? Or have they been around a while, in various hands?'

Annette Dominick's wide mouth was set primly. 'I don't know. But I have a vague suspicion that the one item in particular is special—and it hasn't seen the light of day too long.'

When Arnold saw that Jane was staring at him intently, he knew she had been sharp enough to guess what was going through his mind.

The following day he sought out John Vincent at the field site and asked him, casually, whether he was free to join him for a drink at the end of the day's work. Vincent stared at him with clear, sharp blue eyes for a moment, then glanced towards Dr Ormond, working on her knees to his left. Slowly he nodded. 'That shouldn't provide a problem.'

Still not sure that he was behaving wisely, Arnold went back to the excavation shaft.

At the conference that afternoon Colin Marshall produced the list of catalogued items and asked Mike Swindon to sign it. There was some discussion relating to a clasp and the remains of a leather shoe that had been found that day, and then the meeting broke up. Arnold noticed Dr Ormond talking to Vincent: he was shaking his head gently, and she seemed rather pink-faced. Arnold hoped he hadn't upset any arrangements, but rather guessed he had.

He arrived first at the pub and bought a whisky for himself to steady his nerves, and a pint of beer for Vincent. The man came in to join him some ten minutes later and nodded his thanks. 'Work at the field can give rise to a surprisingly prodigious thirst,' he said.

Arnold nodded. 'I . . . er . . . hope I haven't upset any previous arrangements,' he mumbled.

Vincent regarded him steadily for a little while, and smiled. 'Jill Ormond, you mean? Well, yes, I had arranged to meet her. But it's as I told you—I like women, but duty must always come first. There's an old saying about it— one must leave sweet kisses and the flowing wine if called by the sterner fray of War.' He raised his glass in mock salute. 'So here's to War and Duty!'

'The quotation has a familiar ring,' Arnold remarked.

'It's a very old one. But now then, you didn't bring me to this meeting to talk about quotations. What's the problem?'

Arnold hesitated. 'You asked me—last time we were here

—to keep my eyes and ears open. I have done, but I'm afraid I'm not aware of anything . . . odd, as you suggest, at the site. On the other hand . . .'

Something glittered in Vincent's eyes. He leaned forward slightly, as though poised, and Arnold became aware of the coiled power in the policeman's body.

'It's come to my attention that the dealers' ring in the north-east has been asked to raise a short list of potential buyers for some mediæval artefacts of historical interest and considerable value.'

Vincent said nothing but continued to stare fixedly at Arnold.

'When I last spoke to Frank Lindley,' Arnold went on lamely, 'he made some remark to me about discrepancies . . . an argument he was having with Mike Swindon about artefacts at the site . . . You see, as far as I'm aware there's no other major dig in the north-east at this time which is uncovering mediæval material. And now, suddenly, some valuable items are up for secret auction. Of course, it may be a complete coincidence, but after what Lindley said to me—vague though it was—and then your comments about this site . . .' His voice faded away into uncertainty. 'I guess I'm over-reacting.'

'I'm not so sure,' Vincent said flatly. He sipped at his beer, and continued staring at Arnold but it was as though he did not really see him: there was a faraway look in his eyes, as though he was turning his glance inward, searching out past events, hidden thoughts. 'I'm not so sure . . . I told you, I had my suspicions, myself. Still, the thing is now to be even more watchful. But . . . I'm not sure you shouldn't just leave this to me, now. I'm here in an official capacity, after all. You're not.'

'I just thought you ought to know,' Arnold said lamely.

'And I'm grateful for the information. But you can leave it with me, now.' He smiled suddenly, his mouth lopsided. 'You tangled with Culpeper lately?'

Arnold shook his head. 'I've not seen him, or anyone from Morpeth—except that detective-inspector.'

'Farnsby?' Vincent nodded. 'Mmm. He didn't stay long, though.'

'What did he want?'

Vincent was silent for a moment. 'Police business,' he said shortly. 'Another drink? And then I must go.'

The following day John Vincent did not appear at the site. Jill Ormond seemed preoccupied, and Arnold saw her talking animatedly to Colin Marshall. After she went back to her work, Marshall strolled across to where Arnold was working. 'Nothing to do with me,' he muttered.

'What?'

'Vincent rang in this morning: he's packed in. And apparently didn't tell Her Nibs. So she's upset because she's lost a good worker . . .' He grimaced. 'And the rest. He say anything to you?'

Arnold shook his head.

'Ah well . . . You hear the radio this morning?'

'No.'

'No one here seems to listen to morning radio!' There was a satisfied gleam in Marshall's eyes. 'Anyway, it's great news. The police have made an arrest. As the announcer put it, they've got someone who is helping them with their inquiries . . . into the death of Frank Lindley!'

2

Culpeper went back to his office, removed his handkerchief from his top pocket and mopped his brow. The interview room had been hot, and he was getting frustrated. He slumped in the chair behind his desk and sipped the coffee that had been left there for him. He needed a break: they seemed to be getting nowhere.

The hunt for F. J. Wicklow had been over surprisingly quickly. The man had left his job at Wallsend, it seemed, and headed south, stayed with his sister for some time, where his trial had been picked up, and then had come back north to book a ferry passage on the Hull–Zeebrugge route, presumably hoping to avoid some of the attention that might have been stricter on the south Channel ports.

He'd been unlucky, Culpeper thought sourly. There were still keen young passport control men who checked documents carefully, in spite of the freedom of entry arrangements that were becoming common with movement in Europe. Wicklow had been spotted, detained, and eventually brought back to Northumberland.

But he had proved uncooperative.

Culpeper had questioned him for several hours now. He had managed to establish very little that he didn't know already.

'Well, Fred—you don't mind if I call you Fred?'

Wicklow had shrugged. He was in his early forties, above middle height, thickset, dark-skinned. His eyes were pouched and he needed a shave. He was wearing the jeans and sweatshirt that he had been arrested in, and his manner was truculent. He'd asked for a lawyer but Culpeper had announced that this was just a friendly chat and there was no need for such formalities. Wicklow had accepted the statement, for the moment. Culpeper knew that it would only be a matter of time before the request would be made again.

Accordingly, Culpeper trod softly.

During the first hour he managed to get the man somewhat more relaxed: they talked about Wicklow's job in Wallsend, about the three years he had worked in the northeast, and the other odd jobs he'd undertaken since leaving the Navy. It was when they began to discuss the SBS that Wicklow started to show signs of nervousness.

'You *did* see service in the SBS, didn't you?'

'You should ask the Navy about that.'

'I have—and they say you did. So there's no secret about it.'

Wicklow shrugged, but his dark eyes were watchful.

'That's where you'll have met James Lloyd,' Culpeper went on.

'If you say so.'

'And then there were the others . . . like Leo Chesters,

and . . . well, you know the names better than I. Did you ever come across Michael Jenkins in your travels?'

'I don't know the name.'

'He was Jim Lloyd's uncle.'

'I wouldn't know about that.'

'You ever been to Dunwich?'

'No.'

'And what about Everett Chesters—Leo's father?'

Wicklow hesitated. 'I think I did meet him once. We had a function in London . . . He turned up. Leo introduced me to him.'

'What was your reaction to hearing he'd died?'

'Leo?'

'No,' Culpeper replied patiently. 'Everett Chesters.'

'I didn't know he had died,' Wicklow said warily, but his hands were still in his lap.

'So what about your own father-in-law . . . Sam Conors? It must have been a blow when you heard about his death.'

Wicklow seemed to be about to speak, but then held his peace. Culpeper waited for a few moments, then asked, 'You *did* know he was dead, I imagine.'

The sarcasm was not lost on Wicklow. With a hint of anger, he said, 'I heard he'd been killed. But you'd better know something. I haven't seen my wife for seven years. She didn't like my life in the Navy—and she found someone else while I was on duty in the Mediterranean. And Sam Conors would have enjoyed that. You see, he never approved of me, made no secret of his disapproval of our marriage—and that was OK with me, too. I disliked him intensely.'

'Enough to kill him?' Culpeper asked softly.

Wicklow straightened slowly in his seat. 'That's a stupid question. I had no reason to kill Sam Conors. I heard he died a violent death: I won't pretend I felt any sorrow. I hated his guts—for personal reasons. But he didn't loom large in my life. I was indifferent to whether he lived or died.'

'And Jim Lloyd—were you indifferent to his existence too?'

'We . . . knew each other well. We were in the same unit.'

'You haven't answered the question.'

Wicklow shrugged. 'I hadn't been in touch with Jim since we both left the service.'

'You both lived in the north-east.'

'So what?' Wicklow protested. 'What's wrong with that? I never met him up here, that's for sure.'

'Why were you heading for Zeebrugge?'

'Change of air.'

'Just after Jim Lloyd got killed—and Frank Lindley?'

'I've never even heard of Frank Lindley.'

'But you *must* have seen his name in the papers!' Culpeper asserted. 'And you'll have seen his murder was linked, by the media at least, to Lloyd's killing. And that's when you packed in your job and headed south. Why did you do that, Fred?'

Wicklow shook his head. 'I don't need to give any explanation. And I don't know what you're driving at.'

But there had been something in his eyes that made Culpeper believe he was lying.

'I think we'll take another break, Fred. And what I'm driving at is this. Everett Chesters, Sam Conors, Michael Jenkins and James Lloyd are all dead—murdered in the same way. Lloyd was ex-SBS and the other two were related to SBS men. The service personnel in question were part of a single unit in the service—and it seems you're the only remaining person of that unit still alive. So it looks to me like you've got some answers to give us—not least when you shot off south like a startled rabbit after the Lindley killing came to light.' Wicklow made no reply, and suddenly Culpeper's frustration got the better of him. 'Maybe you didn't have time to do the job properly . . . is that what it is? Not the way you did it with your own father-in-law!'

It had been due to the frustration, but Culpeper had gone too far. Wicklow stiffened. In a slow, deliberate tone, he said, 'Are you seriously suggesting I had something to do with the murder of Jim Lloyd and this man Lindley?'

Angrily Culpeper had said, 'Don't forget the others, Wicklow!'

Wicklow gritted his teeth. 'I had no reason to kill my father-in-law. He was no part of my life. And if you think I had anything to do with Lloyd's murder, you're crazy. In fact . . .' He had hesitated then, pausing while he seemed to be weighing his words carefully. 'I think this has gone far enough. I've done nothing, but you're treating me like a criminal. I've asked you once—now, I'm insisting on it. I want a lawyer present here—I intend answering no more questions until I have legal representation!'

It had taken a couple of hours to arrange. Now, as Culpeper sat in his office with the feeling he had overstepped the mark, the frustration in his chest mounted. He had thought that Wicklow would be the key . . . and yet he had found nothing in what had been said so far that took him any closer to a solution to the problem.

Maybe he'd been asking the wrong questions. Gloomily he stared at the brown envelope on his desk: Commander Askwith at least had come through, with a set of photographs of the SBS unit. He'd show them to Wicklow in due course—stir him up a bit, maybe. But even then, where did Lindley fit into all this?

He called Farnsby into his office. The Detective-Inspector sat down, pale-faced and oddly nervous. Culpeper inspected him critically. 'I went over the notes you made after your visit to the Birley Thore site. You didn't get much at all.'

'There was no one there who seemed to be able to tell me much about Lindley, sir. I tried Dr Ormond, Mr Swindon, even Mr Landon—'

'What about this Colin Marshall character? According to the notes, he knew Lindley well.'

Farnsby hesitated. 'He wasn't able to add much.'

'What was he like?'

Farnsby was silent for a few moments. 'I . . . I didn't actually interview him myself.'

Culpeper looked up from the notes in front of him. 'He wasn't on site?'

'No . . . well, yes, later, but I was leaving, so I got Detective-Constable Stevens to interview him at his home.'

There was something odd in the air: Culpeper felt it, almost palpably. 'Why didn't you wait until he returned to the site? What was so urgent that you had to leave?'

Farnsby was gnawing at his lower lip. He ducked his head awkwardly. 'I had-personal reasons, sir.'

'You were on *duty*, Farnsby!'

Farnsby wriggled unhappily. 'The man was . . . known to me, sir. I'd seen him before.'

Culpeper snorted. 'So what? Was the fact you knew him going to bias your judgement so much that you couldn't talk to him about Frank Lindley, for God's sake?'

Farnsby's face was white and his mouth twisted angrily. 'I'd seen him before, sir, but I didn't know who he was.'

Culpeper groaned theatrically. 'All right, so his identity was important to you. So who the hell was he?'

'The bastard who's been screwing my wife!'

Work at the Birley Thore site continued until six in the evening; dark clouds had gathered over the hills and there was the threat of storms, with the sound of distant rolling thunder. The atmosphere was heavy, the air humid and the conference at the end of the day was brief. Everyone seemed to be in a hurry to pack up and leave and Arnold himself was glad of the opportunity to go down the pub and get himself a drink before driving home to Morpeth.

Dr Jill Ormond was in the lounge bar, seated alone. Arnold considered for a moment, wondering whether he should join her, but eventually thought better of it. He took a seat near the window and ordered a half of lager. It was not long, however, before she presented herself before him.

'Do you mind if I join you for a few minutes?'

'Not at all.'

She seemed tense, and there were dark shadows under

her eyes. She sat down with her gin and tonic and said nothing for a little while.

'Are you pleased the way things are going at the dig?' Arnold asked at last, in an attempt to break the strained silence.

'It's developing well,' she replied in a rush, 'and I'm still expecting some interesting information to emerge . . .' Her voice died away: she could not keep up the pretence any longer. 'You . . . you had a meeting with . . . John Vincent yesterday evening.'

Arnold nodded. 'That's right—here at the pub.'

'What was it about?'

Arnold hesitated. He had no idea how much the policeman had told Dr Ormond, and he did not think it wise to explain what they had discussed. 'Nothing of any consequence, really,' he replied lamely.

'Did it have anything to do with his finishing at the field site?'

Arnold shook his head. 'I'm sure it didn't.'

She didn't believe him. 'So why did he leave the site so abruptly?'

Arnold could guess it was to do with the arrest of the suspect in the Lindley killing—they would have recalled him to Morpeth. But he could not tell her that. He shrugged, and gave her a half truth. 'I really don't know.'

'What do you know about him?' she asked, after a little while.

'I barely know him at all.'

'He keeps very much to himself,' she mused. 'We've become . . . friends, but I have a feeling I've never got to know him. I followed him once . . .' She flushed, as though admitting to a grave weakness. 'I think the least he could have done was to say . . . was to take leave of us all at the site.'

Arnold did not know what to say. It was obvious Vincent had made a deep impression on her in a short while: she was not a woman with a great experience of men—she had concentrated on her work. She would not have made many men friends, and perhaps she had woven dreams around this one. Arnold sat there dumbly, aware of the pain she was feeling for a man she barely knew. He recalled John Vincent's cynical words about Duty.

When he glanced up Dr Ormond was rising to her feet. She clearly regretted speaking to him, demonstrating her weakness. She nodded firmly. 'I'll see you tomorrow, at the site,' she said and left the lounge.

Arnold had the feeling she'd never speak to him of John Vincent again.

The brief discussion left him vaguely on edge. He could not pin down the reason for his being so unsettled, but it was perhaps due to the feeling that he was dealing with situations and emotions that defied categorization. Ever since he had been drafted into this project at Birley Thore he seemed to have been at the periphery of a swirling, only half-understood, sequence of events.

He ordered some pie and chips and another drink at the bar, and settled down to eat a lonely meal.

The lounge bar gradually filled up, but he was left alone at his table. He sat there quietly, thinking of the events of the last few weeks, and guessing that it would not be long now before he would have to return to the office at Morpeth. He was not sure whether the prospect was pleasing or otherwise: the thought demonstrated to him the way he seemed to be drifting at the moment.

The decision to go back to the field site was unreasoning. It may have had something to do with what he had heard from Annette Dominick at the bookshop; it might, on the other hand, have been motivated by his general foot-looseness of purpose. He left the pub and went to his car, manœuvred out of the car park and drove up the hill to the field.

It was almost dark: the sky was heavy with storm, and occasional pale flashes in the distance were followed at intervals by a low unpleasant rumbling. Occasional spots of rain dropped on his windscreen but there was no heavy rainfall: he had no doubt, however, that the storm would

soon break and bring a welcome lightening of the oppres-
sive, humid atmosphere.

Two vehicles were parked at the bottom of the hill, close
under the hedge. Arnold manœuvred his way past them
and drove on up the hill. He stopped the car at the field
gate and made his way through into the field itself. He
could not remember what had been decided about a watchman that evening, but no one seemed to be about. A brief,
crackling flash lit up the site and the wind was beginning
to rise, warm and damp on his face.

He caught the glimpse of a shaded light in the hut and
he stopped in his tracks.

The two vehicles parked at the bottom of the hill were
probably owned by locals hunting rabbits on the fellside.
There was no other car up here at the field, and no sign of
a watchman. Yet someone was in the hut—not openly, not
with the lights on, but furtively, with just occasional gleams
of torchlight—shining through the cracks in the door and
the window.

Arnold recalled Annette Dominick's conversation: it
seemed his own suspicions might have been accurate after
all, and the reason for the quarrel between Mike Swindon
and Frank Lindley lay in the hut. Arnold took a deep
breath, hesitating, not certain what to do and then cautiously he stepped forward towards the hut, moving as
silently as he could. The grass was damp, whispering under
his shoes, and the distant roll of thunder came again,
moving closer across the hills, presaging the storm that was
to come.

When he reached the edge of the hut he realized that the
shutters had been closed at the window. Tiny points of light
crept through cracks in the shutters, but it was impossible
for Arnold to see within. He contemplated entering through
the doorway, but thought better of it: the person inside the
hut clearly wanted to work there unobserved, and would
not welcome intrusion. It seemed a better plan merely to
wait, concealed at the side of the hut, until whoever it was
inside emerged again. Arnold would be able to discover who

it was, hopefully without his own presence being detected.

He leaned against the side of the hut, waiting, aware of the muffled sounds of movement within the hut.

He heard nothing apart from those sounds until a rustling movement behind him made him turn his head. But he was too late. Before he could turn, an arm was looped round his neck, half-stifling him with the ferocity of the pressure.

Arnold's own hands flew up to grasp at the man's muscular, encircling arm, trying to tear free from the choking pressure, but even as he did so something damp was pressed against his mouth and nostrils and he was aware of a sweet, cloying odour, choking him as he struggled. He fought against the restraint, flailing with his arms, trying to kick backwards against the body pressed hard against his, but his limbs seemed heavy, his senses began to swim, and he was unable to breathe. A mist rose about his eyes, and he was barely aware of the hut, and the descending darkness.

He began to lurch, and had the vague impression that the arms around him were now supportive rather than restraining. He began to slide into a blackness deeper and darker than his actual surroundings and his senses faded. He was in a whirling dark hole, in which a slick, slow-moving pool threatened to swallow him completely into its turgid depths.

And then there was nothing.

When he came to his senses again the darkness was still around him.

He was dimly aware of sounds but they seemed to beat and fade and beat again, waves crashing on a shore. There was an ache behind his eyes and his skull was throbbing. He felt nauseous but it was only momentary for soon the blackness came again and he lost consciousness once more.

When he woke again, hours must have passed. There was a foul taste in his mouth and his head was aching fiercely. He tried to move his head and his neck was stiff; sharp pains swept through his throbbing skull and he put his head back, leaning it against the wall for relief.

He was seated, back to the wall, aware now that his hands were bound behind his back.

He flexed his fingers and pins and needles seemed to dig into his hands. The wall behind him felt cold and wet, and the atmosphere itself was cool. He could see nothing, but he was seated on a stone floor, smooth-flagged and damp. The intensity of the darkness and the coldness of the atmosphere meant, at a guess, that he was in an old cellar.

He coughed, and then almost retched: his throat was dry and rasping, but he tried to call out. His voice came out as a croak. After that he stayed silent for a while, swallowing, attempting to overcome the soreness of his throat.

His feet were free: only his hands were bound.

It could have been an hour or more before he tried to move: his head still throbbing painfully, he turned to get his shoulder against the wall, and slowly managed to struggle to an upright position. He placed his thundering forehead against the cool dampness of the stone and tried to think, but his mind was confused, his senses still whirling. He waited, and slowly his head cleared although he was still left with a feeling of sickness in his throat.

With one shoulder braced against the wall he took a step, then another.

Slowly he began to traverse the room in which he was imprisoned, one painful step after another as the blood sang in his head and the ache behind his eyes throbbed painfully. As he moved he concentrated on his surroundings.

It was a cellar, he was certain of it, musty, damp, and probably little used. Step by step he moved along the wall, scrabbling with his fingers as he went, searching for an entrance. He reached the angle in the wall, and moved along.

He calculated the wall had been some fourteen feet in length; now as he moved along he carried on his calculations. This was a shorter wall— perhaps ten feet or so. He turned the angle in the darkness once again and made his slow progress along the damp stone. The same length as the first wall he had encountered, he guessed—he reached the next angle, but it was different.

He leaned his head against the wall but felt nothing: the stone reached up only to his shoulder.

For a moment he was puzzled, and then he visualized the situation: he was standing beside stone-built steps that rose to a height of perhaps five feet. At the top of the steps would be the exit. The thought excited him suddenly, gave him a surge of confidence enough to overcome the painful throbbing in his head.

Hurriedly he moved along beside the steps, seeking the lower one to mount. Then his feet struck something yielding and he lost his balance, fell forward helplessly, unable to protect himself with his hands still roped behind his back.

He careered into the wall opposite and fell, painfully, striking his head on the stone floor. His senses whirled again and he retched violently. He lay there for several minutes, waiting for the ringing in his skull to stop, hardly aware of the cold stone against his cheek and then, painfully, he twisted his body, struggled to a kneeling position, and hobbled towards the wall, until he could get his shoulder against it, and rise to his feet again.

He was a little uncertain about his position, but he guessed he had effectively traversed the room, and was leaning against the wall in roughly the original position in which he had found himself.

The steps would be ahead of him: when he'd started to move he had walked away from them in a circuit of the cellar. Cautiously, he now shuffled forward, seeking the obstruction that had caused him to trip and stumble. After three hesitant steps his foot encountered the heavy, yielding obstruction that had caused him to career into the wall.

Arnold stood stock still. He pushed the object with his foot again, and as it moved he felt cold. He could guess what it was. He dropped to his knees, turned sideways and with trembling fingers pushed against the bonds that restrained him, feeling for what lay beside him.

Cloth. A man's shoulder. A sticky mess.

Shuddering, Arnold stood up. He began to shake. It was partly the result of the shock of his own incarceration, partly that of the discovery at his feet. The man who lay there had lost part of his skull: Arnold had touched blood and shattered bone.

Arnold stood there helplessly, panicked, unable to think straight, uncertain what to do next. The body lay at the foot of the steps: he would have to scramble over it before he could climb those steps. The thought made him nauseous again but he knew that if he was to get out of the cellar, or attract attention, he would have to do it.

He moved forward, shuffling his feet against the corpse on the cellar floor. He was about to step over it, searching for the lowest step, when a sound from above stopped him where he stood.

Someone was moving in the room at the top of the steps.

Arnold waited, hardly breathing, and listened. There was the sound of scraping on the floor, furniture being moved. There was a short delay, a rattling of bolts, and a sudden light flooded from the doorway, down the steps and into the cellar. Momentarily dazzled, Arnold blinked. He peered upwards into the light. A man stood there, framed in the doorway, solid, black, menacing, looking down at Arnold. There was a short silence, and then the man spoke.

'Are you all right?'

There was concern in the man's tone, and its impact on Arnold was almost stunning. He was unable to answer.

'Are you all right?' the man repeated.

A vast feeling of relief flooded through Arnold. 'It's you,' he gasped, almost choking. 'Thank God it's you!'

3

The solicitor was well-known to Culpeper, a small, dapper character addicted to bow ties and a lugubrious expression. His name was Purdy and he tended to specialize in criminal cases: most were of a minor kind and he would be full of self-importance with this one. He had peppery-coloured hair and a grey countenance; thin-lipped, he rarely smiled, and his hooded eyes pronounced a sleepiness that was in ill accord with the sharpness of his intellect. Culpeper knew him for a street-wise performer and he listened to the man with care.

'Well, Chief Inspector, I have now had the opportunity for a discussion with my client.'

Four hours of it, Culpeper thought sourly.

'It's never been Mr Wicklow's intention to refuse to cooperate with the police in ... ah ... whatever investigation they are conducting. Indeed, it is his clear wish to help in any way that he can, and to that end he has now authorized me to speak to you. He is quite prepared to be interviewed again—in my presence, of course— and he will speak freely and frankly. He has explained his reasons to me ... his reasons, that is, for leaving the north-east, and for his ... ah ... nervousness during the first interview with you. But there are certain issues he would not wish to dwell upon ...'

'And you'll be there to keep him on a straight line,' Culpeper suggested.

'That is so, Chief Inspector.' The hooded eyes were thoughtful. 'And I trust, after he has cooperated in the manner I expect, he will be free to leave. No charges have yet been brought, of course ...'

'Not yet,' Culpeper agreed.

'Yes, well, I think perhaps we should proceed with the interview; the earlier my client is able to leave these premises, the better.'

Culpeper led the way back to the interview room, with Purdy stepping briskly behind him.

Wicklow sat upright in the chair behind the desk. He had been furnished with a cup of tea and a cigarette. His eyes were vaguely defiant as he glared at Culpeper; Purdy took a chair and sat just slightly behind his client facing the Chief Inspector. Culpeper had his own support: Detective-Constable Andrew stood behind Culpeper, a brown folder in his hands.

'So,' Culpeper began, 'you've decided to cooperate.'

'My client has never refused to cooperate,' Purdy insisted smoothly.

Culpeper grunted. He had the feeling that if he proceeded along the same tack as previously he'd hit rocks again, so he decided to concentrate on other matters.

'Tell me about your days in the SBS, Mr Wicklow.'

'What do you want to know about them?'

Culpeper shrugged. 'I've had information from the Admiralty, but I'd like to hear from you what it was really like.'

'What "it" are you interested in?' Wicklow replied, almost sneeringly.

'Being a *dreng*,' Culpeper said in a quiet voice.

There was a short silence. 'It just meant you were one of the unit,' Wicklow said at last.

'It was called the Dreng Unit, wasn't it?'

'That's right,' Wicklow replied with reluctance staining his tone.

'Who thought of the term?'

Wicklow shrugged. 'It just happened. It was somebody's idea . . . I don't quite remember who now, maybe it was Sam Elliott, but it gave us a sort of . . . identification.'

'Formal? Emotional?'

'Both.'

'You used a number of Norse terms?'

'I suppose so.'

Culpeper paused. 'Did you use the words *krokr* and *hagr*?'

'I don't recall.'

'You don't know what they mean?'

Carefully, Wicklow replied, 'I might have at some time . . . I've forgotten now.'

Culpeper eyed him coldly. 'I understand that *dreng* means "comrade" and *hird* means "group".'

'I was never into all that detail. Some of the others—Leo Chesters, for instance, and Sam Elliott, they really lived it all, you know what I mean? They took the rigmarole very seriously.' He shrugged. 'Looking back, it was really all a bit childish.'

Purdy almost smirked; his client was cooperating, clearly. Culpeper cleared his throat. 'And what about Bloodeagle?'

'What?'

'Bloodeagle.'

Wicklow licked his lips. He was pale. He shook his head. 'I don't know anything about that.'

'Oh, come on! You were a member of the Dreng unit, you were into Viking identification all the time. It was like a game with you all, wasn't it, as well as a formal identification with the SBS? And you must have played that game even in the field. You were in a violent occupation. Bloodeagle was part of it, surely.'

'I don't know what you're talking about.'

Culpeper knew he was lying. 'All right, but you'll have heard about berserkers.'

'Of course.'

'Did *you* ever get into a berserk rage?'

Purdy leaned forward and touched his client's arm. 'Mr Culpeper doesn't really expect you to answer that question, Mr Wicklow.'

Culpeper grunted. 'Then perhaps he'll tell me about *Godar*.'

Wicklow's eyes were nervous. 'What about it?'

'What's it mean?'

Wicklow shrugged uneasily. He glanced at his solicitor for support. 'Chief. Just . . . chief, that's all.' He hesitated, half turning to Purdy. 'I . . . I think I'd better do what you suggested.'

'And what might that be?' Culpeper asked cynically. 'Stay silent?'

Purdy blinked his hooded eyes. 'On the contrary. Rather than submit to these . . . errant questions, it might be better if Mr Wicklow were to make a statement. Along the lines,' he added in a warning tone to Wicklow, 'he and I have already discussed. It seems to me to be a more sensible way forward.'

'My questions—' Culpeper rumbled.

'May be rendered unnecessary,' Purdy reproved. 'And the statement might prevent you from getting into . . . ah . . . deep water, Chief Inspector.'

Culpeper leaned back in his chair. He stared at Wicklow for several seconds, then glanced at the folder in Detective-Constable Andrew's hands. He considered the matter, then decided he really had nothing to lose. If Wicklow and Purdy thought they could deflect him by some carefully thought out story, they didn't know the man who was facing them. And he'd keep the matter of identification till later.

'All right, let's hear your . . . statement.'

Wicklow took a deep breath. 'I was selected for the SBS while I was in Navy service. It was at the training school that I first met the others. There were eight of us eventually drafted into the unit—and we became good mates. And since all units were encouraged to have a sort of identity, to kind of cement us together, someone came up with the idea of a Viking group. It seemed to all of us to suit, you know what I mean? The kind of work we were expected to do.' He paused. 'And it did work for us. We formed a tight little group—did everything together. Formed close loyalties. We built a bit of a wild reputation, I guess, but we were known as hard men, too. It was a . . . good time.'

Young men engaged in hard, dangerous, physical activity, a group against the world. Culpeper shuffled in his seat. Purdy was watching his client carefully, ready to advise him against any indiscretion.

'We worked together for a couple of years or more—never got split up. We were a good unit: we had a sense of pride. You asked about berserkers—' Purdy leaned forward watchfully. Wicklow hesitated. 'You have to remember, we had some dirty jobs to do. You don't have time to ask questions. You got to act. Follow orders. And we each had to display commitment. That could sometimes mean doing things that—'

'I think the Chief Inspector understands what you're getting at,' Purdy warned.

'Yes, well . . . Anyway, we were a good unit, but then I suppose some of us were already growing away from it, I don't know. Anyway, after the African incident—'

'And what was that?' Culpeper asked.

Purdy raised his hand defensively. 'I don't think my client wants to go into that.'

'*He* mentioned it,' Culpeper complained.

'Yes, but it might be better if *I* explained,' Purdy insisted. 'It would seem that the SBS unit was asked to undertake a certain . . . activity that had possible sensitive political repercussions. It involved the . . . ah . . . presence of his unit in an undercover operation. In a . . . foreign location.' He glanced at his silent client. 'Mr Wicklow feels he cannot go into details.'

'So?' Culpeper rumbled unhappily.

'We'll leave out the background,' Purdy said and nodded to his client.

'It was on the beach that we got decimated,' Wicklow said, almost mumbling. 'We came under heavy fire—our cover had been blown, you see, and they caught us on that bloody beach, just as it was getting dark. Only three of us managed to get off the beach. The other five were killed. It was a . . . bad time.'

Culpeper watched Wicklow carefully: the man was disturbed. The death of his comrades on that beach would have affected him badly at the time, and it clearly still did so. If they had been close comrades, as he said, the incident would haunt his dreams.

'We were debriefed back in Portsmouth some time later. We were offered an assignment to another unit. But it wasn't the same. So all three of us—me, Leo Chesters and Jimmy Lloyd—went back into normal Navy service for a short while. But that wasn't any good either. We'd lost our friends.'

And probably more than friends, Culpeper guessed,

recalling the emphasis that the SBS seemed to have placed upon personal loyalties. 'So what happened then?'

Wicklow shrugged. 'Each of us—we got out. Not together, but within a matter of months, I guess. I heard Jimmy Lloyd was going north to farm but I never saw him again. Me—I sort of drifted around in various jobs until I picked up the Wallsend one. With Leo I think it was a bit different—he found he couldn't settle in civvy life after all. So he went back into the Navy.'

'He was killed in the Gulf War.'

Wicklow nodded. 'I heard about that.'

Culpeper waited. Wicklow now seemed less eager to talk: he hesitated, glanced at Purdy. The solicitor nodded in encouragement.

'I had settled OK; the job was all right. But then I heard that my father-in-law had been murdered. Now I'd never been close to Sam Conors—truth is, I hated the old bastard —so I wasn't too much bothered about his death. It didn't affect me really, at all—I'd been separated from my wife for years anyway. But then a year or so later I saw that Michael Jenkins had been killed in Suffolk.'

'You *did* know Michael Jenkins?' Culpeper asked swiftly.

Wicklow shook his head. 'No, never *met* him. But I occasionally talked among the *drengs* about my feuding with Sam Conors, and Jimmy *had* told me he had an uncle who had never done a thing for him—even though he could have afforded to. Apparently, Jimmy's parents were killed in a car crash but this uncle didn't even put his hand in his pocket. Jimmy thought he was a mean old bastard—it rankled with him, even though he hadn't seen the guy for years. So . . . I never met him, but I knew Jimmy had an uncle called Michael Jenkins.' He paused, wetting his lips nervously. 'So when I read in the newspapers that a Michael Jenkins had been murdered . . . I thought there was a coincidence there. I mean . . . my father-in-law, and Jimmy's uncle.'

There was a short silence. Culpeper sniffed. 'Did you find out how they died?'

'No. Other than that they were murdered. Details about Sam Conors's death were never released, really . . . I wondered about that. Anyway, with Sam Conors and Michael Jenkins murdered . . . it sort of preyed on my mind. It niggled at me; I couldn't get it out of my thoughts. Then I heard Jimmy Lloyd's body had been found at South Middleton.' He raised his left hand and began to pick nervously at his underlip. 'I began to get worried. I suppose it was then I decided to leave the north-east. I didn't know what was going on, but I had a feeling . . . Then on that morning there was an account in the paper—another killing, linked to the murder of Jimmy, with mutilations . . . It meant the guy was still in the area. It was the spur, if you like. I felt I had to get out . . . get away.'

'From what?' Culpeper asked. 'You didn't know Lindley, did you?'

'No. But . . .' Wicklow's voice died away almost to a whisper. 'It was just that coincidences . . . I was scared. I didn't know what the hell was going on, but it worried me. I had a prickly feeling about it . . . So I left.'

There was something the man was not saying; Culpeper felt it, almost palpably, lying between them. 'You were afraid you might be next.'

'Yes.'

'*Why?*'

Purdy leaned forward cautiously. 'I don't think we need go into that at this stage. It is enough that my client felt . . . threatened. That was his reason for leaving the area where his erstwhile comrade had been murdered.'

Culpeper's glance was hostile as he glared at Wicklow. The police forces in France, Switzerland and England had been seeking a connection between these killings, and this man hadn't said a word when his own suspicions were raised. 'Why the hell didn't you go to the police?'

'To say what?' Wicklow flashed. 'I didn't know what was going on. All I knew was I was feeling scared.'

'An ex-SBS man!' Culpeper scoffed.

Wicklow was angry. 'It's one thing to go in with a group

of your mates, face a situation where you can see someone holding a gun in your face . . . but it's different when something's happening you can't explain, when something seems to be creeping up on you. When you think something's happening that you know can't really happen! Go to the police? What could I say? My mucker from the SBS has been killed, and I think I'm next? What credence would you have given me?'

'Why would you think you were next?' Culpeper asked.

Wicklow made no reply.

'Why you? And who would want to come after you, anyway? Who . . . and for what reason?'

Wicklow shook his head, almost angrily.

Culpeper sat still, breathing hard. The *drengs* . . . He cast back to the conversation he had had with Professor Dennis at Durham, and the butterfly danced into his mind again. He almost lost it once more, but suddenly it was there, trapped . . . He stared at the ex-SBS man seated across the table. 'Tell me, in this whole Viking nonsense that you people went along with how much delving did you do? Into the systems, and traditions and so on?'

Wicklow shrugged. 'Me, not so much. But I heard the others talking . . .'

'Did anyone ever talk about blood feuds?'

'Naturally. It didn't apply to us, of course, but we often talked about the way the Vikings killed, about the berserkers and all that. How they settled their quarrels personally—killed their enemies outside any real kind of judicial system, that sort of thing.'

'And family?'

Wicklow hesitated. 'What do you mean?'

'Isn't it true,' Culpeper asked, 'that the Viking warrior in a blood feud would sometimes kill members of the family as well as his personal enemy?'

'I'm not sure—'

'I believe it was a matter of honour, even, to strike at the most senior member of the family instead of, or as well as, killing your enemy. Do you think that's what has been happening here, Wicklow? Because there's another killing you haven't heard about. Everett Chesters, Leo's father, was also murdered. In the same way as your father-in-law, and James Lloyd's uncle. Do you see a pattern here, Wicklow? Is that what's been going on? Some kind of blood feud?'

The man's face was white. He shook his head. 'It isn't *possible*.'

'If it *were* possible, why would it happen?' Culpeper pressed.

Purdy inched his chair forward, scraping the chair leg noisily on the floor. 'My client should not be pressed in this way—'

'Who is it who carries on this Viking tradition, Wicklow? And why is he doing it?'

'But there can't be anyone! They're all dead!'

'Except you!'

Purdy pushed his chair forward more vigorously, until he was seated beside Wicklow. His mouth was thin and tight. 'This isn't a cross-examination, Chief Inspector. This is no courtroom. And no charges have been brought. This flight of fancy you're indulging in is an attempt to implicate my client in a way that is unacceptable. I would recommend moderation.'

'Moderation be damned!' Culpeper swore in frustration at the lawyer's interruption. But it had been effective. It had given Purdy's client pause, the chance to get himself under control. Wicklow was leaning back, his face closing, his emotions shuttered. He wanted to say no more. Culpeper had lost the moment.

Behind them, the door opened and Vic Farnsby came in, to stand beside Detective-Constable Andrew. He whispered something in his ear and took the folder from him. Andrew left the room.

Culpeper glowered at Farnsby. There had been no need for him to relieve Andrew. Farnsby must be feeling a bit left out of things. But it was deliberate. Culpeper had kept him away from the investigation since his outburst earlier,

and had not even shown him the contents of the folder.
Culpeper put out his hand now, and took it from Farnsby.
He opened it, and removed three of the eight photographs
it contained. He spread them in front of Wicklow.

'I've had these sent from the Admiralty. They've been
taken from SBS identity files. It's the members of the Dreng
unit, they say. I want you to confirm who they are . . . one
by one. Who's this?'

'Alan Laurie.'

'Dead?'

Wicklow nodded. 'He was one of the five killed in the
SBS operation.'

'This one?'

'Leo Chesters.'

'And these?'

To the remaining photograph, Culpeper added the rest.
All eight faces stared up from the table. Wicklow looked at
each of them, nodding. His mouth was tight as he stared
at the images of his dead comrades. 'That's the group.'

'Because of something that happened in this group,' Culpeper said quietly, 'or because of someone in this group,
you're suggesting people are still dying.'

'I didn't say—'

'You were scared! You recognized a link in these killings
before we did. You know of some motive, some reason . . .
For God's sake, what the hell do you think's been going
on?'

There was a sibilant hiss from behind Culpeper's shoulder. Irritated, Culpeper glanced back. Farnsby was standing there, leaning forward, his eyes wide and staring.

'What's the matter?' Culpeper snapped.

'That man,' Farnsby said slowly, pointing, his face pale.
'I've seen him.'

Wicklow's mouth sagged, and he stared at Farnsby. He
dragged his gaze back to the photograph and shook his
head wildly. 'That's not possible. He was the *Godar*—'

'What?' Culpeper asked quickly.

'He was the chief . . . he was our leader. But he's *dead.*

He's got to be dead. We left him on the beach—he was one of the five who died!'

'No.' Farnsby's finger was shaking slightly as he pointed to the photograph on the table. 'He's not dead—he's very much alive. I've seen him. He works at the archæological field site at Birley Thore!'

3

The body crumpled at the foot of the cellar steps lay in a huddle. The face was unrecognizable: the bullet which had entered the back of the head had exploded through the front, destroying the face and leaving a mass of shattered bone and blood. The arms were twisted behind his back, bound as Arnold's were. As Arnold was helped up the cellar steps he looked back in horror: for a moment he thought he might see further mutilations, as he had on Frank Lindley's body, but there were none.

Arnold felt weak. He stumbled as he was led across the kitchen and helped into a chair. The bonds were loosened, removed from his wrists, and he leaned forward, elbows on the plain pine table.

'Here—drink this.'

It was hot steaming coffee in a chipped mug. Arnold cupped his shaking hands around the mug, sipped at the coffee. His throat was dry, and he seemed drained of strength—he had no idea how long he had been in the cellar but pangs of hunger gnawed at him, and he still felt nauseous. He had no idea of the time. He glanced through the kitchen window: dusk was falling, but he could make out the outline of hills, hazy against the sky. It meant he must have been in the cellar for almost twenty hours.

'Where are we?'

'My cottage.'

'Who . . . who's that in the cellar?'

'Colin Marshall.'

'But how—'

'I put him there. He was a *nidingr*,' John Vincent said calmly, and sipped his coffee.

Something cold moved in Arnold's chest. Shaken, he stared at the man across the table speechlessly.

John Vincent's eyes narrowed as he contemplated Arnold. 'Him, I could deal with. You . . . now that's a different matter.'

'I don't understand what's going on,' Arnold muttered, shaking his head in stupefaction. 'You've killed Colin Marshall? But you said you were a policeman—'

Vincent smiled thinly, his lopsided mouth dragging at the corner. 'No. *You* said I was a policeman. *You* told me Culpeper had put me in to watch you. I merely went along with it. It served my purpose.'

'What purpose?'

'Finding out who killed Frank Lindley. And visiting justice upon him. Justice, and vengeance.'

Arnold's mind was in a whirl. 'What the hell are you talking about? Looking for Lindley's murderer, and you killed Marshall? Are you seriously suggesting that Colin Marshall murdered Frank Lindley? The man was Lindley's protégé—'

There was a pistol lying on the table between them. Vincent's left hand rested lightly on it while he held his coffee mug in his right hand. He was dressed in a dark sweater and blue shirt. His face seemed thinner, as though tension had fined it down, and his eyes were hard and cynical. He shook his head.

'Protégé, maybe, in Lindley's mind. But Marshall was a weasel. I understand Lindley had helped that young man considerably—gave him money, a job, tried to give him self-respect. Marshall paid him back by smashing in the back of his head.'

'I can't believe it!'

Vincent shrugged disdainfully. 'Please yourself. But he confessed to me eventually . . . last night, after I brought you both back here.'

'But why should Marshall kill Lindley?'

'Greed. A rottenness at the core. Maybe even resentment
at being helped. A confusion of emotions.' Vincent paused,
eyeing Arnold contemplatively. 'You see, Marshall has
been stealing artefacts from the site for the last month. He
was responsible for logging them, but Ormond and Swindon and Lindley himself were remarkably lax: surprising
for archæologists. They left too much in Marshall's hands,
probably because Lindley himself trusted his young protégé. He took just little things at first, but then he started
going up in the evenings, rooting around. It's when he
found this.'

Vincent put down the coffee mug and slipped his hand
into his pocket. He brought out what looked like a small,
dirty medallion, or pendant. It was oval in shape, engraved
with a skeletal figure, badly worn; the figure itself was
framed in lettering Arnold could not make out. Vincent
placed it on the surface of the table and gestured towards
it.

'It's an antique gem,' Vincent said carelessly. 'Marshall
found it, and had made contact with the antiques underground, preparing to put it on the market, it seems. Lindley
came up to the site that evening and caught Marshall rob-
bing the excavation pit on the site. Marshall wasn't terribly
clear telling me what exactly happened: he was somewhat
incoherent when he knew I was going to execute him . . .
Anyway, the guy was greedy, wanted the short route to
success and money, and when he was caught by Lindley he
panicked, hit him when his back was turned. It's possible
he didn't intend to kill him, but when he realized what he'd
done he carried him to his Land-Rover and dumped him
in the cofferdam.'

Arnold's mouth was dry. He shook his head. 'But the
mutilations . . .'

Vincent grimaced. 'That was just to divert suspicion. He
took the body away from the site so that the police wouldn't
spend too much time searching at the field, but after he
dumped him in the cofferdam he was calmer . . . he knew
the police would come questioning him and others on site

so he undertook the mutilations to make the police believe there was a link with the killing of Jimmy Lloyd. That was what I couldn't accept. That was why I had to take a hand.'

'But what did it have to do with *you*?'

Vincent's lopsided mouth was grim. 'It has *always* concerned me. I was *Godar*.'

'The Chief?' Arnold struggled to think back to the meeting in Professor Dennis's room, and Chief Inspector Culpeper's interest in Viking ways of death. 'I don't understand . . .'

Vincent shrugged. 'No reason why you should. No reason why I shouldn't tell you, on the other hand. I killed a man in Basle, and another in Saumur. I killed a man in Dunwich, and I killed Jimmy Lloyd. One for each man who died on a beach. There was one more to go, for me, to end it all—and Marshall interfered.'

'You killed all these people?' Arnold asked in fascinated horror. 'But why?'

Vincent's features were suddenly tense as he looked backwards in his own mind to scenes that had clearly been riveted into his memory. 'Because of Africa, five years ago,' he said slowly. 'The hot darkness of a beach, suddenly lit by gunfire, and five of us pinned down. We were a group, we were a unit, we were the *drengs*, we fought together and we should have died—or lived—together. But there were three of us who were offshore—they had the boat—they could have come back. They *should* have come back. They didn't. They roared off into the darkness: they ran like scared rabbits. They left us to die.' His eyes had a pale sheen as he stared at Arnold, hardly seeing him. 'Four of the men on the beach did die. I didn't. I was wounded, I hid out for three nights in the bush, while they searched for me. But I survived. It took me eight weeks to get back, and I was in bad health. It took me months to get back my strength. But no one knew. I never reported back to the unit. Because I had a job to do. They had betrayed us, those three, done the worst thing a *dreng* could do to his comrades. They had to pay.'

'But killing them! Why didn't you just report back—'

'For them to be court-martialled, stripped of their rank, discharged the service? What sort of punishment was that?' There was a mad, angry light in Vincent's eyes. 'They'd betrayed us, left us to die, run away instead of dying with us. They had to pay, with their lives. I was the *Godar*; I was the Bringer of Justice; I was the Executioner.'

'Lloyd was one of the . . . *drengs*?' Arnold whispered.

'That's right. Another of the three—Leo Chesters—was already killed before I could get to him. But I disposed of his father, the head of his family . . . it was the Viking way, you see, strike at the head of the family, as well as your enemy. That's why Conors and Jenkins died, and on each of them I cut the sign—the bloodeagle.' He paused, reflecting, his hand resting lightly on the pistol. 'And I planned to take the last of the three—Fred Wicklow. I would have done it, I had it planned, and then this *nidingr* Marshall interfered, tried to fool the police into believing that the *Godar* had killed Frank Lindley. It scared Wicklow, made him run. There was no point in my following—easier to let the police find him for me, maybe, or follow his trail later. Meanwhile, I wanted to find the man who had ruined my own vengeance. Marshall.'

'But how could Marshall know about the bloodeagle, and *Godar*?'

Vincent smiled. 'Women . . . It was Dr Ormond who helped me a great deal in working out who killed Lindley. She told me of her own and Mike Swindon's suspicions about the loss of artefacts. And it was a woman who gave Marshall a few details of Lloyd's death. Enough for him to use, to make the police believe the *Godar* killed Lindley.'

'But who—'

Vincent shrugged. 'Marshall's been having an affair with the wife of one of Culpeper's men. Farnsby—the guy who came asking questions at the site. Apparently some of her pillow talk must have been somewhat macabre, talking about her husband's job, complaining about him to her lover. She told Marshall some details of the Lloyd murder.

He used it, to fool the police and keep them away from the field site. Yes . . . he told me all about Mrs Farnsby when I pushed the gun muzzle against the back of his head.'

Arnold recalled the woman he had met with Marshall in Durham, when he had been about to visit Professor Dennis. She had worn a wedding ring—and she had been reluctant to be seen with Marshall. Arnold's hand was shaking slightly as he lifted the mug of coffee. 'You . . . you cut the bloodeagle on Lloyd and the others. But not on Marshall.'

Vincent snorted contemptuously. 'He didn't deserve to die with honour. He was a *nidingr*, the lowest scum. The others, even though they'd betrayed us on the beach, they had to be killed in an honourable way—so it was a clean shot to the head, and a cutting of the bloodeagle. But not for Marshall. He'd killed the man who befriended him. And he was always going to die like a coward. He pleaded with me. I just shot him in the back of the head: an execution.'

'Who *are* you?' asked Arnold quietly, appalled by the coldness of the man. 'And why are you talking to me like this?'

'My name?' Vincent smiled thinly. 'My real name is Sam Elliott. I was the *Godar*—the leader of the *drengs* in our SBS unit. Why do I tell you?' He shrugged. 'It's part of the pattern, you must understand. I explained to each of them, before I killed them. About the reason. About the publicity . . . In the Viking way of death a killing was not honourable unless publicity was given, the enemy identified. I couldn't do that, for obvious reasons, so I did the next best thing. I announced my presence . . . in Saumur, in Basle, in Southwold, and up here at Elsdon. And at the same time I used the names of the *drengs* who died on the beach, as well as an indication of the reason for it all. I've no doubt the police have traced the link by now, so with Lloyd's killing I had to be a little more careful, register at a hotel a bit more remote . . .'

'You intend to kill me?' Arnold asked, his mouth dry.

The hand lay lightly on the pistol.

'What else can I do?' Vincent asked quietly. 'I've nothing

against you, but I have one more step to take. I must get Wicklow, and then it will be over. But you came up to the site last night when I was about to take Marshall—that was him in the hut, still looking for loot. I had to quieten you—and now I have to make sure you stay quiet, so that I can go after Wicklow.'

The hot coffee steamed in Arnold's mug. He glanced at it inadvertently, and the muscles in his arm tensed. John Vincent smiled thinly, guessing his intention. 'Don't even think of it. I can put a bullet in you before you even move.'

Arnold was cold. 'Killing Wicklow . . . that's not going to be easy.'

'He's in police custody.' Vincent shrugged. 'But they'll get around to releasing him . . . there's no reason to hold him. And once he's out and running, I'll get to him. But you . . . for me you pose a problem.'

'I've done nothing to hurt you.'

Vincent nodded. 'Nothing. In fact, you've helped me. But I can't afford to let you live. If I'd finished, if I'd killed Wicklow, it wouldn't have mattered. It would have been over. You could have gone free. But I can't afford to let you live, not now I'd brought you here. And I had no choice other than to bring you. I couldn't leave you at Birley Thore . . . I moved Marshall's Land-Rover and put your car down in the car park. But if they'd found you in the field . . .' He sat frowning, staring at the pistol on the table. 'All I can promise you is that it will be clean and quick. Marshall was different . . . I made him sweat before I killed him.'

'You're crazy! You'll never get away with this!'

'Crazy?' Vincent frowned. 'Maybe. But you don't under-stand what it was like on that beach. We had been the *drengs*; we were bound together; we'd lived and fought and cut bloodeagles together. And those three bastards left us to die . . . I *had* to do this. I had no choice. As for getting away with it . . . once I've taken Wicklow out, I won't care anyway. It'll all be over.'

Arnold began to rise. The pistol muzzle was snapped up, levelling at him. It was then that they both heard the cars in the road, and saw the headlights sweep across the fell slopes.

Once Arnold's hands were bound again, and he had been pushed back on the floor, in the corner of the room, Vincent crossed catlike, swiftly, to the window. He stood with his back to the wall, the pistol raised against his shoulder as he peered out. He muttered something under his breath, cursing, then he turned and moved quickly across the kitchen, out towards the back of the house. The flashing of a blue light began, beating intermittently against the ceiling of the narrow kitchen. Arnold waited, struggling against the thin nylon rope that bound his wrists until he could feel the slipperiness of sweat or blood on his fingers.

John Vincent moved back into the room, almost silently. 'They're at the back as well,' he muttered to Arnold.

'Police?'

'Who else?' Vincent gritted his teeth angrily. 'How the hell did they trace me here?'

Arnold could guess.

An unhappy woman, concerned that the man she was attracted to seemed to be reluctant to talk about himself. A woman who had followed Vincent on one occasion, maybe to check whether he lived alone, or was married . . . Arnold had a swift vision of Dr Ormond's unhappy features in the pub lounge at Birley Thore, and then the voice called out to them from the gathering darkness.

'Elliott? Sam Elliott?'

Vincent stiffened, and stood close to the window, listening, as the man with the megaphone called again.

'We know you're in there. We want to talk to you. Better come out. Let's have no trouble from you.'

'They're crazy if they think I'll just walk out there!'

'You don't stand a chance,' Arnold said quickly.

Vincent swung around, glaring at Arnold. 'I make my *own* luck!' he snapped. 'And if they think I can't get out of here . . .' His eyes hardened, glittered in reflection. 'Particularly with you here.'

He made up his mind surprisingly quickly. He stepped forward, grabbed Arnold's shoulder with his free hand and swung him to his feet. He rammed the muzzle of the pistol against the underside of Arnold's jaw: it brought forth a small trickle of blood. 'You're my passport, Mr Landon. You're going to get me out of here. But first thing, they've got to *see* the ace I've got in the hole!'

He pushed Arnold towards the door, holding the gun against his jawline. He braced himself against the door itself, gripping Arnold's collar, as the blood thundered in Arnold's skull. 'All right, in a second I'm going to open this door and we're going to walk out of here. If you move, or cry out, you'll get a bullet in your brain. You're going to help me cross the yard and you're going to help me get a car. You ready?'

Arnold's heart was thundering in his chest.

He stared at John Vincent desperately. The police would be armed, but they wouldn't open fire while Arnold was held hostage. But if Vincent did get a car and escape with Arnold, what chance would be left then? The man could still kill him, once his usefulness has ended. Oddly, the thought sent a contemptuous anger surging through Arnold. He glared at the man holding him captive. 'So is this what *drengila* means?'

'What?'

'Behaving like a *dreng* . . . behaving like a man. Is *that* what it means?'

Vincent swung Arnold against the wall, painfully, and pushed the gun muzzle hard against Arnold's neck. There was cold fury in his eyes, but Arnold too was angry, and contemptuous.

'So this is the true *Godar*! Using an innocent human shield, someone who's done nothing to hurt you, using him to escape a tight corner? Is that how you escaped that beach? You're no better than the three men who left you for dead! *Dreng*, berserker, *Godar* . . . you've just been playing games. When it comes down to it, you're no better than Lloyd, or the others.'

For a long moment John Vincent stared at Arnold. A pulse beat violently in his temple and his eyes were dark with fury. His grip on the pistol was rigid with tension and Arnold knew that the killing mood was upon him. Arnold remembered what Dennis had said about the berserk rage as he felt the fierce grip on his throat and the cold muzzle of the pistol against his neck. But he kept glaring at Vincent, willing that the words should drill into the man's mind, watching the mad flare of fury in his eyes until, gradually, the grip on his throat slackened.

The moments ticked past, and both men were silent.

John Vincent stood staring at Arnold, his lopsided mouth slack. He blinked as though puzzled, and then slowly the rage diminished, and the confidence seemed to seep back into his face. A slow smile touched his mouth.

'I could have killed you for saying that.'

'You were set to kill me anyway. What did I have to lose?' Arnold challenged him.

The lopsided smile grew broader as John Vincent stepped back. 'You're right—there was nothing to lose—and maybe something to gain.' He shook his head ruefully, eyeing Arnold between narrowed lids. 'I underestimated you. Now . . . I wish we'd had more time together. I wish I'd got to know you better, Mr Landon. You're no fool.'

He stood there thoughtfully for a little while, observing Arnold, and then he loosened his grip on Arnold's collar. He pushed him violently, back across the room. Arnold fell to his knees, hands still bound behind his back. Vincent stood over him, pistol in hand, grinning almost in triumph. 'I guess you're right. I'd almost forgotten who I am,' he said. 'But you've reminded me. You're absolutely right. It's not the way for the *Godar* to go out.'

He moved back away from Arnold, the pistol dangling in his right hand. Someone was calling again, outside the house, but Vincent ignored the words. Instead he left the room briefly: when he returned, he was carrying a small radio and tape-recorder. He smiled grimly at Arnold as he slid a tape into place and switched on the machine.

The voice echoed eerily in the kitchen. Vincent's voice, intoning, deep, excited and vibrant. The sound filled the room and as it did so Vincent seemed to grow taller, bigger, and Arnold knew it was Vincent's own voice on the tape. He could hear the passion in the voice and see the exultation in Vincent's face as he himself listened and was charged with excitement.

'. . . *each man his own leader on the brazen prows. On the one side lions mounted in gold were to be seen on the ships, on the other, birds on the tops of the masts showed by their movements the winds as they blew, or dragons poured fire from their nostrils* . . .'

Vincent stooped over Arnold. He was smiling, but there was excitement in his eyes. 'I got off that beach, and I can get out of this. And if I don't, at least I'm going out like a *dreng*! You were right, Mr Landon. You read me right—and you understand me. So pray to the Gods for me now . . .'

The voice was still booming in the kitchen and darkness was gathering in the hills when the *Godar* slipped out of the back door and ran for the cover of the trees.

5

'He won't get far. He doesn't really stand a chance out there,' Detective Chief Inspector Culpeper said confidently. 'He got by us in the confusion, but he's wounded, and though we lost him in the darkness we know he's somewhere up there in the hills, and we'll get him, eventually.'

'Don't underestimate him,' Arnold said ruefully. 'He escaped that beach, and he could escape you here.'

Culpeper shook his head. 'The whole of the north is looking for him. He'll fall into our net.' He paused. 'We'll be keeping a guard on Fred Wicklow in the meanwhile, just in case. We wouldn't want to be accused of setting him out like a goat, to catch the wandering tiger. And I have a feeling Sam Elliott won't want to give up . . . Anyway, you've finished your statement?'

Arnold nodded. 'The only thing I'd forgotten to mention, really, was that Frank Lindley told me he'd had the feeling someone had been watching the site at night.'

'That would have been Marshall, waiting for his chance once Lindley left. It cost him dearly in the end.' Culpeper's autumn brown eyes were thoughtful. '*You* got out of that cottage all right, at least. Not like Marshall. And . . . I suppose I have an apology to make to you.'

'Apology?'

'About that newspaper thing,' Culpeper replied uncomfortably. 'I had convinced myself it was you or Miss Wilson who talked to the newspapers. It was Marshall, of course. Once he'd decided to smash open Lindley's chest he gave the newspapers an anonymous tip-off.'

'It led to his own death, eventually. And almost cost me my life. Was it Dr Osmond who pointed the way to the cottage?'

Culpeper nodded. 'More or less. We'd got a list of recent lettings, so when we came to the site looking for Vincent, Dr Ormond was able to tell us the valley where he had his cottage and we were able to check it pretty quickly. A somewhat isolated spot.' Culpeper eyed Arnold for a little while. 'Did you see the . . . implements, when he held you at the cottage?'

Arnold shook his head.

Culpeper grimaced. 'There was a heavy, ceremonial sword. An axe—short-handled thing. And one last leaf-shaped spearhead. Ready for Wicklow . . . He was a Viking nut, that one.'

'He was the *Godar*,' Arnold murmured.

'And when we get him he'll spend the rest of his life in Broadmoor.'

With the memory of the gun muzzle pressed against his jaw, Arnold trusted it would be soon.

'But what are they going to do about the artefacts Marshall stole?' Jane Wilson asked Arnold at the Quayside bookshop some days later.

'The ones they can trace they'll return to Mike Swindon.'

'And was Marshall doing it just for the money?'

'Seems so. My own guess is he chafed under Lindley's benevolent eye, felt humiliated by his role with all those experts around him, and saw the chance to make money—and maybe gain an odd sort of prestige—by selling the artefacts under cover. And when Lindley caught him, he panicked, struck out . . .'

'He was calculating enough after that,' Jane muttered. 'That horrible mutilation business . . . and he got the details from Mrs Farnsby, was it?'

'Some details,' Arnold replied. 'The bloodeagle, and the word *Godar*. There were other details, such as the use of the spear that Marshall was hazy about. Culpeper wasn't very precise . . . just said it was a copycat killing but lacking in some details.'

'And what will happen about Mrs Farnsby?'

Arnold shrugged. 'I don't really know. There'll be no charges, of course, but I suppose the rest is up to Farnsby —break with her, or continue to suffer. Culpeper sort of hinted he thought Farnsby would divorce her, but it wasn't something I could ask about.'

'And did you ask about the mediæval pendant?'

Arnold nodded. 'That goes back to the site team with anything else they trace. The police are hanging on to it for the time being. But I had the chance to take a good look at it. Culpeper was . . . amenable for a while.'

'So what exactly was it?'

Slowly Arnold said, 'At first I thought it was a pendant. Vincent called it a mediæval gem . . . maybe it's what Marshall told him. But when I took a close look at it, I realized there was more to it than that. And I realized why there had been the stir in antiques circles that Annette Dominick told us about.'

'How do you mean?'

'It was certainly an antique gem—I wouldn't be able to tell you what the stone was, though. I *can* tell you what was engraved on it.'

'Well?'

'It had the figure of a Roman god or hero . . . possibly Mercury. Or maybe Mars or Perseus. But it wasn't a pendant; it was a seal.'

'You mean—'

'It was a personal seal, probably used as a counterseal on official documents.'

'How do you know that?'

'Because of the lettering on it, carved around the figure of the god.'

'Well,' Jane demanded impatiently, 'what did the letters say?'

Arnold hesitated. He looked at her for a moment thoughtfully. 'Now I don't want you jumping to conclusions . . .'

'You know me better than that! What did it reveal?'

'I mean, although we know it was in Colin Marshall's possession—as far as his killer said—we don't know where Marshall actually *obtained* it. I mean, it is likely it was at the Birley Thore site, but we can't be positive about that. And with its actual location doubtful, it doesn't follow—'

She gripped his wrist fiercely. 'What the hell did it *say?*'

Arnold sighed. 'The legend on the seal was SIGILLUM TOME DEI GRATIA ARCHIEPISCOPI CANTUARIENSIS.'

'*What?*'

'Now I warned you—'

'*The seal of Thomas, by the Grace of God Archbishop of Canterbury!* At Birley Thore?' Jane leapt to her feet in excitement. 'But you know what this means! William Fitzstephen *was* at the site, carrying proof of his identity as Becket's henchman to Hugh le Puiset. He was beset by reivers . . . the seal was lost in the skirmish . . . the reivers buried the dead and with it, inadvertently, the lost seal, while Fitzstephen rode north again to warn the Bishop of Durham of his danger. Arnold—'

'Oh dear, I knew you'd over-react. There's a strong likelihood, I agree, but there's no proof—'

'As I said before—who cares about proof? This is all I need and more. Because of what you've told me, Arnold,

William Fitzstephen can ride north again in my book, while the seal of Becket awaits its finder. Aren't you just *thrilled* about this, Arnold?'

Arnold looked at her, flushed in her excitement, and he smiled wryly. Not quite the word he would have chosen. But, well, yes, he admitted to himself: just thrilled.